EVERYMAN, I will go with thee,

and be thy guide,

In thy most need to go by thy side

HENRIK IBSEN

Born at Skien, Norway, on 20th March
1828. Obtained work in connection with
theatres in Bergen and Christiania. Left
Norway in 1864 and lived abroad—
mostly in Germany—returning to Norway in 1891. Died at Christiania on
23rd May 1906.

HENRIK IBSEN

Hedda Gabler · The Master Builder
TRANSLATED BY EVA LE GALLIENNE

John Gabriel Borkman
TRANSLATED BY NORMAN GINSBURY

INTRODUCTION BY
BRIAN W. DOWNS
D. LITT.

*Emeritus Professor of Scandinavian Studies
in the University of Cambridge*

DENT: LONDON
EVERYMAN'S LIBRARY
DUTTON: NEW YORK

No. 111   Hardback ISBN 0 460 00111 6
No. 1111 Paperback ISBN 0 460 01111 1

INTRODUCTION

Hedda Gabler was published in December 1890, *The Master Builder* (*Bygmester Solness*) in December 1892, *John Gabriel Borkman* in December 1896. They form a sequence which was, however, interrupted in two ways: first, by Ibsen's return in 1891 to live in his native country after twenty-five years' self-imposed exile, and, second, by *Little Eyolf* (December 1894), a low-toned play that nevertheless is at least technically a comedy and meant to be one—in that it shows how good may come out of evil—as the play immediately preceding these, *The Lady from the Sea* (1888), was also, and more recognizably, a comedy. But, even if Ibsen himself never used the term, *Hedda Gabler*, *The Master Builder* and *John Gabriel Borkman* are in the fullest sense tragedies. As their titles proclaim, each is focused on a single personality, whose decline and fall are shown, through the finished mastery with which Ibsen marshalled a vast complex of relevant factors, to be ineluctable.

Hedda Gabler is the only play of its author's to which the adjective slick may be applied. To the taste of today indeed its construction may seem a shade too slick. Hedda Gabler's drawing-room, that had once been that of a cabinet minister's wife, and the elegance of her appearance also made the play outwardly its author's smartest. These are among the reasons for bracketing it, as was often done, with other 'well-made plays' of the time which exhibited *le supplice d'une femme*, more or less genteel blackmail and an 'eternal triangle' (here in fact multiplied by two). For all such recommendations, however, the furore made by the younger Dumas's, Sudermann's or Pinero's productions was never to attend *Hedda Gabler* when it was a novelty. The setting might be attractive, the construction a theatrical masterpiece, the spectacle of a young woman driven to do away with herself one to engage sympathy and compassion; but, behind the façade, all was ugliness, every climax only too plainly brought calamity nearer, and at the very centre of the play there was a puzzle that, far from providing in itself an added source of enjoyment, was a nagging distraction—the enigmatic nature of the heroine's character.

In accordance with his practice, Ibsen was lavish with details of her life, past and present, and dropped abundance of hints at the workings of her mind. But for what sort of woman, essentially, did he intend her to be taken? She has been summed up in endless formulas: as a common or garden society lady, such as one might take down to dinner on ninety-nine evenings out of a hundred; as a bloodless wraith withered in ennui or a specimen of sterile frigidity; as a hysteric, panic-stricken at the thought of imminent child-bearing; as an aristocrat, 'General Gabler's daughter', a noble creature—even a *grande amoureuse manquée*—in the toils of a petty marriage of convenience; as a vicious, dirty-minded *canaille*; and so on.

Behind such infinite variety—which at the hand of ambitious actresses proved the salvation of the play in the long run—we sense an ambivalence of attitude towards Hedda in Ibsen himself, forbidding us to decide whether his estimate of her makes her end a good riddance or a tragic waste, which leaves the puzzle unresolved.

A clue has been sought in Ibsen's biography. If, in fashioning the figure of Hedda, he had a model before him, then what can be discovered about the model might throw some light on the chiaroscuro of the portrait. And such a model has been found: in Emilie Bardach, a very young Austrian lady, of whom Ibsen saw a great deal during his Alpine summer holiday of 1889. But, as regards *Hedda Gabler* (then incubating), the trail does not lead very far. Ibsen was flattered by the attentions of a charming girl and the confidence she showed in unburdening her *Backfisch* soul to him; one may go further and speak of an infatuation on his part. But—is there any trace of infatuation, even of 'loving care', in the delineation of Hedda, and, on the other hand, do the fairly numerous pieces of external evidence anywhere suggest that he sensed in his young friend a highly complex personality which it would be worth his while to unravel? There is only one direct pointer to Emilie Bardach: Ibsen left it on record that he was 'fascinated' to discover in her a 'little bird of prey', whose ambition was set on stealing other women's husbands away from them. This may be the germ, possibly even *the* germ, of Hedda's little game of ruining Thea's relationship with Løvborg. But that is all.

The clue that failed for *Hedda Gabler*, however, leads to the heart of *The Master Builder*. Here Emilie Bardach, the young, the virgin, the vital, may be said to come into her own. That Ibsen had fallen in love with her we need not question. And, whatever else may have to be said about *The Master Builder*, it is a great and poignant love story: Lugné-Poe, Ibsen's most eminent French interpreter, in playing it as such, broke away from the drab, super-naturalistic manner generally thought appropriate for Ibsen performances, with electrifying effect: 'It is the resurrection of my play!' its author exclaimed. Its poignancy lies not so much in its swift, catastrophic ending, as in the apprehension, present from the start and becoming almost unbearable in the visions of the aerial castle the Master Builder is to build for his loved Princess, that, in her words, he is 'attempting the impossible'.

The poignancy takes on a further dimension when 'the mood and personal situation' which, Ibsen himself declared, underlay every one of his works be taken into account. *The Master Builder* is a tragic love story, but the tragic ending also veils a drama of love renounced. The erection of castles in the air is none of the business of an aging contractor who disdains even the title of architect; it is still less the business of the man Henrik Ibsen, at the age of sixty-four working for his royalties in the Victoria Terrasse, Oslo, with a devoted helpmate from whom no little bird of prey must filch him. The radiance of the summer sun at Gossensass may, for once, reflect on the scene, but then, at every cost, it must be forgotten, Fräulein Bardach sent about her business—and so, in effect, she was.

Besides the sense of double guilt—towards Susannah Ibsen and Emilie Bardach—other factors contributed to the mood of sadness, possibly of despair, enveloping the doomful tension of *The Master Builder*. Of one of them more has been made than is warranted. It is suggested by Solness's morbid fear of being crowded out of business by younger competitors. One need not go so far as to dismiss it as a mere technical device for preparing the *coup de théâtre* of Hilda Wangel's first appearance:

> . . . one of these days the younger generation will come knocking at my door . . . That will be the end of Master Builder Solness. . . .
>   [*There is a knock at the door . . . Hilda Wangel enters.*

But at the other extreme there are no good grounds for believing that Ibsen himself suffered from an obsession of this kind. Certainly a new generation was knocking at the door; its most distinguished representative in Norway, Knut Hamsun, had in the autumn of Ibsen's return to Norway been lecturing on the necessity of superseding what he denounced as the utilitarian, stereotyped, peasant-bourgeois literature of his elders—literary naturalism, in short. Ibsen had been there to hear him and had sat unmoved, as well he might: for, if the new literature for which Hamsun called was to disdain the useful and exemplary, the chess-board moves of typical figures in humdrum situations in favour of adventurous psychological delineations, then the creator of Rebekka West, Ellida Wangel and Hedda Gabler need not tremble for his reputation or his royalties. Nor did he tremble. It had never been his nature to 'puff' other authors, but when Gerhart Hauptmann, the man then thought to be his most dangerous rival, came to visit Christiania, Ibsen showed himself unfeignedly friendly.

Nevertheless the rough intimation Knut Hamsun conveyed that, in time at any rate, Ibsen belonged to a bygone generation, must have added to the melancholy he could scarcely escape that autumn, as he saw the red and yellow leaves fall from the trees in the Royal Park just outside his unfamiliar flat, and remembered the ambitions with which he and dead friends had walked the pavements of Christiania when he lived there last, thirty years ago. A sharper reminder of the distant days came to him through the visit of one who had survived, an irruption into his life that bears a much closer resemblance to that of Hilda Wangel into Solness's than any incident with which Emilie Bardach can be associated. The visitor was Laura Kieler, whose fortunes had contributed much to the story of *A Doll's House*, the work on which his great fame had been raised. The whole story is too long and complex to tell here. In brief, Fru Kieler came with a request, passionately urged: she had become embroiled in a public controversy affecting her good name and desired that Ibsen, who—if indirectly—owed so much to her, should now enter the lists in her defence; shaken and weeping, he refused. He had better reasons than his inveterate shrinking from publicity. Nevertheless he could not but feel that he had failed a friend in her distress, irrevocably lost her, and was guilty of leaving undischarged a debt which not she alone thought due to her.

It might not be too fanciful to urge that in precipitating Master Builder Solness from the tower of his new house Ibsen was enacting a vicarious sacrifice in order to set at rest his own 'sickly conscience'. That conscience was to stir again in *When We Dead Awaken*. But in the two intervening plays, *Little Eyolf* and *John*

Gabriel Borkman, he was as little 'committed' as in *Hedda Gabler*. The fact need not altogether rule out considerations of 'mood and personal situation'. Ibsen, now nearer seventy than sixty, would find it no difficulty to put himself into the position of another man brooding through the long, dark Norwegian winter over the end and disappointments of his career. But Borkman is not Ibsen as, by transformation, Solness and Rubek of *When We Dead Awaken* may be held to be. (Even less can Fru Borkman be identified with Fru Ibsen or a 'real-life' parallel to Ella Rentheim and her relationship with John Gabriel be drawn.)

John Gabriel Borkman is (or was) no ordinary man: clearly an *entrepreneur* of great capacity and, what is more, a man of vision not wholly focused on his own enrichment; he came to grief while at the height of his powers and was condemned, first to jail, then to complete inactivity. The caged eagle is an object of compassion; and Ibsen, grimly reticent though he may be, does nothing to forbid such pity or admiration as may be due to him. The portrait, however, is an inimical one; indeed it comes within a hair's breadth of being cruelly sardonic.

For one parallel may easily be drawn: and it is that between Borkman and the man Hinckel to whose betrayal he attributes his downfall. Both were or are tycoons on a large scale, and in their unscrupulous transactions they combined to make a victim of the same woman, Ella Rentheim. For Borkman, Hinckel is the 'super-scoundrel', yet his own villainy in bartering away Ella Rentheim in return for financial accommodation was the blacker. The term is interesting: an adaptation of 'Superman', then so common in the public mouth, and Ibsen's one-word criticism of the Nietzschean 'Will to Power' of which the Superman, Hinckel and Borkman are embodiments. In coining it Ibsen shows himself not so far out of touch with the spirit of the times as Hamsun would have it believed and betrays also his insistence, growing ever more emphatic after *An Enemy of the People*, that grand issues of social improvement, political integrity, industrial development, the future of the race and the like are as nothing in comparison with the happiness of the individual who may be caught up in their meshes.

This happiness is no superficial cheerfulness, complacency or ease of living. Its conditions Ibsen formulated at the end of *The Lady from the Sea*: 'freedom with responsibility'; the formula is an austere one, the freedom envisaged being a liberation to be fought for, the responsibility implying a moral awareness constantly on the alert.

It seems doubly anomalous that the man who won his fame, his notoriety, by his exposure of public evils should have reached the point of putting them by altogether, and that a quest for happiness should underlie four great tragedies, *Hedda Gabler*, *The Master Builder*, *John Gabriel Borkman* and *When We Dead Awaken*. Yet there is an inner consistency. The dramatist, as such concerned with conflict, fastened on the obstacles. First—though never exclusively —he found them in accepted but indefensible abuses and the tyranny of convention; from the time of *Rosmersholm* at any rate he saw that the more serious, the more intractable hindrances, lay within, in the individual's character and the circumstances it had created for itself. They could be overcome, as *The Lady from the Sea* and *Little Eyolf* demonstrated. But there were incurable cases, in which liberation was impossible. The web of circumstances in itself could be too dense to break through—clearly the case in *Hedda Gabler*. An individuality might not only, if infected with the Will to Power, do irreparable damage to others (Hedda to Løvborg, Solness to the Broviks, Borkman to Ella Rentheim), it might hopelessly maim itself. For Solness and Borkman, as for Hedda Gabler, there could be no revivification to freedom and happiness except in sterile and ultimately suicidal dreams. That was their tragedy. General Gabler's pistol, the high tower on Solness's house, the ice and snow round Ella Rentheim's merely write the word 'Finis'.

B. W. D.

1966.

SELECT BIBLIOGRAPHY

SEPARATE PLAYS (titles in English; dates of first Norwegian editions). *Catilina*,
1850; *The Warrior's Barrow*, 1850; *Norma*, 1851; *Olaf Liljekrans*, 1856; *The Feast at
Solhoug*, 1856; *Lady Inger of Østeraad*, 1857; *The Vikings in Helgeland*, 1858; *Love's
Comedy*, 1862; *The Pretenders*, 1864; *Brand*, 1866; *Peer Gynt*, 1867; *The League of
Youth*, 1869; *Emperor and Galilean*, 1873; *Pillars of Society*, 1877; *A Doll's House*,
1879; *Ghosts*, 1881; *An Enemy of the People*, 1882; *The Wild Duck*, 1884; *Rosmersholm*,
1886; *The Lady From the Sea*, 1888; *Hedda Gabler*, 1890; *The Master Builder*, 1892;
Little Eyolf, 1894; *John Gabriel Borkman*, 1896; *When We Dead Awaken*, 1899.

COLLECTED EDITIONS. *The Collected Works of Henrik Ibsen*, edited and translated
by W. Archer, 12 vols., 1906–12; *The Correspondence of Henrik Ibsen*, translated by
Mary Morison, 1905. *Lyrics and Poems from Ibsen*, translated by F. E. Garrett, 1912.

BIOGRAPHY AND CRITICISM. G. B. Shaw, *The Quintessence of Ibsenism*, 1891; ex-
panded 1913: P. H. Wicksteed, *Four Lectures on Henrik Ibsen*, 1892; G. M. C. Brandes,
Henrik Ibsen, Critical Studies, translated by J. Muir, 1899; E. W. Gosse, *Henrik Ibsen*
(Literary Lives Series), 1907; H. J. Weigand, *The Modern Ibsen*, 1926; A. E. Zucker
Ibsen the Master Builder, 1930; H. Koht, *Henrik Ibsen*, 1931; M. C. Bradbrook,
Ibsen the Norwegian, 1946; B. W. Downs, *Ibsen: The Intellectual Background*, 1946;
J. Lavrin, *Ibsen: an Approach*, 1950; B. W. Downs, *A Study of Six Plays by Ibsen*,
1950; J. R. Northam, *Ibsen's Dramatic Method*, 1951; B. Ibsen, *The Three Ibsens*,
translated by G. Schjelderup, 1951; G. Wilson Knight, *Ibsen*, 1962; F. L. Lucas,
The Drama of Ibsen and Strindberg, 1962; M. C. Bradbrook, *Ibsen the Norwegian: A
Revaluation*, 1966; J. W. McFarlane (ed.), *Henrik Ibsen*, 1970; M. Egan (ed.), *Ibsen,
Critical Heritage Series*, 1972; J. Northam, *Ibsen: A Critical Study*, 1973.

CONTENTS

HEDDA GABLER

HEDDA GABLER

ACT I

A large, handsomely furnished drawing-room, decorated in dark colours. In the back wall a wide opening with portières that are drawn back. This opening leads to a smaller room decorated in the same style as the drawing-room. In the right-hand wall of the front room is a folding door leading to the hall. In the wall opposite, on the left, a glass door, its hangings also drawn back. Through the panes can be seen part of a veranda and trees covered in autumn foliage. Standing well forward is an oval table, with a cover on it and surrounded by chairs. By the wall on the right stands a wide stove of dark porcelain, a high-backed armchair, an upholstered footstool and two tabourets. A small sofa fits into the right-hand corner with a small round table in front of it. Down left, standing slightly away from the wall, another sofa. Above the glass door, a piano. On either side of the opening in the back wall two étagères with terra-cotta and majolica ornaments. Against the back wall of the inner room a sofa, a table and a couple of chairs. Above the sofa hangs the portrait of a handsome elderly man in the uniform of a general. Over the table a hanging-lamp with an opalescent glass shade. A number of bouquets of flowers are arranged about the drawing-room in vases and glasses. Others lie on the various tables. The floors in both rooms are covered with thick carpets. It is morning. The sun shines through the glass door.
Miss Julia Tesman, wearing a hat and carrying a parasol, enters from the hall followed by Berta, who carries a bouquet wrapped in paper. Miss Tesman is a good and pleasant-looking lady of about sixty-five. Simply but nicely dressed in a grey tailor-made. Berta is a maid getting on in years, plain and rather countrified in appearance.

MISS TESMAN. [*Stops just inside the door, listens, and says softly*] Good gracious! They're not even up—I do believe!

BERTA. [*Also speaks softly.*] That's what I told you, Miss Julia. The steamer got in so late last night; and the young mistress had such a lot of unpacking to do before she could get to bed.

3

MISS TESMAN. Well—let them sleep as long as they like. But when they do get up, they'll certainly need a breath of fresh air.

[*She goes to the glass door and opens it wide.*

BERTA. [*At the table uncertain what to do with the bouquet in her hand.*] There's not a bit of room left anywhere. I'll just put them down here, Miss Julia.   [*Puts the bouquet down on the piano.*

MISS TESMAN. So now you have a new mistress, Berta. Heaven knows it was hard enough for me to part with you.

BERTA. [*On the verge of tears.*] Don't think it wasn't hard for me too, Miss Julia; after all those happy years I spent with you and Miss Rina.

MISS TESMAN. We'll just have to make the best of it, Berta. Master George needs you—he really does. You've looked after him ever since he was a little boy.

BERTA. That's true, Miss Julia; but I can't help worrying about Miss Rina lying there helpless, poor thing; how *will* she manage? That new maid will never learn to take proper care of an invalid!

MISS TESMAN. I'll soon be able to train her; and until then, I'll do most of the work myself—so don't you worry about my poor sister, Berta.

BERTA. But, there's something else, Miss Julia—you see, I'm so afraid I won't be able to please the young mistress.

MISS TESMAN. Well—there may be one or two things, just at first——

BERTA. She'll be very particular, I expect——

MISS TESMAN. That's only natural—after all, she's General Gabler's daughter. She was used to being spoiled when her father was alive. Do you remember how we used to see her galloping by? How smart she looked in her riding clothes!

BERTA. Indeed I do remember, Miss Julia! Who would ever have thought that she and Master George would make a match of it!

MISS TESMAN. God moves in mysterious ways——! But, by the way, Berta—before I forget—you mustn't say Master George any more—it's Doctor Tesman!

BERTA. I know, Miss Julia. That was one of the very first things the young mistress told me last night. So it's really true, Miss Julia?

MISS TESMAN. Yes, it is indeed! He was made a doctor by one of the foreign universities while he was abroad. It was a great surprise to me; I knew nothing about it until he told me last night on the pier.

BERTA. Well—he's clever enough for anything, he is! But I never thought he'd go in for doctoring people!

MISS TESMAN. It's not *that* kind of a doctor, Berta! [*Nods significantly.*] But later on, you may have to call him something even grander!

BERTA. Really, Miss Julia? Now what could that be?

MISS TESMAN. [*Smiles.*] Wouldn't you like to know! [*Moved.*] I wonder what my poor brother would say if he could see what a great man his little boy has become. [*Looking around.*] But, what's this, Berta? Why have you taken all the covers off the furniture?

BERTA. The young mistress told me to. She said she couldn't bear them.

MISS TESMAN. Perhaps she intends to use this as the living-room?

BERTA. I think maybe she does, Miss Julia; though Master George —I mean the Doctor—said nothing about it.

[*George Tesman enters the inner room from right, singing gaily. He carries an unstrapped empty suitcase. He is a young-looking man of thirty-three, medium height. Rather plump, a pleasant, round, open face. Blond hair and beard, wears spectacles. Rather carelessly dressed in comfortable lounging clothes.*]

MISS TESMAN. Good morning—good morning, my dear George!

TESMAN. [*At the opening between the rooms.*] Aunt Julia! Dear Aunt Julia! [*Goes to her and shakes her warmly by the hand.*] Way out here —so early in the morning—eh?

MISS TESMAN. I had to come and see how you were getting on.

TESMAN. In spite of going to bed so late?

MISS TESMAN. My dear boy—as if that mattered to me!

TESMAN. You got home all right from the pier—eh?

MISS TESMAN. Quite all right, dear, thank you. Judge Brack was kind enough to see me safely to my door.

TESMAN. We were so sorry we couldn't give you a lift—but Hedda had such a fearful lot of luggage——

MISS TESMAN. Yes—she did seem to have quite a bit!

BERTA. [*To Tesman.*] Should I ask the Mistress if there's anything I can do for her, sir?

TESMAN. No, thank you, Berta—there's no need. She said she'd ring if she wanted anything.

BERTA. [*Starting right.*] Very good, sir.

TESMAN. [*Indicates suitcase.*] You might just take that suitcase with you.

BERTA. [*Taking it.*] Yes, sir. I'll put it in the attic.

[*She goes out by the hall door.*

TESMAN. Do you know, Aunt Julia—I had that whole suitcase full of notes? It's unbelievable how much I found in all the archives I examined; curious old details no one had any idea existed.

MISS TESMAN. You don't seem to have wasted your time on your wedding-trip!

TESMAN. Indeed I haven't!—But do take off your hat, Aunt Julia—let me help you—eh?

MISS TESMAN. [*While he does so.*] How sweet of you! This is just like the old days when you were still with us!

TESMAN. [*He turns the hat round in his hands looking at it admiringly from all sides.*] That's a very elegant hat you've treated yourself to.

MISS TESMAN. I bought that on Hedda's account.

TESMAN. On Hedda's account—eh?

MISS TESMAN. Yes—I didn't want her to feel ashamed of her old aunt—in case we should happen to go out together.

TESMAN. [*Patting her cheek.*] What a dear you are, Aunt Julia— always thinking of everything! [*Puts the hat down on the table.*] And now let's sit down here on the sofa and have a cosy little chat till Hedda comes.

[*They sit down. She leans her parasol in the corner of the sofa.*

MISS TESMAN. [*Takes both his hands and gazes at him.*] I can't tell you what a joy it is to have you home again, George.

TESMAN. And it's a joy for me to see you again, dear Aunt Julia. You've been as good as a father and mother to me—I can never forget that!

MISS TESMAN. I know, dear—you'll always have a place in your heart for your poor old aunts.

TESMAN. How *is* Aunt Rina—eh? Isn't she feeling a little better?

MISS TESMAN. No, dear. I'm afraid she'll never be any better, poor thing! But I pray God I may keep her with me a little longer—for now that I haven't you to look after any more, I don't know what will become of me when she goes.

TESMAN. [*Pats her on the back.*] There, there, there!

MISS TESMAN. [*With a sudden change of tone.*] You know, I can't get used to thinking of you as a married man, George. And to think that you should have been the one to carry off Hedda Gabler— the fascinating Hedda Gabler—who was always surrounded by so many admirers!

TESMAN. [*Hums a little and smiles complacently.*] Yes—I wouldn't be surprised if some of my friends were a bit jealous of me—eh?

MISS TESMAN. And then this wonderful wedding trip! Five—nearly six months!

TESMAN. Of course, you must remember, the trip was also of great value to me in my research work. I can't begin to tell you all the archives I've been through—and the many books I've read!

MISS TESMAN. I can well believe it! [*More confidently, lowering her voice.*] But, George dear, are you sure you've nothing—well—nothing *special* to tell me?

TESMAN. About our trip?

MISS TESMAN. Yes.

TESMAN. I can't think of anything I didn't write you about. I had a doctor's degree conferred on me—but I told you that last night.

MISS TESMAN. Yes, yes—you told me about that. But what I mean is —haven't you any—well—any expectations?

TESMAN. Expectations?

MISS TESMAN. Yes, George. Surely you can talk frankly to your old aunt?

TESMAN. Well, of course I have expectations!

MISS TESMAN. Well?

TESMAN. I have every expectation of becoming a professor one of these days!

MISS TESMAN. A professor—yes, yes, I know, dear—but——

TESMAN. In fact I'm certain of it. But you know that just as well as I do, Aunt Julia.

MISS TESMAN. [*Chuckling.*] Of course I do, dear—you're quite right. [*Changing the subject.*] But we were talking about your journey— it must have cost a great deal of money, George!

TESMAN. Well, you see, the scholarship I had was pretty ample— that went a good way.

MISS TESMAN. Still—I don't see how it could have been ample enough for two—especially travelling with a lady—they say that makes it ever so much more expensive.

TESMAN. It does make it a bit more expensive—but Hedda simply had to have this trip—she really had to—it was the fashionable thing to do.

MISS TESMAN. I know—nowadays it seems a wedding has to be followed by a wedding-trip. But tell me, George—have you been over the house yet?

TESMAN. I have indeed! I've been up since daybreak!

MISS TESMAN. What do you think of it?

TESMAN. It's splendid—simply splendid! But it seems awfully big —what on earth shall we do with all those empty rooms?

MISS TESMAN. [*Laughingly.*] Oh, my dear George—I expect you'll find plenty of use for them—a little later on.

TESMAN. Yes, you're right, Aunt Julia—as I get more and more books—eh?

MISS TESMAN. Of course, my dear boy—it was your books I was thinking of!

TESMAN. I'm especially pleased for Hedda's sake. She had her heart set on this house—it belonged to Secretary Falk you know—even before we were engaged, she used to say it was the one place she'd really like to live in.

MISS TESMAN. But I'm afraid you'll find all this very expensive, my dear George—very expensive!

TESMAN. [*Looks at her a little despondently.*] Yes, I suppose so. How much do you really think it will cost? I mean approximately—eh?

MISS TESMAN. That's impossible to say until we've seen all the bills.

TESMAN. Judge Brack wrote Hedda that he'd been able to secure very favourable terms for me.

MISS TESMAN. But you mustn't worry about it, my dear boy—for one thing, I've given security for all the furniture and the carpets.

TESMAN. Security? You, dear Aunt Julia? What sort of security?

MISS TESMAN. A mortgage on our annuity.

TESMAN. [*Jumps up.*] What!

MISS TESMAN. I didn't know what else to do.

TESMAN. [*Standing before her.*] You must be mad, Aunt Julia—quite mad! That annuity is all that you and Aunt Rina have to live on!

MISS TESMAN. Don't get so excited about it! It's only a matter of form, Judge Brack says. He was kind enough to arrange the whole matter for me.

TESMAN. That's all very well—but still——!

MISS TESMAN. And from now on you'll have your own salary to depend on—and even if we should have to help out a little, just at first—it would only be the greatest pleasure to us!

TESMAN. Isn't that just like you, Aunt Julia! Always making sacrifices for me.

MISS TESMAN. [*Rises and places her hands on his shoulders.*] The only happiness I have in the world is making things easier for you, my dear boy. We've been through some bad times, I admit—but now we've reached the goal and we've nothing to fear.

TESMAN. [*Sits down beside her again.*] Yes—it's amazing how everything's turned out for the best!

MISS TESMAN. Now there's no one to stand in your way—even your most dangerous rival has fallen. Well, he made his bed—let him lie on it, poor misguided creature.

TESMAN. Has there been any news of Eilert—since I went away, I mean?

MISS TESMAN. They say he's supposed to have published a new book.

TESMAN. Eilert Løvborg! A new book? Recently—eh?

MISS TESMAN. That's what they say—but I shouldn't think any book of his would be worth much. It'll be a very different story when *your* new book appears. What's it to be about, George?

TESMAN. It will deal with the Domestic Industries of Brabant during the Middle Ages.

MISS TESMAN. Fancy being able to write about such things!

TESMAN. Of course it'll be some time before the book is ready—I still have to arrange and classify all my notes, you see.

MISS TESMAN. Yes—collecting and arranging—no one can compete with you in that! You're not your father's son for nothing!

TESMAN. I can't wait to begin! Especially now that I have my own comfortable home to work in.

MISS TESMAN. And best of all—you have your wife! The wife you longed for!

TESMAN. [*Embracing her.*] Yes, you're right, Aunt Julia—Hedda! She's the most wonderful part of it all! [*Looks towards opening between the rooms.*] But here she comes—eh?

[*Hedda enters from the left through the inner room. She is a woman of twenty-nine. Her face and figure show breeding and distinction. Her complexion is pale and opaque. Her eyes are steel grey and express a cold, unruffled repose. Her hair is an agreeable medium brown, but not especially abundant. She wears a tasteful, somewhat loose-fitting negligee.*]

MISS TESMAN. [*Goes to meet Hedda.*] Good morning, Hedda dear—and welcome home!

HEDDA. [*Gives her her hand.*] Good morning, my dear Miss Tesman. What an early visitor you are—how kind of you!

MISS TESMAN. [*Seems slightly embarrassed.*] Not at all. And did the bride sleep well in her new home?

HEDDA. Thank you—fairly well.

TESMAN. [*Laughing.*] Fairly well! I like that, Hedda! You were sleeping like a log when I got up!

HEDDA. Yes—fortunately. You know, Miss Tesman, one has to adapt oneself gradually to new surroundings. [*Glancing towards the left.*] Good heavens—what a nuisance! That maid's opened the window and let in a whole flood of sunshine!

MISS TESMAN. [*Starts towards door.*] Well—we'll just close it then!

HEDDA. No, no—don't do that! George dear, just draw the curtains, will you? It'll give a softer light.

TESMAN. [*At the door.*] There, Hedda! Now you have both shade and fresh air!

HEDDA. Heaven knows we need some fresh air, with all these stacks of flowers! But do sit down, my dear Miss Tesman.

MISS TESMAN. No—many thanks! Now that I know everything's all right here, I must be getting home to my poor sister.

TESMAN. Do give her my best love, Aunt Julia—and tell her I'll drop in and see her later in the day.

MISS TESMAN. Yes, dear, I'll do that. . . . Oh! I'd almost forgotten [*feeling in the pocket of her dress*] I've brought something for you!

TESMAN. What can that be, Aunt Julia—eh?

MISS TESMAN. [*Produces a flat parcel wrapped in newspaper and presents him with it.*] Look, dear!

TESMAN. [*Opens the parcel.*] Oh, Aunt Julia! You really kept them for me! Isn't that touching, Hedda—eh?

HEDDA. [*By the étagère on the right.*] Well, what is it, dear?

TESMAN. My slippers, Hedda! My old bedroom slippers!

HEDDA. Oh yes—I remember. You often spoke of them on our journey.

TESMAN. I can't tell you how I've missed them! [*Goes up to her.*] Do have a look at them, Hedda——

HEDDA. [*Going towards stove.*] I'm really not very interested, George——

TESMAN. [*Following her.*] Dear Aunt Rina embroidered them for me during her illness. They have so many memories for me——

HEDDA. [*At the table.*] Scarcely for me, George.

MISS TESMAN. Of course not, George! They mean nothing to Hedda.

TESMAN. I only thought, now that she's one of the family——

HEDDA. [*Interrupting.*] We shall never get on with this servant, George!

MISS TESMAN. Not get on with Berta?

TESMAN. Hedda, dear, what do you mean?

HEDDA. [*Pointing.*] Look! She's left her old hat lying about on the table.

TESMAN. [*Flustered—dropping the slippers on the floor.*] Why—Hedda——!

HEDDA. Just imagine if someone were to come in and see it!

TESMAN. But, Hedda! That's Aunt Julia's hat!

HEDDA. Oh! Is it?

MISS TESMAN. [*Picks up the hat.*] Yes, indeed it is! And what's more it's not old—little Mrs Tesman!

HEDDA. I really didn't look at it very closely, Miss Tesman.

MISS TESMAN. [*Puts on the hat.*] This is the very first time I've worn it!

TESMAN. And it's a lovely hat too—quite a beauty!

MISS TESMAN. Oh, it isn't as beautiful as all that. [*Looking round.*] Where's my parasol? [*Takes it.*] Ah—here it is! [*Mutters.*] For this is mine too—not Berta's.

TESMAN. A new hat and a new parasol—just think, Hedda!

HEDDA. Most handsome and lovely, I'm sure!

TESMAN. Yes—isn't it, eh? But do take a good look at Hedda—see how lovely *she* is!

MISS TESMAN. Hedda was always lovely, my dear boy—that's nothing new.   [*She nods and goes towards the right.*

TESMAN. [*Following her.*] But don't you think she's looking especially well? I think she's filled out a bit while we've been away.

HEDDA. [*Crossing the room.*] Oh, do be quiet! . . .

MISS TESMAN. [*Who has stopped and turned towards them.*] Filled out?

TESMAN. Of course, you can't notice it so much in that loose dress —but I have certain opportunities——

HEDDA. [*Stands at the glass door—impatiently.*] You have no opportunities at all, George——

TESMAN. I think it must have been the mountain air in the Tyrol——

HEDDA. [*Curtly interrupting.*] I'm exactly as I was when we left!

TESMAN. That's what you say—but I don't agree with you! What do you think, Aunt Julia?

MISS TESMAN. [*Gazing at her with folded hands.*] Hedda is lovely—lovely! [*Goes to her, takes her face in her hands and gently kisses the top of her head.*] God bless and keep you, Hedda Tesman, for George's sake!

HEDDA. [*Quietly freeing herself.*] Please! Oh, please let me go!

MISS TESMAN. [*With quiet emotion.*] I shan't let a day pass without coming to see you!

TESMAN. That's right, Aunt Julia!

MISS TESMAN. Goodbye, dearest Hedda—goodbye!

[*She goes out by the hall door. Tesman sees her out. The door remains half open. Tesman can be heard repeating his greetings to Aunt Rina and his thanks for the bedroom slippers. Meanwhile Hedda paces about the room, raises her arms and clenches her hands as though in desperation. She flings back the curtains of the glass door and stands gazing out. In a moment Tesman returns and closes the door behind him.*

TESMAN. [*Picking up the slippers from the floor.*] What are you looking at, Hedda?

HEDDA. [*Once more calm and controlled.*] I'm just looking at the leaves—they're so yellow—so withered.

TESMAN. [*Wraps up the slippers and puts them on the table.*] Well, we're well into September now.

HEDDA. [*Again restless.*] God, yes! September—September already!

TESMAN. Didn't you think Aunt Julia was a little strange? Almost solemn, I thought. What do you suppose was the matter with her—eh?

HEDDA. Well, you see, I scarcely know her. Isn't she always like that?

TESMAN. No, not as she was today.

HEDDA. [*Leaving the glass door.*] Perhaps she was annoyed about the hat.

TESMAN. Oh, not specially—perhaps just for a moment——

HEDDA. [*Crosses over towards the fireplace.*] Such a peculiar way to behave—flinging one's hat about in the drawing-room—one doesn't do that sort of thing.

TESMAN. I'm sure Aunt Julia won't do it again.

HEDDA. I shall manage to make my peace with her. When you see her this afternoon, George, you might ask her to come and spend the evening here.

TESMAN. Yes, I will, Hedda. And there's another thing you could do that would give her so much pleasure.

HEDDA. Well—what's that?

TESMAN. If you could only be a little more affectionate with her—just for my sake—eh?

HEDDA. I shall try to call her aunt—but that's really all I can do.

TESMAN. Very well. I just thought, now that you belong to the family——

HEDDA. I really don't see why, George——

[She goes towards the centre opening.

TESMAN. [*After a short pause.*] Is there anything the matter with you, Hedda, eh?

HEDDA. No, nothing. I'm just looking at my old piano. It doesn't seem to fit in with the rest of the furniture.

TESMAN. The first time I draw my salary, we'll see about exchanging it.

HEDDA. Exchange it! Why exchange it? I don't want to part with it. Why couldn't we put it in the inner room and get a new one for here? That is, of course, when we can afford it.

TESMAN. [*Slightly taken back.*] Yes, I suppose we could do that.

HEDDA. [*Takes up the bouquet from the piano.*] These flowers weren't here last night when we arrived.

TESMAN. I expect Aunt Julia brought them for you.

HEDDA. [*Examines the bouquet.*] Here's a card. [*Takes out a card and reads it.*] 'Shall return later in the day.' Can you guess who it's from?

TESMAN. No. Tell me.

HEDDA. From Mrs Elvsted.

TESMAN. Really! Sheriff Elvsted's wife. The former Miss Rysing.

HEDDA. Exactly. The girl with that irritating mass of hair—she was always showing off. I've heard she was an old flame of yours, George?

TESMAN. [*Laughs.*] Oh, that didn't last long, and it was before I met you, Hedda. Fancy her being in town.

HEDDA. Funny that she should call on us. I haven't seen her for years. Not since we were at school together.

TESMAN. I haven't seen her either for ever so long. I wonder how she can stand living in that remote, dreary place.

HEDDA. I wonder! [*After a moment's thought, says suddenly*] Tell me, George, doesn't Eilert Løvborg live somewhere near there?

TESMAN. Yes, I believe he does. Somewhere in that neighbourhood.

BERTA. [*Enters by the hall door.*] That lady, ma'am, who left some flowers a little while ago is back again. [*Pointing.*] The flowers you have in your hand, ma'am.

HEDDA. Oh, is she? Very well, ask her to come in.

[*Berta opens the door for Mrs Elvsted and exits. Thea Elvsted is a fragile woman with soft pretty features. Her large, round, light blue eyes are slightly prominent and have a timid, questioning look. Her hair is unusually fair, almost white gold and extremely thick and wavy. She is a couple of years younger than Hedda. She wears a dark visiting dress, in good taste but not in the latest fashion.*

HEDDA. [*Graciously goes to meet her.*] How do you do, my dear Mrs Elvsted? How delightful to see you again after all these years.

THEA. [*Nervously, trying to control herself.*] Yes, it's a very long time since we met.

TESMAN. [*Gives her his hand.*] And we haven't met for a long time either, eh?

HEDDA. Thank you for your lovely flowers.

THEA. Oh, don't mention it. I would have come to see you yesterday, but I heard you were away.

TESMAN. Have you just arrived in town, eh?

THEA. Yes, I got here yesterday morning. I was so upset not to find you at home.

HEDDA. Upset! But why, my dear Mrs Elvsted?

TESMAN. But, my dear Mrs Rysing—er—Mrs Elvsted, I mean——

HEDDA. I hope you're not in any trouble.

THEA. Well, yes I am, and I know no one else in town that I could possibly turn to——

HEDDA. [*Puts the bouquet down on the table.*] Come, let's sit down here on the sofa——

THEA. I'm really too nervous to sit down.

HEDDA. Of course you're not. Come along now——

[*She draws Mrs Elvsted down to the sofa and sits beside her.*

TESMAN. Well, Mrs Elvsted?

HEDDA. Has anything gone wrong at home?

THEA. Well—er—yes and no. I do hope you won't misunderstand me.

HEDDA. Perhaps you'd better tell us all about it, Mrs Elvsted.

TESMAN. I suppose that's what you've come for, eh?

THEA. Yes, of course. Well, first of all—but perhaps you've already heard—Eilert Løvborg is in town too.

HEDDA. Løvborg!

TESMAN. What! Eilert Løvborg has come back! Think of that, Hedda!

HEDDA. Good heavens, yes, I heard it!

THEA. He's been here for a week. A whole week. I'm so afraid
he'll get into trouble——

HEDDA. But, my dear Mrs Elvsted, why should you be so worried
about him?

THEA. [*Gives her a startled look and speaks hurriedly.*] Well, you see—
he's the children's tutor.

HEDDA. Your children's?

THEA. No. My husband's. I have none.

HEDDA. Oh, your stepchildren's then?

THEA. Yes.

TESMAN. [*With some hesitation.*] Was he—I don't quite know how
to put it—was he dependable enough to fill such a position,
eh?

THEA. For the last two years his conduct has been irreproachable.

TESMAN. Has it really? Think of that, Hedda!

HEDDA. Yes, yes, yes! I heard it.

THEA. Irreproachable in every respect, I assure you, but still I know
how dangerous it is for him to be here in town all alone, and he
has quite a lot of money with him. I can't help being worried to
death about him.

TESMAN. But why did he *come* here? Why didn't he stay where he
was? With you and your husband, eh?

THEA. After his book was published he felt too restless to stay on
with us.

TESMAN. Oh yes, of course. Aunt Julia told me he had published a
new book.

THEA. Yes, a wonderful book. A sort of outline of civilization. It
came out a couple of weeks ago. It's sold marvellously. Made
quite a sensation.

TESMAN. Has it really? Then I suppose it's something he wrote
some time ago—during his better years.

THEA. No, no. He's written it all since he's been with us.

TESMAN. Well, isn't that splendid, Hedda? Think of that!

THEA. Yes, if only he'll keep it up.

HEDDA. Have you seen him here in town?

THEA. Not yet. I had great trouble finding out his address, but this
morning I got it at last.

HEDDA. [*Gives her a searching look.*] But doesn't it seem rather odd of
your husband to——

THEA. [*With a nervous start.*] Of my husband—what?

HEDDA. Well—to send you on such an errand. Why didn't he come himself to look after his friend?

THEA. Oh no. My husband is much too busy. And besides, I had some shopping to do.

HEDDA. [*With a slight smile.*] Oh, I see!

THEA. [*Rising quickly and uneasily.*] I implore you, Mr Tesman, be good to Eilert Løvborg if he should come to see you. I'm sure he will. You were such great friends in the old days, and after all you're both interested in the same studies. You specialize in the same subjects—as far as I can understand.

TESMAN. Yes, we used to, at any rate.

THEA. That's why I'd be so grateful if you too would—well—keep an eye on him. You will do that, won't you, Mr Tesman?

TESMAN. I'd be delighted to, Mrs Rysing.

HEDDA. Elvsted!

TESMAN. I'd be delighted to do anything in my power to help Eilert. You can rely on me.

THEA. [*Presses his hands.*] Oh, how very kind of you! I can't thank you enough. . . . [*Frightened.*] You see, my husband is so very fond of him.

HEDDA. [*Rises.*] Yes—I see. I think you should write to him, George. He may not care to come of his own accord.

TESMAN. Perhaps that would be the right thing to do, Hedda, eh?

HEDDA. Yes. The sooner the better. Why not at once?

THEA. [*Imploringly.*] Oh yes, please do!

TESMAN. I'll write him this minute. Have you his address, Mrs Ry—Elvsted?

THEA. [*Takes a slip of paper from her pocket and gives it to him.*] Here it is.

TESMAN. Splendid. Then I'll go in. [*Looks around.*] Oh—I mustn't forget my slippers. Ah, here they are.

[*Takes the parcel and starts to go.*

HEDDA. Mind you write him a nice friendly letter, George, and a good long one too.

TESMAN. I most certainly will.

THEA. But don't let him know that I suggested it!

TESMAN. Of course not! That goes without saying, eh?

[*He goes out right, through the inner room.*

HEDDA. [*Smilingly goes to Mrs Elvsted and says in a low voice*] There! Now we've killed two birds with one stone.

THEA. What do you mean?

HEDDA. Couldn't you see that I wanted to get rid of him?

THEA. Yes, to write the letter.

HEDDA. And so that I could talk to you alone.

THEA. [*Bewildered.*] About the same thing?

HEDDA. Precisely.

THEA. [*Apprehensively.*] But there's nothing else to tell, Mrs Tesman. Absolutely nothing.

HEDDA. Of course there is. I can see that. There's a great *deal* more to tell. Come along. Sit down. We'll have a nice friendly talk.

[*She forces Mrs Elvsted down into the armchair by the stove and seats herself on one of the tabourets.*]

THEA. [*Anxiously looking at her watch.*] But really, Mrs Tesman, I was just thinking of going——

HEDDA. Oh, you can't be in such a hurry. Come along now—I want to know all about your life at home.

THEA. I prefer not to speak about that.

HEDDA. But to me, dear! After all, we went to school together.

THEA. Yes, but you were in a higher class, and I was always so dreadfully afraid of you then.

HEDDA. Afraid of me!

THEA. Yes, dreadfully. When we met on the stairs you always used to pull my hair.

HEDDA. Did I really?

THEA. Yes. And once you said you were going to burn it all off.

HEDDA. I was just teasing you of course!

THEA. I was so silly in those days, and afterwards we drifted so far apart. We lived in such different worlds. . . .

HEDDA. Well, then we must drift together again. At school we always called each other by our first names. Why shouldn't we now?

THEA. I think you're mistaken——

HEDDA. Of course not. I remember it distinctly. We were *great* friends! [*Draws her stool near to Mrs Elvsted and kisses her on the cheek.*] So you must call me Hedda.

THEA. [*Pressing her hands and patting them.*] You're so kind and understanding. I'm not used to kindness.

HEDDA. And I shall call you my darling little Thora.

THEA. My name is Thea.

HEDDA. Yes, yes, of course, I meant Thea! [*Looking at her*

compassionately.] So my darling little Thea—you mean they're not kind to you at home?

THEA. If only I had a home! But I haven't. I never had one.

HEDDA. [*Gives her a quick look.*] I suspected something of the sort.

THEA. [*Gazing helplessly before her.*] Ah!

HEDDA. Tell me, Thea—I'm a little vague about it. When you first went to the Elvsteds' you were engaged as housekeeper, weren't you?

THEA. I was supposed to go as governess, but Mrs Elvsted—the first Mrs Elvsted, that is—was an invalid and rarely left her room, so I had to take charge of the house as well.

HEDDA. And eventually you became mistress of the house?

THEA. [*Sadly.*] Yes, I did.

HEDDA. How long ago was that?

THEA. That I married him?

HEDDA. Yes.

THEA. Five years ago.

HEDDA. Yes, that's right.

THEA. Oh, those five years, especially the last two or three of them —if only you knew, Mrs Tesman!

HEDDA. [*Slaps her lightly on the hand.*] Mrs Tesman! Thea!

THEA. I'll try—you have no idea, Hedda——

HEDDA. [*Casually.*] Eilert Løvborg's lived near you about three years, hasn't he?

THEA. [*Looks at her doubtfully.*] Eilert Løvborg? Why, yes, he has.

HEDDA. Had you met him before, here in town?

THEA. No, not really—I knew him by his name, of course.

HEDDA. But I suppose up there you saw a good deal of him.

THEA. Yes, he came to our house every day. He gave the children lessons, you see. I had so much to do; I couldn't manage that as well.

HEDDA. No. Of course not. And I suppose your husband's away from home a good deal.

THEA. Yes. Being sheriff, he often has to travel about his district.

HEDDA. [*Leans against the arm of the chair.*] Now, my dear darling little Thea, I want you to tell me everything—exactly as it is.

THEA. Well, then you must question me.

HEDDA. Tell me—what sort of a man is your husband, Thea? To live with, I mean. Is he kind to you?

THEA. [*Evasively.*] He probably thinks he is.

HEDDA. But isn't he much too old for you, dear? There must be at least twenty years between you.

THEA. [*Irritably.*] Yes, that makes it all the harder. We haven't a thought in common. Nothing, in fact.

HEDDA. But I suppose he's fond of you in his own way.

THEA. Oh, I don't know. I think he finds me useful. And then it doesn't cost much to keep me. I'm not expensive.

HEDDA. That's stupid of you.

THEA. [*Shakes her head.*] It couldn't be otherwise. Not with him. I don't believe he really cares about anyone but himself. And perhaps a little for the children.

HEDDA. And for Eilert Løvborg, Thea?

THEA. [*Looking at her.*] Eilert Løvborg? What makes you say that?

HEDDA. Well, it's obvious!—After all, he's sent you all this way into town, simply to look for him!—[*With the trace of a smile.*] Wasn't that what you told George?

THEA. [*With a nervous twitch.*] Yes, I suppose I did. [*Vehemently but in a low voice*] Oh, I might as well tell you the truth. It's bound to come out sooner or later.

HEDDA. What——?

THEA. Well then—my husband knew nothing about my coming here.

HEDDA. Your husband didn't know!

THEA. No, of course not. He was away himself at the time. I couldn't stand it any longer, Hedda. I simply couldn't. I felt so alone, so deserted——

HEDDA. Yes, yes—well?

THEA. So I packed a few of my things—just those I needed most— I didn't say a word to anyone. I simply left the house.

HEDDA. Just like that!

THEA. Yes, and took the next train to town.

HEDDA. But, Thea, my darling! How did you dare do such a thing?

THEA. [*Rises and walks about the room.*] What else could I possibly do?

HEDDA. But what will your husband say when you go home again?

THEA. [*At the table, looks at her.*] Back to him!

HEDDA. Well, of course.

THEA. I shall never go back to him again.

HEDDA. [*Rises and goes towards her.*] You mean you've actually left your home for *good*?

THEA. I saw nothing else to do.

HEDDA. But to leave like that, so openly——

THEA. You can't very well *hide* a thing like that!

HEDDA. But what will people say about you, Thea?

THEA. They can say whatever they like. [*Sits on the sofa wearily and sadly.*] I only did what I had to do.

HEDDA. [*After a short silence.*] What are your plans now?

THEA. I don't know yet. All I know is that I must live near Eilert Løvborg, if I'm to live at all.

HEDDA. [*Takes a chair from the table, sits down near Mrs Elvsted and strokes her hands.*] Tell me, Thea—how did this friendship start between you and Eilert Løvborg?

THEA. It grew gradually. I began to have a sort of power over him.

HEDDA. Really?

THEA. Yes. After a while he gave up his old habits. Oh, not because I asked him to—I never would have dared do that. But I suppose he realized how unhappy they made me, and so he dropped them.

HEDDA. [*Concealing a scornful smile.*] So, my darling little Thea, you've actually reformed him!

THEA. Well, *he* says so, at any rate, and in return he's made a human being out of me. Taught me to think and understand so many things.

HEDDA. Did he give you lessons too then?

THEA. Not lessons, exactly, but he talked to me, explained so much to me—and the most wonderful thing of all was when he finally allowed me to share in his work. Allowed me to help him.

HEDDA. He did, did he?

THEA. Yes. He wanted me to be a part of everything he wrote.

HEDDA. Like two good comrades!

THEA. [*Brightly.*] Comrades! Why, Hedda, that's exactly what *he* says! I ought to be so happy, but somehow I'm not. I'm so afraid it may not last.

HEDDA. You're not very sure of him, then?

THEA. [*Gloomily.*] I sometimes feel a shadow between Løvborg and me—a woman's shadow.

HEDDA. [*Looks at her intently.*] Who could that be?

THEA. I don't know. Someone he knew long ago. Someone he's never been able to forget.

HEDDA. Has he told you anything about her?

THEA. He spoke of her once—quite vaguely.

HEDDA. What did he say?

THEA. He said that when they parted she threatened to shoot him.

HEDDA. [*With cold composure.*] What nonsense! No one does that sort of thing here!

THEA. I know. That's why I think it must have been that red-haired cabaret singer he was once——

HEDDA. Very likely.

THEA. They say she used to go about with loaded pistols.

HEDDA. Then of course it must have been she.

THEA. [*Wringing her hands.*] But, Hedda, they say she's here now—in town again! I'm so worried I don't know what to do!

HEDDA. [*With a glance towards inner room.*] Sh! Here comes Tesman. Not a word to him. All this is between us.

THEA. [*Jumps up.*] Yes, yes, of course.

[*George Tesman, a letter in his hand, enters from the right through the inner room.*

TESMAN. Well, here is the letter signed and sealed!

HEDDA. Splendid! Mrs Elvsted was just leaving, George. Wait a minute! I'll go with you as far as the garden gate.

TESMAN. Do you think Berta could post this for me, dear?

HEDDA. [*Takes the letter.*] I'll tell her to.   [*Berta enters from the hall.*

BERTA. Judge Brack wishes to know if you will see him, ma'am.

HEDDA. Yes. Show him in. And post this letter, will you?

BERTA. [*Taking the letter.*] Certainly, ma'am.

[*She opens the door for Judge Brack and goes out. The Judge is a man of forty-five. Thick-set but well built and supple in his movements. His face is rounded and his profile aristocratic. His short hair is still almost black and carefully dressed. His eyes are bright and sparkling. His eyebrows thick. His moustache also thick with short-cut ends. He wears a smart walking-suit, slightly youthful for his age. He uses an eyeglass, which he lets drops from time to time.*

BRACK. [*Bowing, hat in hand.*] May one venture to call so early in the day?

HEDDA. Of course one may.

TESMAN. [*Shakes hands with him.*] You know you're always welcome. [*Introduces him.*] Judge Brack, Miss Rysing.

HEDDA. Ah!

BRACK. [*Bows.*] Delighted.

HEDDA. [*Looks at him and laughs.*] What fun to have a look at you by daylight, Judge.

BRACK. Do you find me—altered?

HEDDA. A little younger, I think.

BRACK. [*Laughs and goes down to fireplace.*] I thank you, most heartily.

TESMAN. But what do you say to Hedda, eh? Doesn't she look flourishing? She's positively——

HEDDA. For heaven's sake, leave me out of it, George! You'd far better thank Judge Brack for all the trouble he's taken.

BRACK. Oh, don't mention it. It was a pleasure, I assure you.

HEDDA. Yes, you're a loyal soul; but I mustn't keep Mrs Elvsted waiting. Excuse me, Judge. I'll be back directly.

   [*Exchange of greetings. Mrs Elvsted and Hedda go out through the hall door.*

BRACK. Well, I hope your wife's pleased with everything.

TESMAN. We really can't thank you enough. Of course she wants to rearrange things a bit, and she talks of buying a few additional trifles.

BRACK. Is that so?

TESMAN. But you needn't bother about that. Hedda will see to that herself. Why don't we sit down, eh?

BRACK. [*Sits at table.*] Thanks. Just for a moment—there's something I must talk to you about, my dear Tesman.

TESMAN. Yes, the expenses, eh? [*Sits down.*] I suppose it's time we got down to business.

BRACK. Oh, that's not so very pressing. Though perhaps it would have been wiser to be a bit more economical.

TESMAN. But that would have been out of the question. You know Hedda, Judge. After all, she's been used to a certain standard of living——

BRACK. Yes, that's just the trouble.

TESMAN. Fortunately it won't be long before I receive my appointment.

BRACK. Well, you see—such things sometimes hang fire.

TESMAN. Have you heard anything further, eh?

BRACK. Nothing really definite. [*Interrupts himself.*] But, by the way, I have one bit of news for you.

TESMAN. Well?

BRACK. Your old friend Eilert Løvborg is back in town.

TESMAN. I've heard that already.

BRACK. Really? Who told you?

TESMAN. That lady who went out with Hedda.

BRACK. Oh yes, what was her name? I didn't quite catch it.

TESMAN. Mrs Elvsted.

BRACK. Oh yes, the sheriff's wife. Of course. Løvborg's been living near them these past few years.

TESMAN. And, just think, I'm delighted to hear he's quite a reformed character.

BRACK. Yes, so they say.

TESMAN. And he's published a new book, eh?

BRACK. Indeed he has.

TESMAN. I hear it's made quite a sensation.

BRACK. A most unusual sensation.

TESMAN. Think of that. I'm delighted to hear it. A man of such extraordinary gifts. I felt so sorry to think he'd gone completely to rack and ruin!

BRACK. Well—everybody thought so.

TESMAN. I wonder what he'll do now—how on earth will he manage to make a living?

[*During these last words Hedda has re-entered by the hall door.*

HEDDA. [*To Brack with a scornful laugh.*] Isn't that just like Tesman, Judge? Always worrying about how people are going to make their living.

TESMAN. We were just talking about Eilert Løvborg, dear.

HEDDA. [*Giving him a quick glance. Seats herself in the armchair by the stove and asks casually.*] What's the matter with him?

TESMAN. That money he inherited—he's undoubtedly squandered that long ago. And he can't very well write a new book every year, eh? So why shouldn't I wonder what's to become of him?

BRACK. Perhaps I can give you some information on the subject.

TESMAN. Indeed?

BRACK. You must remember that his relatives have a great deal of influence.

TESMAN. But they washed their hands of him long ago.

BRACK. At one time he was considered the hope of the family.

TESMAN. At one time, perhaps. But he soon put an end to that.

HEDDA. Who knows? [*With a slight smile.*] I hear they've quite reformed him up at the Elvsteds'.

BRACK. And then there's his new book of course.

TESMAN. Yes, that's true. Let's hope things will turn out well for him. I've just written him a note. I asked him to come and see me this evening, Hedda dear.

BRACK. But you're coming to my stag party this evening. You promised me last night on the pier.

HEDDA. Had you forgotten, Tesman?

TESMAN. Yes, I really had.

BRACK. In any case, I think you can be pretty sure he won't come.

TESMAN. Why shouldn't he?

BRACK. [*With a slight hesitation, rises and leans against the back of the chair.*] My dear Tesman, and you, too Mrs Tesman, I think it's only right that I should inform you of something that——

TESMAN. That concerns Eilert, eh?

BRACK. Yes, you as well as him.

TESMAN. [*Jumps up anxiously.*] But, my dear Judge, what is it?

BRACK. I think you should be prepared to find your appointment deferred—rather longer than you desired or expected.

TESMAN. Has anything happened to prevent it, eh?

BRACK. The nomination may depend on the result of a competition.

TESMAN. A competition! Think of that, Hedda. But who would my competitor be? Surely not——?

BRACK. Yes. Eilert Løvborg. Precisely.

       [*Hedda leans farther back in the armchair with an ejaculation.*

TESMAN. No, no! It's impossible! It's utterly inconceivable, eh?

BRACK. It may come to that, all the same.

TESMAN. But, Judge Brack, this would be incredibly unfair to me. [*Waving his arms.*] Just think, I'm a married man! We married on these prospects, Hedda and I. Think of the money we've spent, and we've borrowed from Aunt Julia too! Why, they practically promised me the appointment, eh?

BRACK. Don't get so excited. You'll probably get the appointment all the same, only you'll have to compete for it.

HEDDA. [*Sits motionless in the armchair.*] Just think, George, it will have quite a sporting interest.

TESMAN. Dearest Hedda, how can you be so indifferent about it?

HEDDA. [*As before.*] Indifferent! I'm not in the least indifferent. I can hardly wait to see which of you will win.

BRACK. In any case I thought it better to warn you, Mrs Tesman! Perhaps under the circumstances, you'd better go easy on those 'additional trifles' you're thinking of buying.

HEDDA. I don't see how this could possibly make any difference, my dear Judge.

BRACK. Really? Then I've no more to say. Goodbye. I'll call for you later on my way back from my afternoon walk.

TESMAN. Yes, yes—I'm so upset—my head's in a whirl!

HEDDA. [*Still reclining holds out her hand to him.*] I shall hope to see you later, Judge.

BRACK. Thank you, Mrs Tesman. Goodbye.

TESMAN. [*Accompanies him to the door.*] Goodbye, my dear Judge. You really must excuse me——

[*Judge goes out by the hall door.*

TESMAN. [*Pacing the room.*] Oh, Hedda, Hedda, one should never rush into adventures, eh?

HEDDA. [*Looks at him and smiles.*] Do you do that, George?

TESMAN. What else can you call it? To get married and settle down on mere expectations, eh?

HEDDA. You may be right.

TESMAN. Well, at least we have our lovely home, Hedda, eh? The home we both dreamt of.

HEDDA. [*Rises slowly and wearily.*] I'd counted on doing a lot of entertaining. That was part of the agreement, I thought. We were to keep open house.

TESMAN. I'd been so looking forward to it, Hedda dear. To see you, a brilliant hostess, surrounded by distinguished guests—well, we'll just have to make the best of it for the time being, dear. Be happy in one another. We can always invite Aunt Julia in now and then. But I wanted it to be so different for you, Hedda. So very different.

HEDDA. I suppose this means I'll have to do without my butler.

TESMAN. Yes, I'm afraid a butler is quite out of the question!

HEDDA. You promised me a saddle-horse, remember? I suppose *that*'s out of the question too?

TESMAN. I'm afraid so, Hedda.

HEDDA. [*Walks about the room.*] Well, at least I have one thing to amuse myself with.

TESMAN. [*Beaming.*] Thank heaven for that. What is it, Hedda, eh?

HEDDA. [*At centre opening—looks at him with suppressed scorn.*] My pistols, George.

TESMAN. Your pistols!

HEDDA. [*With cold eyes.*] General Gabler's pistols.

[*She goes out through the inner room to the left.*

TESMAN. [*Rushes to the centre opening and calls after her.*] Oh, Hedda, darling, please don't touch those dangerous things. For my sake, Hedda, eh?

END OF ACT I

ACT II

The room at the Tesmans' as in the first act. Only the piano has been removed and replaced by an elegant little writing-table with bookshelves. A smaller table has been placed by the sofa left. Most of the bouquets have been removed. Mrs Elvsted's bouquet stands on the large table downstage. It is afternoon.

Hedda, dressed to receive callers, is alone in the room. She stands by the open glass door loading a pistol. The matching pistol lies in an open pistol case on the writing-table.

HEDDA. [*Looks down into the garden and calls out.*] Welcome back, Judge!

BRACK. [*Is heard calling below at a distance.*] Thank you, Mrs Tesman.

HEDDA. [*Raises the pistol and takes aim.*] Now, I'm going to shoot you, Judge!

BRACK. [*From below.*] No, no, don't aim at me like that!

HEDDA. That's what you get for sneaking in the back way. [*She fires.*]

BRACK. [*Nearer.*] Have you gone quite mad?

HEDDA. So sorry. Did I hit you by any chance?

BRACK. [*Still from outside.*] I wish you'd stop all this nonsense.

HEDDA. Come along, Judge, I'll let you pass.

[*Judge Brack, dressed as for a men's party, comes in through the glass door. Over his arm he carries a light overcoat.*

BRACK. So you're still fooling with those pistols. What are you shooting at?

HEDDA. Just killing time. Shooting up into the blue.

BRACK. [*Gently takes the pistol out of her hand.*] Allow me. [*Examines it.*] H'm . . . I know this pistol . . . I've seen it before. [*Looks around.*] Where's the case for it? Ah, here! [*Places the pistol in its case and closes it.*] So that game is finished for today.

HEDDA. What in heaven's name am I to do with myself all day long!

BRACK. Haven't you had any visitors?

HEDDA. [*Closing the glass door.*] Not one. I suppose all our friends are still out of town.

26

BRACK. Isn't Tesman home?

HEDDA. [*At the writing-table. Putting the pistol case away in a drawer.*] No. He rushed off to his aunts' directly after lunch. He didn't expect you so early, Judge.

BRACK. Fancy my not thinking of that—That was stupid of me.

HEDDA. [*Turns her head and looks at him.*] Why stupid?

BRACK. Because I should have come even earlier.

HEDDA. [*Crossing the room.*] Then you'd have found no one to receive you, for I've been dressing ever since lunch.

BRACK. But isn't there a little crack in the door through which one might converse?

HEDDA. No. You forgot to provide one, Judge.

BRACK. Again stupid of me.

HEDDA. We must just sit here and wait until Tesman comes. He may not be back for some time.

BRACK. Never mind. I shan't be impatient.

[*Hedda sits in the corner of the sofa. Brack lays his overcoat over the back of the nearest chair and sits down, but keeps his hat in his hand. A short pause. They look at each other.*

HEDDA. Well?

BRACK. [*In the same tone.*] Well?

HEDDA. I spoke first.

BRACK. [*Slightly bending forward.*] Let's have a really pleasant little talk, Mrs—Hedda.

HEDDA. [*Leaning farther back on the sofa.*] It seems ages since our last one, doesn't it, Judge? Of course I don't count the few words we had last night and this morning.

BRACK. I know—you mean a *real* talk. Just a 'twosome'.

HEDDA. Yes, that's it.

BRACK. Every single day I've wished you were home again.

HEDDA. I've wished that too.

BRACK. You have? Really, Mrs Hedda? And I thought you were having such a good time on your journey.

HEDDA. Ha!

BRACK. Tesman's letters led me to think so.

HEDDA. Oh well, Tesman! You know Tesman, my dear Judge! His idea of bliss is grubbing about in a lot of dirty bookshops and making endless copies of antiquated manuscripts.

BRACK. [*With a touch of malice.*] Well, after all, that's his vocation in life, you know. Or a large part of it.

HEDDA. Yes, if it's one's vocation, I suppose that makes it different, but as for me! Oh, my dear Judge, I can't tell you how bored I've been!

BRACK. [*Sympathetically.*] Are you really serious?

HEDDA. Of course. Surely you can understand? How would *you* like to spend six whole months without meeting a soul you could really talk to?

BRACK. I shouldn't like it at all.

HEDDA. But the most unendurable thing of all was——

BRACK. What?

HEDDA. To be everlastingly with one and the same person.

BRACK. [*With a nod of agreement.*] Morning, noon and night, at all possible times.

HEDDA. I said 'everlastingly'.

BRACK. But with our good Tesman, I should have thought one might——

HEDDA. Tesman is a specialist, my dear Judge.

BRACK. Undeniably.

HEDDA. And specialists are not amusing travelling companions—not for long, at any rate.

BRACK. Not even the specialist you happen to love?

HEDDA. Ugh! Don't use that revolting word!

BRACK. [*Startled.*] What? What's that, Mrs Hedda?

HEDDA. [*Half laughing, half in irritation.*] Just you try it! Nothing but the history of civilization morning, noon and night.

BRACK. Everlastingly.

HEDDA. And then all this business about the domestic industries of Brabant during the Middle Ages. That's the most maddening part of it all.

BRACK. [*Looks at her searchingly.*] But, tell me, in that case, how did it happen that you——?

HEDDA. Married Tesman, you mean? Is there anything so very odd in that?

BRACK. Both yes and no, Mrs Hedda.

HEDDA. I had danced myself tired, my dear Judge—and I wasn't getting any younger. [*With a slight shudder.*] But I won't talk about that. I won't even think about it.

BRACK. You certainly have no cause.

HEDDA. [*Watching him intently.*] And one must admit that George Tesman is a thoroughly worthy man.

BRACK. A worthy, dependable man. There can be no question of that.

HEDDA. And I don't see anything especially—*funny* about him, do you?

BRACK. Funny? No-o—not really. No, I wouldn't say that.

HEDDA. After all, he's a distinguished scholar. Who knows? He may still go far.

BRACK. [*Looks at her uncertainly.*] I thought you believed like everyone else that some day he'd become a really famous man.

HEDDA. [*In a tired voice.*] Yes, so I did. And then since he was so absolutely bent on supporting me, I really didn't see why I shouldn't accept his offer.

BRACK. No, if you look at it from that point of view——

HEDDA. Well, that was more than some of my other admirers were prepared to do, my dear Judge.

BRACK. [*Laughs.*] I can't answer for the others, of course. You know that, generally speaking, I have a great respect for the state of matrimony, but I confess that, as an individual——

HEDDA. [*Jokingly.*] I never had any hopes as far as you were concerned.

BRACK. All I ask of life is to know a few people intimately. A few nice people whom I can help and advise, in whose houses I can come and go as a trusted friend.

HEDDA. Of the—master of the house, you mean?

BRACK. [*With a bow.*] Well, preferably, of the mistress. But of the master too of course! I find such a triangular friendship, if I may call it so, a great convenience to all concerned.

HEDDA. Yes, God knows, a third person would have been welcome on our journey. Oh, those infernal tête-à-têtes!

BRACK. Cheer up! Your wedding trip is over now.

HEDDA. [*Shaking her head.*] Not by a long shot. No, we've only stopped at a station on the line.

BRACK. Then the thing to do is to jump out and stretch oneself a bit, Mrs Hedda.

HEDDA. I never jump out.

BRACK. Why not?

HEDDA. There's always someone there waiting to——

BRACK. [*Laughing.*] Stare at your legs, you mean?

HEDDA. Precisely.

BRACK. Well, good heavens——

HEDDA. [*With a gesture of distaste.*] I don't like that sort of thing. I'd rather keep my seat and continue the tête-à-tête.

BRACK. But if a third person were to jump *in* and join the couple?

HEDDA. Ah! But *that* 's quite a different thing!

BRACK. A trusted, understanding friend.

HEDDA. Gay and entertaining in a variety of ways?

BRACK. And not a bit of a specialist.

HEDDA. [*With an audible sigh.*] That would certainly be a great relief!

BRACK. [*Hears the front door open and glances in that direction.*] The triangle is completed.

HEDDA. [*In a half-tone.*] And on goes the train.

[*George Tesman enters from the hall. He wears a grey walking-suit and a soft felt hat. He carries a great number of paper-bound books under his arm and in his pockets.*

TESMAN. [*Goes up to the table beside the corner sofa.*] Pooh! It's a warm job to carry all these books, Hedda. [*Puts them down.*] I'm positively perspiring! [*Hedda makes a scarcely audible ejaculation:* '*How charming, George!*' *Tesman puts some of the books down on the table.*] Oh, you're here already, Judge. Berta didn't tell me.

BRACK. [*Rising.*] I came in through the garden.

HEDDA. What are all those books, George?

TESMAN. [*Thumbing through the books.*] They're some new books on my special subject. I simply had to have them.

HEDDA. Your special subject, George?

BRACK. On his special subject, Mrs Tesman.

[*Brack and Hedda exchange a confidential smile.*

HEDDA. Do you need still more books on your special subject, George?

TESMAN. One can never have too many, Hedda. One *must* keep up with all the new publications.

HEDDA. Yes, I suppose one must.

TESMAN. [*Searching among the books.*] Look, I got Eilert Løvborg's new book, too. [*Offers it to her.*] Would you care to have a look at it, Hedda, eh?

HEDDA. No, thank you—well, perhaps a little later, George.

TESMAN. I glanced through it on my way home.

BRACK. What do you think of it? As a specialist, I mean.

TESMAN. He handles his subject with the greatest restraint. That is what struck me most. It's quite remarkable. He never wrote like that before. [*Gathers the books together.*] I'll just take these into my study. I'm longing to cut the leaves. And then I suppose I'd better change, though we needn't go just yet, eh?

BRACK. Oh, no. There's not the slightest hurry.

TESMAN. Then I'll take my time. [*Starts to go out with the books but stops and turns at centre opening.*] Oh, by the way, Hedda, Aunt Julia is afraid she can't come to see you this evening.

HEDDA. Oh? Why not? Is she still annoyed about the hat?

TESMAN. Of course not. That wouldn't be a bit like her! No, but you see Aunt Rina's very ill.

HEDDA. She always is.

TESMAN. Yes, but today she's worse than ever, poor thing!

HEDDA. Then she'll need her sister with her. That's only natural. I shall have to try and bear it.

TESMAN. I can't tell you how delighted Aunt Julia was to see you looking so well, so positively flourishing.

HEDDA. [*In a half-tone, rising.*] Oh, those eternal aunts!

TESMAN. What did you say, dear?

HEDDA. [*Going to the glass door.*] Nothing. Nothing. Nothing!

TESMAN. Very well, Hedda—eh?

[*He goes out right, through the inner room.*

BRACK. What was that you said about a hat?

HEDDA. Oh, it was just something that happened this morning. Miss Tesman had taken off her hat and put it down on the table. [*Looks at him and smiles.*] And I pretended to think it was the servant's.

BRACK. [*Shakes his head.*] Why, my dear Mrs Hedda. How could you do such a thing to that nice old lady?

HEDDA. [*Walks nervously about the room.*] My dear Judge, I really don't know. I suddenly get impulses like that and I simply can't control them. [*Flings herself down in the armchair by the stove.*] I don't know how to explain it myself.

BRACK. [*Behind the armchair.*] You're not really happy. I think that's the explanation.

HEDDA. [*Gazing straight before her.*] I can't imagine why I should be—happy? Can you tell me?

BRACK. Well, to begin with; here you are, in the very house you always longed to live in.

HEDDA. [*Looks up at him and laughs.*] You really believe in that fairy-tale?

BRACK. Wasn't it true, then?

HEDDA. I'll tell you how it happened: last summer I made use of
  Tesman to see me home from parties.

BRACK. Unfortunately my way lay in a different direction.

HEDDA. Yes, you were going in a different direction then, weren't
  you, Judge?

BRACK. [*Laughs.*] Shame on you, Mrs Hedda! And so you and
  Tesman——?

HEDDA. Well, one evening we happened to pass by this house.
  Tesman, poor thing, was turning and twisting and couldn't
  think of anything to say. I really felt sorry for the poor learned
  wretch.

BRACK. [*Smiles sceptically.*] Sorry! You!

HEDDA. Yes, I really did. I felt sorry for him. And so just to make
  conversation, to help him out a bit, I was foolish enough to say
  what a charming house this was, and how I should love to live
  in it.

BRACK. No more than that?

HEDDA. Not *that* evening.

BRACK. But afterwards?

HEDDA. Afterwards! Afterwards my foolishness was not without
  consequences, my dear Judge.

BRACK. Yes. Unfortunately, that happens all too often.

HEDDA. Thanks! So you see it was this fictitious enthusiasm for
  Secretary Falk's villa that really brought Tesman and me
  together. It was the immediate cause of our engagement, our
  wedding, our wedding journey and all the rest of it. Well, my
  dear Judge, they say as you make your bed, so you must lie.

BRACK. This is really priceless! So I suppose you didn't really care
  a rap about the house?

HEDDA. No, God knows I didn't!

BRACK. Still, now that we've made it so attractive and comfortable
  for you——

HEDDA. To me it smells of lavender and dried rose leaves. What
  might be called the 'Aunt Julia atmosphere'.

BRACK. [*Laughs.*] No. That's probably a legacy from the late Mrs
  Falk.

HEDDA. Yes! Yes, you're right! There is a touch of decay about it.
  [*She clasps her hands behind her head, leans back in the chair and looks
  at him*]. Oh, my dear Judge, my dear Judge! How incredibly I
  shall bore myself here!

BRACK. Why shouldn't you too find some sort of vocation in life, Mrs Hedda?

HEDDA. A vocation—that would attract me?

BRACK. Preferably, yes.

HEDDA. God only knows what kind of a vocation that would be! I often wonder whether—— [*Breaks off.*] But that wouldn't be any good either.

BRACK. What? Tell me.

HEDDA. I was wondering whether I could get George to go into politics.

BRACK. [*Laughs.*] Tesman? No, really! I'm afraid political life would be the last thing in the world for him.

HEDDA. I know you're probably right; but I could try and get him into it all the same.

BRACK. But what satisfaction would it be to you unless he were successful at it? Why should you want to drive him into it?

HEDDA. Because I'm *bored*, I tell you. [*After a pause.*] So you think it quite out of the question for George to become—let's say— Secretary of State?

BRACK. Ha, ha! Mrs Hedda. You must remember, apart from anything else, to become anything of that sort he'd have to be a fairly rich man.

HEDDA. [*Rises impatiently.*] There you are. Money! Always money! [*Crosses the room.*] It's this genteel poverty that makes life so hideous, so utterly ludicrous.

BRACK. Now I should say the fault lies elsewhere.

HEDDA. Where then?

BRACK. I don't believe you've ever really been stirred by anything in life.

HEDDA. Anything serious, you mean?

BRACK. If you like. But I expect it will come.

HEDDA. [*Tossing her head.*] If you're thinking about that ridiculous professorship, that's George's own affair. I assure you I shan't give a thought to that!

BRACK. I dare say. But suppose you should suddenly find yourself faced with what's known in solemn language, as a grave responsibility—[*smiling*] a *new* responsibility, Mrs Hedda.

HEDDA. [*Angrily.*] Be quiet! Nothing of that sort will ever happen to me.

BRACK. [*Cautiously.*] We'll talk of this again a year from now, at the very latest.

HEDDA. [*Curtly.*] That sort of thing doesn't appeal to me, Judge. I'm not fitted for it. No responsibilities for me!

BRACK. What makes you think you're less fitted than the majority of women? Why should you deliberately turn away from duties——?

HEDDA. [*At the glass door.*] Be quiet, I tell you! I sometimes think there's only one thing in this world I'm really fitted for.

BRACK. [*Nearer to her.*] What's that, if I may ask?

HEDDA. [*Looking out.*] Boring myself to death! Now you know it. [*Turns, looks towards the inner room, and laughs.*] Ah! I thought so— here comes the professor!

BRACK. [*Softly, warningly.*] Now, now, Mrs Hedda!

[*George Tesman, dressed for the party, his gloves and hat in his hands, enters from the right through the inner room.*

TESMAN. Oh, Hedda, has any message come from Eilert, eh?

HEDDA. No.

TESMAN. Then he'll be here presently, you'll see.

BRACK. You really think he'll come?

TESMAN. I'm almost sure of it. What you told us this morning was probably just a rumour.

BRACK. Do you think so?

TESMAN. At any rate, Aunt Julia didn't believe for a moment that he would ever stand in my way again. Think of that!

BRACK. Well, then, there's nothing to worry about.

TESMAN. [*Puts his hat and gloves down on a chair, right.*] I'd like to wait for him as long as possible though.

BRACK. We've plenty of time. My guests won't arrive before seven or half past.

TESMAN. Meanwhile we can keep Hedda company and see what happens, eh?

HEDDA. [*Puts Brack's overcoat and hat on the corner sofa.*] And if the worst comes to the worst, Mr Løvborg can spend the evening with me.

BRACK. What do you mean by 'the worst'?

HEDDA. I mean—if he refuses to go with you and Tesman.

TESMAN. [*Looks at her dubiously.*] But, Hedda, dear, do you think it would be quite the thing for him to stay here with you, eh? Remember, Aunt Julia isn't coming.

HEDDA. No, but Mrs Elvsted is. We three can have a cup of tea together.

TESMAN. Oh well, then it would be *quite* all right.

BRACK. [*Smiling.*] It might perhaps be the best thing for him too.

HEDDA. Why the 'best thing', Judge?

BRACK. Well you know how rude you are about my stag parties, Mrs Tesman. You always say they're only safe for men of the strictest principles.

HEDDA. I'm sure Mr Løvborg's principles are strict enough now. A converted sinner—

[*Berta appears at the hall door.*

BERTA. There's a gentleman asking to see you, ma'am.

HEDDA. Oh yes—show him in.

TESMAN. [*Softly.*] It must be Eilert. Think of that!

[*Eilert Løvborg enters from the hall. He is slim and lean. The same age as Tesman, he looks older, as though worn out by life. Hair and beard dark brown; a long pale face, but with patches of colour on the cheekbones; he wears a well-cut black visiting suit, obviously new. He carries dark gloves and a silk hat. He stands near the door and makes a rapid bow. He seems slightly embarrassed.*

[*Goes to him and shakes him by the hand.*] Welcome, my dear Eilert. So at last we meet again!

LØVBORG. [*Speaking in a hushed voice.*] Thanks for your letter, George. [*Approaches Hedda.*] May I shake hands with you, too, Mrs Tesman?

HEDDA. [*Takes his hand.*] How do you do, Mr Løvborg, I'm delighted to see you. [*She motions with her hand.*] I don't know if you two gentlemen——

LØVBORG. [*With a slight bow.*] Judge Brack, I believe.

BRACK. [*Bows likewise.*] Yes, I've had the pleasure, some years ago.

TESMAN. [*To Løvborg, with his hands on his shoulders.*] And now, Eilert, you must make yourself at home, mustn't he, Hedda? I hear you're going to settle in town again, eh?

LØVBORG. Yes, I am.

TESMAN. Well, that's splendid. I just got your new book, Eilert, but I haven't had time to read it yet.

LØVBORG. I wouldn't bother to, if I were you.

TESMAN. Why, what do you mean?

LØVBORG. It's pretty thin stuff.

TESMAN. Just think! How can you say that?

BRACK. It's been enormously praised, I hear.

LØVBORG. That was exactly what I wanted, so I put nothing in it that anyone could take exception to.

BRACK. Very wise of you.

TESMAN. But my dear Eilert——

LØVBORG. You see, I'm determined to make a fresh start; to win a real position for myself.

TESMAN. [*Slightly embarrassed.*] Oh, so that's what you plan to do, eh?

LØVBORG. [*Smiles, puts down his hat, and takes a parcel wrapped in paper from his coat pocket.*] But when this one appears, George Tesman, you'll have to read it, for this is a real book. Every ounce of my true self is in this.

TESMAN. Really! What's it about?

LØVBORG. It's the sequel.

TESMAN. Sequel! Sequel of what?

LØVBORG. Of the other book.

TESMAN. You mean, the new one?

LØVBORG. Yes, of course.

TESMAN. But, my dear Eilert, surely that comes right down to our time, doesn't it?

LØVBORG. Yes, but this deals with the future.

TESMAN. With the future. But good heavens, we know nothing about the future!

LØVBORG. There's a thing or two to be said about it all the same. [*Opens the parcel.*] Look here——

TESMAN. That's not your handwriting.

LØVBORG. No, I dictated it. [*Thumbs through the pages.*] It falls into two sections. The first deals with the civilizing forces of the future and the second [*turning to the pages towards the end*] forecasts the probable lines of development.

TESMAN. How remarkable! I should have never thought of writing anything of that sort.

HEDDA. [*At the glass door, drumming on the pane.*] No, I dare say not.

LØVBORG. [*Puts the manuscript back in its wrapping and lays it on the table.*] I brought it with me; I thought I might read you a bit of it this evening.

TESMAN. That was very kind of you, Eilert, but this evening—— [*Glancing at Brack.*] I don't see how we can manage it——

LØVBORG. Well, then some other time. There's no hurry.

BRACK. The fact is, Mr Løvborg, I'm giving a little party this evening to celebrate Tesman's return.

LØVBORG. [*Looking for his hat.*] Oh, then I mustn't detain you.

BRACK. No, but wait. I'd be delighted if you would give me the pleasure of your company.

LØVBORG. [*Curtly and decisively.*] I'm sorry. I can't. Thank you very much.

BRACK. Oh, nonsense! Do come. We shall be quite a select little circle, and I can assure you, we shall have a 'jolly time' as Mrs Hed—Mrs Tesman puts it.

LØVBORG. I don't doubt that, but nevertheless——

BRACK. And you could bring your manuscript with you and read it to Tesman at my house. I could give you a room all to yourselves.

TESMAN. Yes, think of that, Eilert. Why shouldn't you do that, eh?

HEDDA. [*Interposing.*] But, George dear, if Mr Løvborg says he doesn't want to go, I'm sure Mr Løvborg would much prefer to stay here and have supper with me.

LØVBORG. [*Looking at her.*] With you, Mrs Tesman?

HEDDA. Mrs Elvsted will be here too.

LØVBORG. Oh. [*Casually.*] I saw her for a moment today.

HEDDA. Oh, did you? Well, she's spending the evening here. So you see, you're almost obliged to stay, Mr Løvborg. Otherwise Mrs Elvsted will have no one to see her home.

LØVBORG. That's true. Many thanks. In that case, I will stay, Mrs Tesman.

HEDDA. Splendid! I'll just give one or two orders to the servant.
    [*She goes to the hall door and rings. Berta enters. Hedda talks to her in a whisper and points to the inner room. Berta nods and goes out.*

TESMAN. [*During the above, to Eilert Løvborg.*] Tell me, Eilert, is it this new subject, the future, that you are going to lecture about?

LØVBORG. Yes.

TESMAN. They told me at the book store that you were planning a series of lectures.

LØVBORG. Yes, I am. I hope you've no objection.

TESMAN. No, of course not, but——

LØVBORG. I can quite see that it might interfere with your plans.

TESMAN. [*Depressed.*] I can't very well expect you, out of consideration for *me*, to——

LØVBORG. But, of course, I'll wait until you receive your appointment.

TESMAN. What! You'll wait! Then—then you're not going to compete with me, eh?

LØVBORG. No. I only want people to realize that I *could* have—a sort of moral victory, if you like.

TESMAN. Why bless my soul, then Aunt Julia was right after all! I was sure of it. Hedda, just think, Eilert is not going to stand in our way!

HEDDA. [*Curtly.*] Our way! Do please leave me out of it, George.
[*She goes up towards the inner room where Berta is arranging a tray with decanters and glasses on the table. Hedda nods approvingly and comes forward again. Berta goes out.*

TESMAN. [*During the above.*] What do you say to this, Judge, eh?

BRACK. Well, I say a moral victory may be all very fine but——

TESMAN. Yes, certainly, but all the same——

HEDDA. [*Looks at Tesman with a cold smile.*] You stand there looking absolutely thunderstruck, George.

TESMAN. Well, you know, I almost believe I am.

HEDDA. [*Pointing to the inner room.*] And now, gentlemen, won't you have a glass of cold punch before you go?

BRACK. [*Looks at his watch.*] A sort of stirrup cup, you mean. Yes, that's not a bad idea.

TESMAN. A capital idea, Hedda. Just the thing. Now that a heavy weight has been lifted off my mind——

HEDDA. You'll join them, Mr Løvborg?

LØVBORG. [*With a gesture of refusal.*] No, thank you, nothing for me.

BRACK. Why, surely, cold punch is not poison.

LØVBORG. Perhaps not for everyone.

HEDDA. Well, then, you two go in and I'll sit here and keep Mr Løvborg company.

TESMAN. Yes, do, Hedda, dear.
[*He and Brack go into the inner room, sit down, drink punch, smoke cigarettes, and carry on an animated conversation during the following. Eilert Løvborg remains standing by the stove. Hedda goes to the writing-table.*

HEDDA. [*In a raised voice.*] Perhaps you'd like to look at some snapshots, Mr Løvborg. You know, Tesman and I did some sightseeing in the Tyrol, on our way home. I'd so love to show you——

[*She brings over an album which she lays on the table by the sofa, in the farther corner of which she seats herself. Eilert Løvborg approaches, then stops and stands looking at her. He then takes a chair and sits on her left with his back to the inner room.*

[*She opens the album.*] Do you see this group of mountains, Mr Løvborg? It's the Ortlar group. Oh yes, Tesman has written the name underneath: 'The Ortlar group near Meran.'

LØVBORG. [*Who has never taken his eyes off her, says softly and slowly.*] Hedda Gabler——

HEDDA. [*Gives him a hasty look.*] Sh!

LØVBORG. [*Repeats softly.*] Hedda Gabler——

HEDDA. [*Looking at the album.*] That was my name in the old days, when you and I knew each other.

LØVBORG. Then I must learn never to say Hedda Gabler again? Never as long as I live?

HEDDA. [*Turning over the pages.*] Yes, I'm afraid you must.

LØVBORG. [*In an indignant tone.*] Hedda Gabler married! And married to George Tesman!

HEDDA. Such is life!

LØVBORG. Oh, Hedda, Hedda, how could you throw yourself away like that?

HEDDA. [*Looks at him sharply.*] I won't have you say such things.

LØVBORG. Why shouldn't I?

[*Tesman comes into the room and goes towards the sofa.*

HEDDA. [*Hears him coming and says in a casual tone.*] And this, Mr Løvborg, is a view from the Ampezzodalen. Just look at those peaks. [*Looks up at Tesman affectionately.*] Oh, George dear, what's the name of these curious peaks?

TESMAN. Let me see—oh, those are the Dolomites.

HEDDA. Oh yes, those are the Dolomites, Mr Løvborg.

TESMAN. Hedda dear, are you sure you wouldn't like me to bring some punch? For yourself, at any rate, eh?

HEDDA. Yes, I think I will have some, dear. And perhaps a few biscuits.

TESMAN. A cigarette?

HEDDA. No, I think not, dear.

TESMAN. Very well.

[*He goes into the inner room again and out to the right. Brack sits in the inner room, occasionally keeping an eye on Hedda and Løvborg.*

LØVBORG. [*Softly as before.*] Answer me, Hedda. How could you do it?

HEDDA. [*Apparently absorbed in the album.*] If.you go on calling me Hedda, I won't talk to you.

LØVBORG. Can't I say Hedda even when we're alone?

HEDDA. No. You may think it, but you mustn't say it.

LØVBORG. I understand. It offends your love for George Tesman.

HEDDA. [*Glances at him and smiles.*] Love? How funny you are!

LØVBORG. It's not love, then?

HEDDA. All the same, no unfaithfulness, remember.

LØVBORG. Hedda, answer me just one thing.

HEDDA. Sh!

[*Tesman comes from the inner room carrying a small tray.*

TESMAN. Here you are! Doesn't this look tempting!

[*He puts the tray down on the table.*

HEDDA. Why do you bring it yourself, George?

TESMAN. [*Filling the glasses.*] I think it's such fun to wait on you, Hedda.

HEDDA. But you've poured out two glasses. Mr Løvborg said he wouldn't have any.

TESMAN. I know. But Mrs Elvsted will be here soon, won't she?

HEDDA. Oh yes, of course, Mrs Elvsted——

TESMAN. Have you forgotten her, eh?

HEDDA. Yes, you know we were so engrossed in these photographs. Oh, George dear, do you remember this little village?

TESMAN. Yes, of course I do. It's the one just below the Brenner Pass. Don't you remember? We spent the night there.

HEDDA. Oh yes. And met that gay party of tourists.

TESMAN. Yes, that was the place. Just think, if only we could have had you with us, Eilert, eh?

[*He goes back to the inner room and sits down with Judge Brack.*

LØVBORG. Answer me this one thing, Hedda.

HEDDA. Well?

LØVBORG. Was there no love in your feeling for *me*, either? Not the slightest touch of love?

HEDDA. I wonder. To me it seems that we were just two good comrades, two thoroughly intimate friends. [*Smiles.*] You especially were exceedingly frank!

LØVBORG. It was you who made me so.

HEDDA. You know, as I look back on it all I realize there was something very beautiful, something fascinating, something daring—yes, daring—in that secret intimacy, that comradeship no living soul suspected.

LØVBORG. Yes, there was, wasn't there, Hedda? Do you remember when I used to come to your home in the afternoon and the General sat over at the window reading his paper, with his back towards us——

HEDDA. We two sat on the corner sofa——

LØVBORG. Always the same illustrated paper before us——

HEDDA. For want of an album, yes!

LØVBORG. Do you remember, Hedda, all those wild things I confessed to you? Things no one suspected at this time—my days and nights of passion and frenzy, of drinking and madness—— How did you make me talk like that, Hedda? By what power?

HEDDA. Power?

LØVBORG. Yes. How else can one explain it? And all those devious questions you used to ask——

HEDDA. Questions you understood so perfectly——

LØVBORG. How could you bring yourself to ask such questions? So candidly, so boldly?

HEDDA. In a devious way, if you please.

LØVBORG. Yes, but boldly, all the same.

HEDDA. How could you bring yourself to answer them, Mr Løvborg?

LØVBORG. That's just what I can't understand. There must have been love at the bottom of it. Perhaps you felt that by making me confess like that you were somehow washing away my sins.

HEDDA. No, not quite.

LØVBORG. What was your motive then?

HEDDA. Isn't it quite easy to understand, that a young girl, especially if it can be done in secret——

LØVBORG. Well?

HEDDA. Should be tempted to investigate a forbidden world—a world she's supposed to know nothing about?

LØVBORG. So that was it.

HEDDA. That had a lot to do with it, I think.

LØVBORG. I see; we were both greedy for life. That made us comrades. But why did it end?

HEDDA. You were to blame for that!

LØVBORG. You broke with me.

HEDDA. I realized the danger; you wanted to spoil our intimacy—
to drag it down to reality. You talk of my boldness, my candour
—why did you try to abuse them?

LØVBORG. [*Clenching his hands.*] Why didn't you do as you said?
Why didn't you shoot me?

HEDDA. Because . . . I have such a fear of scandal.

LØVBORG. Yes, Hedda, you are a coward at heart.

HEDDA. A terrible coward. [*With a change of tone.*] But after all, it
was a lucky thing for you. You found ample consolation at the
Elvsteds'.

LØVBORG. I know Thea has confided in you.

HEDDA. And I suppose you've confided in her—about us?

LØVBORG. Not a word. She's too stupid to understand that.

HEDDA. Stupid?

LØVBORG. About that sort of thing—yes.

HEDDA. And I am a coward. [*Leans towards him, without looking him
in the eye, says softly.*] Now I'll confide something to you.

LØVBORG. [*Intensely.*] Well?

HEDDA. My not daring to shoot you——

LØVBORG. Yes?

HEDDA. That was not my greatest cowardice that evening.

LØVBORG. [*Looks at her a moment, understands, and whispers passionately.*] Oh, Hedda, Hedda Gabler! I begin to understand the real
meaning of our comradeship. You and I!—— You see, it *was*
your craving for life——

HEDDA. [*Softly, with a keen look.*] Be careful! Believe nothing of the
sort. [*It has begun to get dark. The hall door is opened by Berta.*]
[*Hedda closes the album with a bang and calls out smiling*] At last!
Thea darling! [*Mrs Elvsted enters from the hall. She is in evening
dress. The door is closed behind her. Hedda, still on the sofa, stretches
out her arms towards her.*] Darling little Thea, I thought you were
never coming!

[*In passing, Mrs Elvsted lightly greets the gentlemen in the inner
room, then goes to the table and gives Hedda her hand. Eilert
Løvborg rises. He and Mrs Elvsted greet each other with a silent
nod.*

THEA. Shouldn't I go and say good evening to your husband?

HEDDA. [*Puts her arm round Thea and leads her towards sofa.*] No, we
needn't bother about them. I expect they'll soon be off.

THEA. Are they going out?

HEDDA. Yes. To a wild party!

THEA. [*Quickly. To Løvborg.*] You're not going, are you?

LØVBORG. No.

HEDDA. No. Mr Løvborg is staying here with us.

[*Løvborg sits down again on the sofa.*

THEA. [*Takes a chair and starts to sit beside him.*] Oh, how nice it is to be here!

HEDDA. No, no, little Thea, not there! You be a good girl and sit here, next to me. I'll sit between you.

THEA. Just as you like.

[*She goes round the table and sits on the sofa to Hedda's right. Løvborg sits down again.*

LØVBORG. [*To Hedda, after a short pause.*] Isn't she lovely to look at?

HEDDA. [*Lightly stroking her hair.*] Only to look at?

LØVBORG. We're two real comrades, she and I. We have absolute faith in each other. We can talk with perfect frankness.

HEDDA. Not in a devious way, Mr Løvborg.

LØVBORG. Well——

THEA. [*Softly, clinging to Hedda.*] Oh, I'm so happy, Hedda! You know—he actually says I've inspired him in his work.

HEDDA. [*Looks at her and smiles.*] Does he really, dear?

LØVBORG. And then she has such courage, Mrs Tesman.

THEA. Good heavens, courage!

LØVBORG. Tremendous courage where your comrade is concerned.

HEDDA. God, yes, courage! If one only had that!

LØVBORG. What then?

HEDDA. Then life might perhaps be endurable, after all. . . . [*With a sudden change of tone.*] Now, my darling little Thea, you must have a nice glass of cold punch.

THEA. No, thank you. I never take anything like that.

HEDDA. Then how about you, Mr Løvborg?

LØVBORG. I don't either, thank you.

THEA. No, he doesn't either.

HEDDA. [*Looks at him intently.*] But if I want you to.

LØVBORG. It makes no difference.

HEDDA. [*Laughs.*] Poor me! Have I no power over you at all then?

LØVBORG. Not in that respect.

HEDDA. No, but seriously. I really think you ought to take it for your own sake.

THEA. Why, Hedda——

LØVBORG. How do you mean?

HEDDA. People might begin to suspect that you weren't quite sure, quite confident of yourself.

THEA. [*Softly.*] Don't, Hedda.

LØVBORG. People may suspect whatever they like.

THEA. [*Happily.*] Yes, let them.

HEDDA. You should have seen Judge Brack's face a moment ago. . . .

LØVBORG. Indeed?

HEDDA. His contemptuous smile when you didn't dare join them in there.

LØVBORG. Didn't dare! I simply preferred to stay here and talk to you.

THEA. That's natural enough, Hedda.

HEDDA. That's not what Judge Brack thought. You should have seen him smile and look at Tesman when you didn't dare go to his ridiculous little party.

LØVBORG. Didn't dare! You say I didn't dare!

HEDDA. No, *I* don't say it—but that's how Judge Brack looks at it.

LØVBORG. Well, let him.

HEDDA. So you're not going with them?

LØVBORG. No, I'm staying here with you and Thea.

THEA. Yes, Hedda, of course he is.

HEDDA. [*Smiles and nods approvingly to Løvborg.*] There, you see! Firm as a rock. Faithful to all good principles now and for ever. That's how a man should be. [*Turns to Mrs Elvsted and says with a caress*] What did I tell you this morning, Thea? Didn't I tell you not to be upset?

LØVBORG. [*Amazed.*] Upset?

THEA. [*Terrified.*] Hedda——! *Please*, Hedda!

HEDDA. You see? Now are you convinced? You haven't the slightest reason to be so anxious and worried. . . . There! Now we can all three enjoy ourselves.

LØVBORG. [*With a start.*] What does all this mean, Mrs Tesman?

THEA. Oh, God! What are you doing, Hedda?

HEDDA. Be careful! That horrid Judge is watching you.

LØVBORG. So you were anxious and worried on my account?

THEA. [*Softly, miserably.*] Oh, Hedda, you've ruined everything.

LØVBORG. [*Looks at her intently for a moment. His face is distorted.*] Well, my comrade! So that's all your faith amounts to!

THEA. [*Imploringly.*] You *must* listen to me, Eilert——

LØVBORG. [*Takes one of the glasses of punch, and says in a low, hoarse voice*] Your health, Thea!

        [*He empties the glass, puts it down, and takes the second one.*

THEA. [*Softly.*] Hedda, Hedda, how could you do this?

HEDDA. I do it? I? Are you crazy?

LØVBORG. And your health too, Mrs Tesman. Thanks for the truth. Long live the truth!

        [*He empties the glass and is about to fill it again.*

HEDDA. [*Lays her hand on his arm.*] There, there! No more for the present. You're going to the party, remember.

LØVBORG. [*Putting down the glass.*] Now, Thea, be honest with me.

THEA. Yes?

LØVBORG. Did your husband know you came after me?

THEA. [*Wringing her hands.*] Eilert! . . .

LØVBORG. It was arranged between you, wasn't it, that you should come to town and keep an eye on me. I dare say the old man suggested it himself. No doubt he needed my help in the office. Or perhaps it was at the card table he missed me.

THEA. [*Softly, in great distress.*] Eilert! Eilert!

LØVBORG. [*Seizes the glass and is about to fill it.*] Let's drink to the old sheriff too!

HEDDA. [*Preventing him.*] No more now. Remember you're going to read your manuscript to George.

LØVBORG. [*Calmly, putting down the glass.*] I'm behaving like a fool, Thea. Try and forgive me, my dear, dear comrade. You'll see—I'll prove to you—I'll prove to everyone, that I'm all right again. I'm back on my feet. Thanks to you, Thea.

THEA. [*Radiant.*] Oh, thank God!

    [*In the meantime Brack has looked at his watch. He and Tesman rise and come into the drawing-room.*

BRACK. [*Takes up his hat and overcoat.*] Well, Mrs Tesman, it's time to go.

HEDDA. I suppose it is, Judge.

LØVBORG. [*Rising.*] I've decided to join you, Judge.

THEA. [*Softly, imploringly.*] Oh, Løvborg, don't!

HEDDA. [*Pinching her arm.*] Sh! They'll hear you.

LØVBORG. [*To Brack.*] Since you were kind enough to invite me.

BRACK. You've changed your mind?

LØVBORG. Yes, if you don't mind.

BRACK. I'm delighted.

LØVBORG. [*Putting the manuscripts in his pocket, to Tesman.*] I should like to show you one or two things before the manuscript goes to press.

TESMAN. Just think, how delightful! But, Hedda dear, in that case, how is Mrs Elvsted to get home?

HEDDA. Oh, we shall manage somehow.

LØVBORG. [*Looking towards the ladies.*] Mrs Elvsted? Of course, I'll come back and fetch her. [*Comes nearer.*] Around ten o'clock, Mrs Tesman, Will that do?

HEDDA. That will be splendid, Mr Løvborg.

TESMAN. Well, then that's settled. But you mustn't expect me so early, Hedda.

HEDDA. Oh, you can stay as long as you like, George.

THEA. [*With suppressed anxiety.*] Well then, Mr Løvborg, I'll wait here till you come.

LØVBORG. [*With his hat in his hand.*] That's understood, Mrs Elvsted.

BRACK. Well, gentlemen, shall we start? I hope we're going to have a very jolly time, as a certain fair lady puts it.

HEDDA. If only the fair lady could be there, unseen, Judge.

BRACK. Why unseen?

HEDDA. So as to share a little in your unbridled fun.

BRACK. [*Laughs.*] I shouldn't advise the fair lady to try it.

TESMAN. [*Also laughing.*] Come. You're a nice one, Hedda. Think of that!

BRACK. Well, goodbye. Goodbye, ladies!

LØVBORG. [*Bowing.*] About ten o'clock then.

HEDDA. Yes, Mr Løvborg!

> [*Brack, Løvborg and Tesman go out by the hall door. Simultaneously Berta comes in from the inner room with a lighted lamp which she puts on the drawing-room table; she goes out again through the inner room.*

THEA. [*Who has risen and paces restlessly about the room.*] Hedda, what will come of all this!

HEDDA. At ten o'clock he will be here, with vine leaves in his hair. Flushed and fearless!

THEA. If I could only believe that——

HEDDA. And then, you see, he will have regained confidence in himself. He'll be a free man for ever and ever.

THEA. Pray God you may be right.

HEDDA. I am right! It will be as I say. [*Rises and approaches her.*] Doubt him as much as you like. I believe in him. Now we shall see——

THEA. You have some hidden reason for all this, Hedda.

HEDDA. Yes, I have. For once in my life I want the power to shape a human destiny.

THEA. But surely, you have that?

HEDDA. I haven't. I never have had.

THEA. But what about your husband?

HEDDA. Do you think he's worth bothering about! If you could only understand how poor I am; and that you should be allowed to be so rich! [*She flings her arms round her passionately.*] I think I shall have to burn your hair off after all!

THEA. Let me go! Let me go! I'm afraid of you, Hedda!

BERTA. [*At the centre opening.*] Supper's ready, ma'am.

HEDDA. Very well, we're coming.

THEA. No, no! I'd rather go home alone. Now—at once!

HEDDA. Nonsense! You'll do nothing of the sort, you silly little thing. You'll have some supper and a nice cup of tea and then at ten o'clock Eilert Løvborg will be here with vine leaves in his hair—— [*She almost drags Mrs Elvsted towards the centre opening.*

END OF ACT II

The room at the Tesmans'. The portières of the centre opening are closed as well as the curtains of the glass door. The shaded lamp on the table is turned low. In the stove, of which the door stands open, there has been a fire which is now nearly burnt out.

Mrs Elvsted, wrapped in a large shawl, reclines in the armchair close to the stove with her feet on a footstool. Hedda lies asleep on the sofa, covered with a rug.

THEA. [*After a pause, suddenly straightens up in her chair and listens eagerly. Then she sinks back wearily and says softly and plaintively*] Not yet. Oh, God! Oh, God! Not yet——

    [*Berta slips cautiously in by the hall door. She has a letter in her hand.*

THEA. [*Turns and whispers eagerly.*] Did someone come?

BERTA. [*Softly.*] A girl just brought this letter, ma'am.

THEA. [*Quickly, stretching out her hand.*] A letter! Give it to me!

BERTA. It's for Dr Tesman, ma'am.

THEA. Oh.

BERTA. Miss Tesman's maid brought it. I'll just put it on the table.

THEA. Yes, do.

BERTA. [*Puts down the letter.*] I think I'd better put out the lamp, ma'am.

THEA. You might as well—it must be nearly daylight.

BERTA. [*Puts out the lamp.*] It *is* daylight, ma'am.

THEA. So it is! Broad daylight—and no one's come home yet!

BERTA. Lord bless you, ma'am—I thought something like this would happen.

THEA. You did?

BERTA. Yes—when I saw them go off with a—certain gentleman, last night—we used to hear plenty about him in the old days.

THEA. Sh! Not so loud! You'll wake Mrs Tesman——

BERTA. [*Looks towards the sofa and sighs.*] Yes, you're right—let her sleep, poor thing. Shall I make up the fire, ma'am?

THEA. Thank you—you needn't trouble——

BERTA. Very well, ma'am.   [*She goes out softly by the hall door.*

HEDDA. [*Wakes at the closing of the door and looks up.*] What—what was that?

THEA. It was just the maid——

HEDDA. [*Looks round her.*] What are we doing in here? Oh yes! Now I remember! [*She sits up on the sofa, stretches herself, and rubs her eyes.*] What's the time, Thea?

THEA. [*Looks at her watch.*] It's past seven.

HEDDA. When did George get home?

THEA. He hasn't come.

HEDDA. Not home yet?

THEA. [*Rising.*] No one has come.

HEDDA. And we were fools enough to sit up half the night—watching and waiting!

THEA. [*Wringing her hands.*] And waiting in such terrible anxiety!

HEDDA. [*Yawns, and says with her hand in front of her mouth*] Well— we might have spared ourselves the trouble.

THEA. Did you manage to get a little sleep?

HEDDA. Yes, I believe I slept quite well—didn't you?

THEA. I couldn't, Hedda—I couldn't possibly!

HEDDA. [*Rises and goes towards her.*] There, there! There's nothing to worry about! It's easy to see what's happened.

THEA. What—tell me!

HEDDA. Brack's party probably dragged on for hours——

THEA. I expect that's true, but still——

HEDDA. —and probably Tesman didn't want to come home and wake me up in the middle of the night—perhaps he was in no condition to show himself, after the famous party.

THEA. But where could he have gone?

HEDDA. To his aunts', of course! I expect he went there to sleep it off. They always keep his old room ready for him.

THEA. No, he can't be there. That letter just came for him, from Miss Tesman.

HEDDA. Letter? [*Looks at the address.*] Oh yes! It's from Aunt Julia. Well—then I suppose he stayed at Judge Brack's. As for Eilert Løvborg—he is sitting with vine leaves in his hair, reading his manuscript.

THEA. You're talking nonsense, Hedda! You know you don't believe a word of it——

HEDDA. What a little ninny you are, Thea!

THEA. Yes, I'm afraid I am——

HEDDA. And how dreadfully tired you look!

THEA. I am—dreadfully tired.

HEDDA. Now you do exactly as I tell you! You go into my room—lie down on the bed—and get a little rest.

THEA. No, no! I'd never be able to sleep.

HEDDA. Of course you would.

THEA. Besides, your husband should be back soon; I must find out at once——

HEDDA. I'll tell you the moment he arrives——

THEA. You promise, Hedda?

HEDDA. Yes—you can count on me. Go on in now, and have a good sleep.

THEA. Thanks—I will try. 　　　[*She goes out through the inner room.*

　　[*Hedda goes to the glass door and opens the curtains. Bright daylight streams into the room. She takes a small mirror from the writing-table, looks at herself in it, and tidies her hair. Then she goes to the hall door and rings the bell. A few moments later Berta appears at the hall door.*

BERTA. Did you ring, ma'am?

HEDDA. Yes—do something to the fire—I'm absolutely frozen.

BERTA. Certainly, ma'am—I'll make it up at once. [*She rakes the embers together and puts on a piece of wood. She stops and listens.*] That was the front door, ma'am.

HEDDA. See who it is—I'll look after the fire.

BERTA. It'll soon burn up, ma'am.

　　[*She goes out by the hall door. Hedda kneels on the footstool and puts several pieces of wood in the stove. After a short pause George Tesman comes in from the hall. He looks tired and rather serious. He tiptoes up towards the centre opening and is about to slip through the curtains.*

HEDDA. [*At the stove, without looking up.*] Good morning, George!

TESMAN. [*Turns.*] Hedda! [*Approaches her.*] Good heavens—are you up so early, eh?

HEDDA. Yes, I'm up very early today, George.

TESMAN. And I was sure you'd still be sound asleep—think of that, Hedda!

HEDDA. Sh! Don't talk so loud. You'll wake Mrs Elvsted.

TESMAN. Did Mrs Elvsted stay here all night?

HEDDA. Naturally—since no one came to call for her.

TESMAN. No—I suppose not——

HEDDA. [*Closes the stove door and rises.*] Well—did you enjoy your-selves?

TESMAN. Were you worried about me, Hedda, eh?

HEDDA. That would never occur to me—I asked if you'd enjoyed yourselves?

TESMAN. Yes, we really did, Hedda. Especially at first—you see, Eilert read me part of his book. We got there quite early, think of that—and Brack had all sorts of arrangements to make, so Eilert read to me.

HEDDA. [*Sits to the right of table.*] Yes? Well?

TESMAN. [*Sits on a stool near the stove.*] Hedda, you can't conceive what a book it will be! I believe it's one of the most remarkable things that have ever been written. Think of that!

HEDDA. I'm really not very interested, George.

TESMAN. I've something to confess, Hedda—after he'd finished reading, I had such a horrid feeling——

HEDDA. A horrid feeling, George?

TESMAN. Yes. I felt quite jealous of Eilert, because he'd been able to write such a book. Just think, Hedda.

HEDDA. Yes, yes! I *am* thinking!

TESMAN. It's really appalling that he, with all his great gifts, should be so utterly incorrigible!

HEDDA. Because he has more daring than any of the rest of you?

TESMAN. It's not that, Hedda—he's utterly incapable of moderation.

HEDDA. Well—tell me what happened.

TESMAN. There's only one word to describe it, Hedda—it was an orgy!

HEDDA. Did he have vine leaves in his hair?

TESMAN. Vine leaves? No, I didn't see any vine leaves—but he made a long incoherent speech in honour of the woman who had inspired him in his work—that was the phrase he used.

HEDDA. Did he mention her name?

TESMAN. No, he didn't. But I can't help thinking he meant Mrs Elvsted—just you see!

HEDDA. Where did you part?

TESMAN. When the party finally broke up—there were only a few of us left—so we came away together. Brack came with us too—he wanted a breath of fresh air; and then we decided we had better take Eilert home—he was in pretty bad shape, you see.

HEDDA. Yes, I dare say.

TESMAN. And then, the strangest thing happened, Hedda—the most tragic thing! I'm really almost ashamed to tell you about it—for Eilert's sake——

HEDDA. Oh, do go on, George!

TESMAN. Well—as we were nearing town, you see—I happened to drop a little behind the others—only for a minute or two—think of that!

HEDDA. Yes, yes! Well?

TESMAN. And then, as I hurried after them, what do you think I found on the sidewalk, eh?

HEDDA. How should I know?

TESMAN. You mustn't say a word about it to anyone, Hedda—do you hear? Promise me—for Eilert's sake.

HEDDA. Yes, George!

TESMAN. [*Takes a parcel wrapped in paper from his pocket.*] Just think, dear—I found this.

HEDDA. Isn't that the parcel he had with him yesterday?

TESMAN. Yes. It's his precious, irreplaceable manuscript. He had lost it, and hadn't even noticed it. Isn't it tragic, Hedda, that——

HEDDA. Why didn't you give it back to him at once?

TESMAN. I didn't dare trust him with it, in the condition he was in.

HEDDA. Did you tell any of the others you'd found it?

TESMAN. Certainly not! I didn't want them to know—for Eilert's sake, you see.

HEDDA. Then no one knows that Eilert Løvborg's manuscript is in your possession?

TESMAN. No—and no one must know it.

HEDDA. What did you say to him afterwards?

TESMAN. I didn't get a chance to talk to him again; he and two or three of the others gave us the slip and disappeared—think of that!

HEDDA. I suppose they took him home then.

TESMAN. Yes, I suppose they did—and Brack went home too.

HEDDA. And where have you been gallivanting ever since?

TESMAN. Someone suggested we should go back to his house and have an early breakfast there—or perhaps it should be called a late supper—eh? And now—as soon as I have had a little rest and poor Eilert has had a chance to recover himself a bit—I must take this back to him.

HEDDA. [*Stretching out her hand for the parcel.*] No, George—don't give it back to him—not right away, I mean. Let me read it first.

TESMAN. No, dearest Hedda, I daren't do that. I really dare not.

HEDDA. You dare not, George?

TESMAN. Think of the state he'll be in when he wakes up and can't find his manuscript! There's no copy of it, Hedda—think of that! He told me so himself.

HEDDA. [*Looks at him searchingly.*] Tell me, George—would it be quite impossible to write such a thing over again?

TESMAN. Oh, I should think so, Hedda. You see, it's the inspiration. . . .

HEDDA. Yes, of course—the inspiration. . . . I suppose it depends on that. [*Lightly.*] By the way, George, here's a letter for you.

TESMAN. Just think——

HEDDA. [*Hands it to him.*] It came just a little while ago.

TESMAN. It's from Aunt Julia, Hedda! What can it be? [*He puts the parcel down on the other stool, opens the letter, glances through it, and jumps up.*] Oh, Hedda—she says Aunt Rina is dying, poor thing.

HEDDA. Well—we were expecting that.

TESMAN. And that I must hurry, if I want to see her again—I'll just run over and see them at once.

HEDDA. [*Suppressing a smile.*] Will you run, George?

TESMAN. Oh, my dearest Hedda—if you could only bring yourself to come with me! Just think!

HEDDA. [*Rising. Rejects the idea wearily.*] No, no! Don't ask me to do that! I'll have nothing to do with sickness or death. I loathe anything ugly.

TESMAN. Well then, in that case—— [*Rushing about.*] My hat? My overcoat? Oh, in the hall. I do hope I won't be too late, Hedda —eh?

HEDDA. Well, after all—if you run, George——!

[*Berta enters by the hall door.*

BERTA. Judge Brack is here, sir—and wishes to know if you'll see him?

TESMAN. At this hour? No, no! I can't possibly——

HEDDA. But I'll see him. [*To Berta.*] Ask him to come in, Berta.

[*Berta goes.*

[*Rapidly, in a whisper*] George—the manuscript!

[*She snatches it up from the stool.*

TESMAN. Yes, give it to me!

HEDDA. No, no. I'll keep it here till you come back.

[*She goes over to the writing-table and puts it in the bookcase. Tesman in a frenzy of haste can't get his gloves on. Brack enters from the hall.*

HEDDA. [*Nodding to him.*] You're certainly an early bird, Judge.

BRACK. I am, aren't I? [*To Tesman.*] Where are you off to in such a hurry?

TESMAN. I must rush off to my aunts'. Just think, Aunt Rina is dying, poor thing.

BRACK. Dear me, is she? Then don't let me detain you; every moment may be precious.

TESMAN. Yes, I really must run—goodbye, goodbye, Hedda——

[*He rushes out by the hall door.*

HEDDA. [*Approaching Brack.*] I hear the party was more than usually jolly last night, Judge.

BRACK. Yes, I've been up all night—haven't even changed my clothes.

HEDDA. So I see——

BRACK. What has Tesman told you of last night's adventures?

HEDDA. Oh, nothing much; some dreary tale about going to someone's house and having breakfast.

BRACK. Yes, I've heard about that breakfast party—but Eilert Løvborg wasn't with them, was he?

HEDDA. No—he'd been escorted home.

BRACK. By Tesman, you mean?

HEDDA. No—by some of the others.

BRACK. [*Smiling.*] George Tesman is certainly a naïve creature, Mrs Hedda.

HEDDA. Yes, God knows he is! But, you're very mysterious— what else happened last night?

BRACK. Oh, a number of things——

HEDDA. Do sit down, Judge, and tell me all about it! [*She sits to the left of the table. Brack sits near her, at the long side of the table.*] Well?

BRACK. I had special reasons for keeping an eye on my guests—or rather some of my guests—last night.

HEDDA. One of them being Eilert Løvborg, I suppose.

BRACK. Frankly—yes.

HEDDA. This sounds quite thrilling, Judge!

BRACK. Do you know where he and some of the others spent the rest of the night?

HEDDA. No. Do tell me—if it's not quite unmentionable!

BRACK. No. It's by no means unmentionable. Well—they turned up at an extremely gay party.

HEDDA. A *very* jolly party, Judge?

BRACK. An excessively jolly one!

HEDDA. Do go on!

BRACK. Løvborg, as well as the others, had been invited some time ago. I knew all about it. But he had refused the invitation, for he had become a reformed character, as you know——.

HEDDA. At the Elvsteds', yes. But he went all the same?

BRACK. Well, you see, Mrs Hedda, he became somewhat inspired at my place last night——

HEDDA. Yes. I heard he was . . . inspired.

BRACK. Rather violently inspired, in fact—and so, he changed his mind. We men are not always as high principled as perhaps we should be.

HEDDA. I'm sure you are an exception, Judge. But to get back to Eilert Løvborg——

BRACK. So—to make a long story short—he did finally turn up at Mademoiselle Diana's residence.

HEDDA. Mademoiselle Diana?

BRACK. Yes, it was she who was giving the party—to a very select circle of her friends and admirers.

HEDDA. Is she that red-haired woman?

BRACK. Precisely.

HEDDA. A sort of . . . singer?

BRACK. Yes—in her leisure moments. She is also a mighty huntress —of men. You must have heard of her, Mrs Hedda. In the days of his glory Eilert Løvborg was one of her most enthusiastic protectors.

HEDDA. But how did all this end, Judge?

BRACK. In a none-too-friendly fashion, it seems. After greeting him most tenderly, Mademoiselle finally proceeded to tear his hair out!

HEDDA. What? Løvborg's?

BRACK. Yes. It seems he accused her, or her friends, of having robbed him. He kept insisting some valuable notebook had disappeared—as well as various other things. In short, he raised quite a terrific row.

HEDDA. What did all this lead to?

BRACK. It led to a general free-for-all, in which the women as well as the men took part. Fortunately the police at last appeared on the scene.

HEDDA. The police?

BRACK. Yes. I'm afraid it may prove an expensive amusement for Eilert Løvborg—crazy lunatic that he is!

HEDDA. How?

BRACK. They say he made a violent resistance—half killed one policeman, and tore another one's coat off his back. So they marched him off to the police station.

HEDDA. Where did you hear all this?

BRACK. From the police themselves.

HEDDA. [*Gazing straight before her.*] So that's what happened! Then, after all, he had no vine leaves in his hair!

BRACK. Vine leaves, Mrs Hedda?

HEDDA. [*With a change of tone.*] Tell me, Judge—why should you be so interested in spying on Løvborg in this way?

BRACK. In the first place—I am not entirely indifferent to the fact that during the investigation it will be known that he came directly from my house.

HEDDA. You mean, the case will go to court?

BRACK. Naturally. However—be that as it may. But I felt it my duty, as a friend of the family, to give you and Tesman a full account of his nocturnal exploits.

HEDDA. For what reason, Judge?

BRACK. Because I have a shrewd suspicion that he means to use you as a sort of . . . screen.

HEDDA. Whatever makes you think that?

BRACK. After all—we're not completely blind, Mrs Hedda. You watch! This Mrs Elvsted—she'll be in no great hurry to leave town.

HEDDA. Well—supposing there were something between them—there must be plenty of other places where they could meet.

BRACK. Not a single *home*. From now on, every respectable house will be closed to Eilert Løvborg.

HEDDA. And mine ought to be too, you mean?

BRACK. Yes. I admit it would be more than painful to me if he should be welcome here. If this undesirable and superfluous person should be allowed to force his way into the——

HEDDA. —the triangle?

BRACK. Precisely. It would simply mean that I should find myself homeless.

HEDDA. [*Looks at him with a smile.*] I see. So you want to be cock-of-the-walk, Judge. That is your aim.

BRACK. [*Nods slowly and speaks in a low voice*] Yes—that is my aim; and for that I will fight with every weapon I can command.

HEDDA. [*Her smile vanishing.*] I wonder, Judge, now one comes to think of it, if you're not rather a dangerous person.

BRACK. Do you think so?

HEDDA. I'm beginning to think so. And I'm exceedingly glad that you have no sort of hold over me.

BRACK. [*Laughs ambiguously.*] Well, well, Mrs Hedda—perhaps you're right. If I had, who knows what I might be capable of?

HEDDA. Come now! Come, Judge! That sounds almost like a threat.

BRACK. [*Rising.*] Not at all! For the triangle, it seems to me, ought, if possible, to be based on mutual understanding.

HEDDA. There I entirely agree with you.

BRACK. Well—now I've said all I had to say—I'd better be off. Goodbye, Mrs Hedda.   [*Crossing towards the glass door.*

HEDDA. [*Rising.*] Are you going through the garden, Judge?

BRACK. Yes, it's a short cut for me.

HEDDA. Yes—and then it's the back way, isn't it?

BRACK. Very true; I've no objection to back ways. They are rather intriguing at times.

HEDDA. When there's shooting going on, you mean?

BRACK. [*At the glass door, laughingly.*] People don't shoot their tame poultry, I fancy.

HEDDA. [*Also laughing.*] And certainly not the cock-of-the-walk, Judge! Goodbye!——

[*They exchange laughing nods of farewell. He goes. She closes the glass door after him. Hedda, now serious, stands looking out. She goes up and peeps through the portières into the inner room. Then goes to the writing-table, takes Løvborg's parcel from the bookcase, and is about to examine it. Berta is heard speaking loudly in the hall. Hedda turns and listens. She hurriedly locks the parcel in the drawer and puts the key on the inkstand. Eilert Løvborg, wearing his overcoat and carrying his hat in his hand, tears open the hall door. He looks somewhat confused and excited.*

LØVBORG. [*Turns towards the hall.*] I will go in, I tell you!

[*He closes the door, turns, sees Hedda, at once controls himself and bows.*

HEDDA. [*At the writing-table.*] Well, Mr Løvborg! Isn't it rather late to call for Thea?

LØVBORG. And rather early to call on you—forgive me.

HEDDA. How do you know Thea's still here?

LØVBORG. They told me at her lodgings, she'd been out all night.

HEDDA. [*Goes to the table.*] Did you notice anything odd in their manner when they told you that?

LØVBORG. [*Looks at her inquiringly.*] Anything odd?

HEDDA. Didn't they seem to think it—a little—queer?

LØVBORG. [*Suddenly understanding.*] Oh, of course! I see what you mean. I suppose I'm dragging her down with me—— However, I didn't notice anyting. I suppose Tesman isn't up yet?

HEDDA. No—I don't think so——

LØVBORG. When did he get home?

HEDDA. Oh, very late.

LØVBORG. Did he tell you anything?

HEDDA. He just said it had all been very jolly at Judge Brack's.

LØVBORG. Nothing else?

HEDDA. No, I don't believe so. In any case, I was so dreadfully sleepy——

[*Mrs Elvsted comes in through the portières from the inner room. She goes to him.*

THEA. Eilert! At last!

LØVBORG. Yes—at last—and too late!

THEA. [*Looks at him anxiously.*] What is too late?

LØVBORG. Everything's too late now—it's all up with me.

THEA. No, no! You mustn't say that!

LØVBORG. You'll say the same when you hear——

THEA. I don't want to hear anything!

HEDDA. Perhaps you'd rather talk to her alone? I'll leave you.

LØVBORG. No! Stay, please—I beg of you!

THEA. But I don't want to hear anything, I tell you.

LØVBORG. I don't intend to talk about last night, Thea——

THEA. No?

LØVBORG. No. I just want to tell you that now we must part.

THEA. Part?

HEDDA. [*Involuntarily.*] I knew it!

LØVBORG. I no longer have any use for you, Thea.

THEA. How can you say that! No more use for me? You'll let me go on helping you—we'll go on working together, Eilert?

LØVBORG. I shall do no more work, from now on.

THEA. [*Despairingly.*] Then, what shall I have to live for?

LØVBORG. You must try and live as though you'd never known me.

THEA. But you know I can't do that!

LØVBORG. You must try, Thea. You must go home again.

THEA. [*Protesting vehemently.*] Never! I won't leave you! I won't allow you to drive me away. We must be together when the book appears.

HEDDA. [*Whispers, in suspense.*] Ah yes—the book!

LØVBORG. [*Looks at her.*] My book and Thea's—for that's what it is.

THEA. Yes—that's true; I feel that. That's why we must be together when it's published. I want to see you showered with praise and honours—and, the joy! I want to share that with you too!

LØVBORG. Our book will not be published, Thea.

THEA. Not published?

LØVBORG. No. It never can be.

THEA. [*Anxiously, with foreboding.*] Løvborg—what have you done with the manuscript?

HEDDA. [*Watches him intently.*] Yes—the manuscript?

THEA. Where is it?

LØVBORG. Thea! Don't ask me about it!

THEA. Yes—I must know—I have a right to know.

LØVBORG. Very well, then! I've torn it into a thousand pieces!

THEA. [*Cries out.*] No—no!

HEDDA. [*Involuntarily.*] But that's not——

LØVBORG. [*Looks at her.*] Not true, you think?

HEDDA. [*Controlling herself.*] Of course it must be—if you say so! But it sounds so utterly incredible!

LØVBORG. It's true all the same.

THEA. [*Wringing her hands.*] Torn his own work to pieces! Oh, God, Hedda!

LØVBORG. I've torn my life to pieces—why shouldn't I tear up my work as well!

THEA. And you did this last night?

LØVBORG. Yes. I tore it into a thousand pieces. I scattered them far out on the fiord. I watch them drift on the cool sea water—drift with the current and the wind. In a little while they'll sink, deeper and deeper—just as I shall, Thea.

THEA. Løvborg—this thing you've done to the book—it's as though you'd killed a little child.

LØVBORG. You're right—it was child murder.

THEA. Then—how could you?—it was my child too.

HEDDA. [*Almost inaudibly.*] The child——

THEA. [*Breathes heavily.*] It's all over then—I'll go now, Hedda.

HEDDA. But you won't be leaving town?

THEA. I don't know what I'll do—there's nothing but darkness before me.   [*She goes out by the hall door.*

HEDDA. [*Stands waiting a moment.*] Then—you're not going to see her home, Mr Løvborg?

LØVBORG. I?—— Do you want people to see her with *me*?

HEDDA. Of course, I don't know what else may have happened last night—but is it so utterly irreparable?

LØVBORG. It won't end with last night—I know that only too well; and the trouble is, that kind of life no longer appeals to me. I have no heart to start it again—she's somehow broken my courage—my defiant spirit!

HEDDA. [*Gazes before her.*] To think that that pretty little fool should have influenced a man's destiny! [*Looks at him.*] Still, I don't see how you could be so heartless.

LØVBORG. Don't say that!

HEDDA. What do you expect me to say! You've destroyed her whole purpose in life—isn't that being heartless?

LØVBORG. Hedda—to you I can tell the truth.

HEDDA. The truth?

LØVBORG. First, promise me—give me your word—that Thea will never know.

HEDDA. I give you my word.

LØVBORG. Good. There was no truth in what I said just now——

HEDDA. You mean—about the manuscript?

LØVBORG. Yes. I didn't tear it to pieces or scatter it on the fiord——

HEDDA. Where is it then?

LØVBORG. But I have destroyed it, Hedda—utterly destroyed it!

HEDDA. I don't understand.

LØVBORG. Just now, Thea said I had killed our child——

HEDDA. Yes—so she did——

LØVBORG. One can do worse things to a child than kill it—I wanted to spare Thea the truth——

HEDDA. What do you mean?

LØVBORG. I couldn't bring myself to tell her; I couldn't say to her: Thea, I spent last night in a frenzy of drinking—I took our child with me, dragged it round with me to all sorts of obscene and loathsome places—and I lost our child—lost it! God only knows what's become of it—or who's got hold of it!

HEDDA. But, when you come right down to it, this was only a book——

LØVBORG. Thea's pure soul was in that book.

HEDDA. Yes—so I understand.

LØVBORG. Then you must also understand why no future is possible for us.

HEDDA. What will you do now?

LØVBORG. Nothing. I want to make an end of it. The sooner the better.

HEDDA. [*Takes a step towards him.*] If you do make an end of it, Eilert Løvborg—let it be beautiful!

LØVBORG. [*Smiles.*] Beautiful! Shall I put vine leaves in my hair, as you wanted me to in the old days?

HEDDA. No—I don't believe in vine leaves any more. But—for once—let it be beautiful! Goodbye—you must go now—you mustn't come here any more.

LØVBORG. Goodbye, Mrs Tesman. Remember me to George Tesman.   [*He's on the point of going.*

HEDDA. No, wait!—I want you to take something of mine with you—as a token——

[*She goes to the writing-table, opens the drawer, and the pistol case. Goes back to Løvborg, carrying one of the pistols.*

LØVBORG. [*Looks at her.*] This? Is this the token?

HEDDA. [*Nods slowly.*] Do you remember it? It was aimed at you once.

LØVBORG. You should have used it then.

HEDDA. Take it! Use it now!

LØVBORG. [*Puts the pistol in his inner pocket.*] Thanks.

HEDDA. But let it be—beautiful, Eilert Løvborg! Promise me that!

LØVBORG. Goodbye, Hedda Gabler.

[*He goes out by the hall door. Hedda listens at the door a moment. Then she goes to the writing-table and takes out the parcel with the manuscript, peeps inside the cover, half takes out a few sheets of paper and looks at them. Then she takes the parcel over to the*

armchair by the stove and sits down. She has the parcel in her lap.
In a moment she opens the stove door, then opens the parcel.

HEDDA. [*She throws part of the manuscript in the fire and whispers to*
herself.] Your child, Thea—your child and Eilert Løvborg's.
Darling little Thea, with the curly golden hair. [*Throws more of the*
manuscript into the stove.] I'm burning your child, Thea. [*Throws*
in the rest of the manuscript.] I'm burning it—burning it——

CURTAIN

ACT IV

The same room at the Tesman's. It is evening. The drawing-room is dark. In the inner room the hanging lamp over the table is lighted. The curtains are drawn over the glass doors. Hedda, dressed in black, paces back and forth in the dark room. Then she goes up into the inner room and off left. A few chords are heard on the piano. She appears again and returns to the drawing-room. Berta enters from the right, through the inner room, carrying a lighted lamp which she puts down on the table by the corner sofa in the drawing-room. Her eyes are red with weeping and she has black ribbons on her cap. She goes out right, quietly and circumspectly. Hedda goes to the glass door, pulls the curtains aside a little, and peers out into the darkness. After a moment Miss Tesman comes in from the hall. She is in mourning and wears a hat and veil. Hedda goes towards her and holds out her hand.

MISS TESMAN. Well, Hedda, here I am, all dressed in black! My poor sister has found rest at last!

HEDDA. As you see, I have heard already. Tesman sent me a note.

MISS TESMAN. He promised he would. I wish Rina hadn't left us just now—this is not the time for Hedda's house to be a house of mourning.

HEDDA. [*Changing the subject.*] It is good to know she died peacefully, Miss Tesman.

MISS TESMAN. Yes, her end was so calm, so beautiful. And thank heaven, she had the joy of seeing George once more—and bidding him goodbye. He is not home yet?

HEDDA. No. He wrote me he might be detained. But do sit down, Miss Tesman.

MISS TESMAN. No, thank you, my dearest Hedda. I should like nothing better, but I have so much to do. I must prepare my darling sister for her burial. She must look her very sweetest when they carry her to her grave.

HEDDA. Can I do anything to help?

MISS TESMAN. Oh no, you mustn't think of that! This is no time for Hedda Tesman to take part in such sad work. Nor let her thoughts dwell on it either——

HEDDA. H'm—one's thoughts——!

MISS TESMAN. [*Continuing the theme.*] How strange life is! At home we shall be sewing a shroud; and soon I expect there will be sewing here, too—but of a different kind, thank God!

[*George Tesman enters by the hall door.*

HEDDA. Well! Here you are at last!

TESMAN. You here, Aunt Julia? With Hedda? Think of that!

MISS TESMAN. I am just going, my dear boy. Did you get everything done?

TESMAN. I'm afraid I forgot half of it. I'll have to run over and see you in the morning. Today my brain's in a whirl! I can't keep my thoughts together.

MISS TESMAN. But, my dear George, you mustn't take it so much to heart.

TESMAN. How do you mean?

MISS TESMAN. We must be glad for her sake—glad that she has found rest at last.

TESMAN. Oh yes, of course—you are thinking of Aunt Rina.

HEDDA. I'm afraid it will be very lonely for you now, Miss Tesman.

MISS TESMAN. It will be at first—but I won't let poor Rina's room stay empty for long.

TESMAN. Really? Who will you put in it—eh?

MISS TESMAN. One can always find some poor invalid who needs to be taken care of.

HEDDA. Would you really take such a burden on yourself again?

MISS TESMAN. A burden? Heaven forgive you, child, it has been no burden to me.

HEDDA. But it's different with a stranger!

MISS TESMAN. I simply must have someone to live for—and one soon makes friends with sick folks; and perhaps some day there may be something in this house to keep an old aunt busy.

HEDDA. Oh, please don't trouble about us!

TESMAN. Just think! What a wonderful time we three might have together if——

HEDDA. If——?

TESMAN. [*Uneasy.*] Nothing. Let's hope things will work out for the best—eh?

MISS TESMAN. Well, well, I dare say you two want to have a little talk. [*Smiling.*] And perhaps Hedda may have something to tell you, George. Goodbye! I must go home to poor Rina. [*Turning at the door.*] How strange it is to think that now Rina is with my poor brother, as well as with me.

TESMAN. Yes, think of that, Aunt Julia! Eh?

[*Miss Tesman goes out by the hall door.*

HEDDA. [*Gives Tesman a cold, searching look.*] Aunt Rina's death seems to affect you more than it does Aunt Julia.

TESMAN. Oh, it's not that alone. It's Eilert I am so terribly upset about.

HEDDA. [*Quickly.*] Have you heard anything new?

TESMAN. I called on him this afternoon. I wanted to tell him the manuscript was safe.

HEDDA. Did you see him?

TESMAN. No, he wasn't home. But later, I met Mrs Elvsted and she said he had been here, early this morning.

HEDDA. Yes, directly after you had left.

TESMAN. And he said that he had torn his manuscript to pieces, eh?

HEDDA. That is what he said.

TESMAN. Good heavens, he must have gone completely mad! I suppose in that case you didn't dare give it back to him, Hedda.

HEDDA. No, he didn't get it.

TESMAN. But of course you told him that we had it?

HEDDA. No. Did you tell Mrs Elvsted?

TESMAN. No, I thought I had better not. But you ought to have told him. Just think—he might do himself some injury. Give me the manuscript. I'll run over with it at once. Where is it, Hedda? Eh?

HEDDA. [*Cold and motionless, leaning against the armchair.*] I haven't got it any longer.

TESMAN. Haven't got it? What in the world do you mean?

HEDDA. I've burnt it—every word of it.

TESMAN. [*Starts up in terror.*] Burnt! Burnt Eilert's manuscript!

HEDDA. Don't shout so loud. The servants might hear you.

TESMAN. Burnt! Why, good God——! No, no, no! It's utterly impossible!

HEDDA. It's true, all the same.

TESMAN. Do you realize what you have done, Hedda? It is unlawful appropriation of lost property. Think of that! Just ask Judge Brack—he will tell you what that means.

HEDDA. It would be wiser not to speak of it—either to Judge Brack or to anyone else.

TESMAN. But how could you do anything so unheard of? What put it into your head? What possessed you? Do answer me——

HEDDA. [*Suppressing a scarcely perceptible smile.*] I did it for your sake, George!

Sarcasy

TESMAN. For my sake!

HEDDA. This morning when you told me that he had read it to you——

TESMAN. Yes, yes—what then?

HEDDA. You admitted that you were jealous of his work.

TESMAN. Of course, I didn't mean that literally.

HEDDA. All the same—I could not bear the thought of anyone putting you in the shade.

TESMAN. [*In an outburst of mingled doubt and joy.*] Hedda? Is this true? But—but—I have never known you to show your love like that before. Think of that!

HEDDA. Then—perhaps I'd better tell you that—just now—at this time—— [*Violently breaking off.*] No, no; ask Aunt Julia. She will tell you all about it.

TESMAN. Oh, I almost think I understand, Hedda. [*Clasping his hands together.*] Great heavens! Do you really mean it, eh?

HEDDA. Don't shout so loud. The servants will hear——

TESMAN. [*Laughing with irrepressible joy.*] The servants——? Why how absurd you are, Hedda! It is only my dear old Berta! Why, I'll run out and tell her myself!

HEDDA. [*Clenching her hands in despair.*] Oh, God, I shall die—I shall die of all this——!

TESMAN. Of what, Hedda? What is it? Eh?

HEDDA. [*Coldly, controlling herself.*] It's all so ludicrous—George!

TESMAN. Ludicrous! That I should be overjoyed at the news? Still, after all, perhaps I had better not tell Berta.

HEDDA. Why not that—with all the rest?

TESMAN. No, no, I won't tell her yet. But I must certainly tell Aunt Julia. Oh, she will be so happy—so happy!

HEDDA. When she hears that I've burnt Eilert Løvborg's manuscript—for your sake?

TESMAN. No, of course not—nobody must know about the manuscript. But I will certainly tell her how dearly you love me, Hedda. She must share that joy with me. I wonder, now, whther this sort of thing is usual in young wives? Eh?

HEDDA. Why not ask Aunt Julia that, too?

TESMAN. I will, indeed, some time or other. [*Again agitated and concerned.*] But the manuscript. Good God—the manuscript! I can't bear to think what poor Eilert will do now!

[*Mrs Elvsted, dressed as on her first visit, wearing a hat and coat, comes in from the hall door.*]

THEA. [*She greets them hurriedly, and says in evident agitation*] Hedda, dear—please forgive my coming back so soon.

HEDDA. What is it, Thea? What has happened?

TESMAN. Is it something to do with Eilert Løvborg, eh?

THEA. Yes; I am terribly afraid he has met with some accident.

HEDDA. [*Seizes her arm.*] Ah! You think so?

TESMAN. Why should you think that, Mrs Elvsted?

THEA. When I got back to my lodgings—I heard them talking about him. There are all sorts of strange rumours——

TESMAN. Yes, I've heard them, too! And yet I can bear witness that he went straight home last night. Think of that!

HEDDA. What sort of things did they say?

THEA. Oh, I couldn't quite make it out. Either they knew nothing definite or—in any case, they stopped talking the moment I came in, and I didn't dare question them.

TESMAN. [*Moving about the room uneasily.*] We must only hope you misunderstood them, Mrs Elvsted.

THEA. No, I am sure they were talking about him—they said something about a hospital or——

TESMAN. Hospital?

HEDDA. No, no! That's impossible!

THEA. Oh, I am so terribly afraid for him. I finally went to his house to ask after him!

HEDDA. You went there yourself, Thea?

THEA. What else could I do? I couldn't bear the suspense any longer.

TESMAN. But you didn't find him—eh?

THEA. No. And the people there knew nothing about him. They said he hadn't been home since yesterday afternoon.

TESMAN. Yesterday! Just think—how could they say that?

THEA. I am sure something terrible must have happened to him!

TESMAN. Hedda dear—supposing I run over and make some inquiries——?

HEDDA. No, no! Please don't mix yourself up in this affair.

[*Judge Brack, hat in hand, enters by the hall door which Berta opens and closes behind him. He looks grave and bows silently.*]

TESMAN. Oh, it's you, my dear Judge—eh?

BRACK. Yes, it's imperative that I see you at once.

TESMAN. I can see you have heard the news about Aunt Rina?

BRACK. Yes, that among other things.

TESMAN. Isn't it sad? Eh?

BRACK. Well, my dear Tesman, that depends on how you look at it.

TESMAN. [*Looks at him doubtfully.*] Has anything else happened?

BRACK. Yes.

HEDDA. [*Intensely.*] Anything sad, Judge?

BRACK. That, too, depends on how you look at it, Mrs Tesman.

THEA. [*In an involuntary outburst.*] Oh! It's something about Eilert Løvborg!

BRACK. [*Glancing at her.*] What makes you think that, Mrs Elvsted? Perhaps you have already heard something——?

THEA. [*Confused.*] No, no, nothing at all—but——

TESMAN. Well, for heaven's sake, tell us. What is it?

BRACK. [*Shrugging his shoulders.*] Well, I am sorry to say, Eilert Løvborg has been taken to the hospital—they say he is dying.

THEA. [*Cries out.*] Oh, God! God!

TESMAN. To the hospital! And dying——

HEDDA. [*Involuntarily.*] So soon then——

THEA. [*Tearfully.*] And we parted in anger, Hedda!

HEDDA. [*In a whisper.*] Thea—Thea—be careful!

THEA. [*Not heeding her.*] I must go to him! I must see him alive!

BRACK. I'm afraid it is useless, Mrs Elvsted. No one is allowed to see him.

THEA. But at least tell me what happened to him? What is it?

TESMAN. He didn't try to kill himself—eh?

HEDDA. Yes—I am sure he did!

TESMAN. Hedda, how can you——?

BRACK. [*Not taking his eyes off her.*] Unfortunately you have guessed quite correctly, Mrs Tesman.

THEA. Oh, how horrible!

TESMAN. Killed himself! Think of that!

HEDDA. Shot himself!

BRACK. You are right again, Mrs Tesman.

THEA. [*Trying to control herself.*] When did it happen, Judge Brack?

BRACK. This afternoon—between three and four.

TESMAN. But, where did it happen? Eh?

BRACK. [*With a slight hesitation.*] Where? Well—I suppose at his lodgings.

THEA. No, it couldn't have been there—for I was there myself between six and seven.

BRACK. Well, then, somewhere else—I don't know exactly. I only know that he was found—he had shot himself . . . through the heart.

THEA. How horrible! That he should die like that!

HEDDA. [*To Brack.*] Through the heart?

BRACK. Yes—as I told you.

HEDDA. Through the heart——

TESMAN. It's absolutely fatal, you say?

BRACK. Absolutely! Most likely it is already over.

THEA. Over—all over—oh, Hedda!

TESMAN. You're quite positive of this? Who told you—eh?

BRACK. [*Curtly.*] One of the police.

HEDDA. [*Loud.*] At last, a deed worth doing!

TESMAN. [*Terrified.*] Good heavens, what are you saying, Hedda?

HEDDA. I say, there is beauty in this.

BRACK. H'm, Mrs Tesman——

TESMAN. Beauty! Think of that!

THEA. Oh, Hedda, how can you talk of beauty in such a case?

HEDDA. Eilert Løvborg has made up his own account with life. He had the courage to do—the one right thing.

THEA. No, no! You mustn't believe that! He did it in delirium!

TESMAN. In despair.

HEDDA. No! No! He didn't—I'm sure of that!

THEA. I tell you he must have been delirious—as he was when he tore up our manuscript!

BRACK. [*With a start.*] The manuscript? He tore up the manuscript?

THEA. Yes. Last night.

TESMAN. [*In a low whisper.*] Oh, Hedda, we'll never get over this!

BRACK. H'm—how very extraordinary.

TESMAN. [*Pacing the room.*] To think of Eilert dead! And his book destroyed too—his book that would have made him famous!

THEA. If only there were some way of saving it——

TESMAN. Yes, if only there were! There's nothing I wouldn't give——

THEA. Perhaps there is a way, Mr Tesman.

TESMAN. What do you mean?

THEA. [*Searches in the pocket of her dress.*] Look! I have kept all the notes he used to dictate from——

HEDDA. [*Takes a step towards her.*] Ah——!

TESMAN. You have, Mrs Elvsted? Eh?

THEA. Yes. I took them with me when I left home—they're here in my pocket——

TESMAN. Do let me see them!

THEA. [*Hands him a bundle of scraps of paper.*] I'm afraid they are dreadfully mixed up——

TESMAN. Perhaps, together, we might be able to sort them out—just think!

THEA. We could try at any rate——

TESMAN. We'll do it!—we *must* do it—I'll devote my life to it!

HEDDA. You, George? Your life?

TESMAN. Or at least, all the time I can spare. My own work will simply have to wait—I owe this to Eilert's memory . . . you understand, Hedda, eh?

HEDDA. You may be right.

TESMAN. Now, my dear Mrs Elvsted, we must pull ourselves together—it is no good brooding over what has happened. Eh? We must try and control our grief as much as possible——

THEA. Yes, you're right, Mr Tesman, I *will* try——

TESMAN. That's splendid! Now then, let's see—we must go through the notes at once. Where shall we sit? Here? No, no, we'd better go in there—excuse me, Judge. Come along, Mrs Elvsted!

THEA. Oh! If only it were possible——

[*Tesman and Mrs Elvsted go into the inner room. She takes off her hat and coat. They sit at the table under the hanging lamp and become absorbed in examining the papers. Hedda goes towards the stove and sits down in the armchair. After a moment Brack joins her.*

HEDDA. [*In a low voice.*] Oh, what a sense of freedom there is in this act of Eilert Løvborg's.

BRACK. Freedom, Mrs Hedda? Of course, it is freedom for him.

HEDDA. I mean for me. It gives me a sense of freedom to know that an act of deliberate courage is still possible in this world—an act of spontaneous beauty.

BRACK. [*Smiles.*] H'm—my dear Mrs Hedda——

HEDDA. Oh, I know what you are going to say. For you are a specialist too, in a way—just like—well, you know.

BRACK. [*Looks at her intently.*] Eilert Løvborg meant more to you than you are willing to admit—even to yourself. Or am I mistaken?

HEDDA. I don't answer such questions. I know that Eilert Løvborg had the courage to live his life as he saw it—and to end it in beauty. He had the strength and the will to break with life—while still so young.

BRACK. It pains me to do so, Mrs Hedda—but I fear I must rob you of this beautiful illusion.

HEDDA. Illusion?

BRACK. It would soon be destroyed, in any case.

HEDDA. What do you mean?

BRACK. He did not shoot himself—of his own accord.

HEDDA. Not of his own——?

BRACK. No; the thing did not happen exactly as I told it.

HEDDA. [*In suspense.*] You've concealed something? What is it?

BRACK. For poor Mrs Elvsted's sake, I slightly changed the facts.

HEDDA. What are the facts then?

BRACK. First, that he is already dead.

HEDDA. At the hospital.

BRACK. Yes—without regaining consciousness.

HEDDA. What else have you concealed?

BRACK. That—the tragedy did not happen at his lodgings——

HEDDA. That makes no difference——

BRACK. Doesn't it? Not even if I tell you that Eilert Løvborg was found shot in—in Mademoiselle Diana's boudoir?

HEDDA. [*Attempts to jump up but sinks back again.*] That is impossible, Judge. He couldn't have gone there again today.

BRACK. He was there this afternoon. He went there to claim something he said they had taken from him—talked wildly about a lost child——

HEDDA. Ah—that was why——

BRACK. I thought he must have meant the manuscript. But now I hear he destroyed that himself. So I suppose it must have been his pocketbook.

HEDDA. Yes—probably. So, he was found—there.

BRACK. Yes. With a discharged pistol in his breast pocket. He had wounded himself mortally.

HEDDA. Through the heart!—Yes!

BRACK. No—in the bowels.

HEDDA. [*Looks at him with an expression of loathing.*] How horrible! Everything I touch becomes ludicrous and despicable! It's like a curse!

BRACK. There is something else, Mrs Hedda—something rather ugly——

HEDDA. What is that?

BRACK. The pistol he carried——

HEDDA. [*Breathless.*] What of it?

BRACK. He must have stolen it.

HEDDA. [*Leaps up.*] That is not true! He didn't steal it!

BRACK. No other explanation is possible. He *must* have stolen it—hush!

[*Tesman and Mrs Elvsted have risen from the table in the inner room and come into the drawing-room.*

TESMAN. [*His hands full of papers.*] Hedda dear, it is almost impossible to see under that lamp. Just think!

HEDDA. Yes, I am thinking.

TESMAN. Do you think you'd let us use your desk, eh?

HEDDA. Of course—no, wait! Just let me clear it first.

TESMAN. Oh, you needn't trouble, Hedda. There's plenty of room.

HEDDA. No, no! Let me do as I say. I will put all these things on the piano.

[*She has taken something covered with sheet music from under the bookcase, puts some added pieces of music on it, and carries the whole lot into the inner room and off left. Tesman arranges the scraps of paper on the writing-table and moves the lamp from the corner table over to it. He and Mrs Elvsted sit down and resume their work. Hedda returns.*

HEDDA. [*Stands behind Mrs Elvsted's chair, gently ruffling her hair.*] Well, darling little Thea—how are you getting on with Eilert Løvborg's memorial?

THEA. [*Looks up at her with a disheartened expression.*] I'm afraid it's all very difficult——

TESMAN. We *must* manage it. We've simply got to do it! And you know sorting out and arranging other people's papers—that's something I'm particularly good at——

[*Hedda crosses to the stove and sits down on one of the stools. Brack stands over her leaning on the armchair.*

HEDDA. [*In a whisper.*] What was that you said about the pistol?

BRACK. [*Softly.*] That he must have stolen it.

HEDDA. Why stolen?

BRACK. Because any other explanation ought to be out of the question, Mrs Hedda.

HEDDA. Indeed?

BRACK. [*Glancing at her.*] Of course, Eilert Løvborg was here this morning. Wasn't he?

HEDDA. Yes.

BRACK. Were you alone with him?

HEDDA. Yes—for a little while

BRACK. Did you leave the room while he was here?

HEDDA. No.

BRACK. Try to remember. Are you *sure* you didn't leave the room —even for a moment?

HEDDA, I might have gone into the hall—just for a moment——

BRACK. And where was your pistol case?

HEDDA. It was put away in——

BRACK. Well, Mrs Hedda?

HEDDA. It was over there on the desk.

BRACK. Have you looked since to see if both pistols are there?

HEDDA. No.

BRACK. Well, you needn't. I saw the pistol Løvborg had with him, and I recognized it at once as the one I had seen yesterday—and before that too.

HEDDA. Have you got it by any chance?

BRACK. No, the police have it.

HEDDA. What will the police do with it?

BRACK. Search until they find the owner.

HEDDA. Do you think they will succeed?

BRACK. [*Bends over her and whispers.*] No, Hedda Gabler, not so long as I keep silent.

HEDDA. [*Gives him a frightened look.*] And if you do *not* keep silent— what then?

BRACK. [*Shrugs his shoulders.*] One could always declare that the pistol was stolen.

HEDDA. [*Firmly.*] It would be better to die!

BRACK. [*Smiling.*] One *says* such things—but one doesn't *do* them.

HEDDA. [*Without answering.*] And if the pistol were not stolen and the police find the owner? What then?

BRACK. Well, Hedda—then—think of the scandal!

HEDDA. The scandal!

BRACK. The scandal, yes—of which you are so terrified. You'd naturally have to appear in court—both you and Mademoiselle Diana. She would have to explain how the thing happened—whether it was an accident or murder. Did he threaten to shoot her, and did the pistol go off then—or did she grab the pistol, shoot him, afterwards putting it back into his pocket. She might have done that, for she is a hefty woman, this—Mademoiselle Diana.

HEDDA. What have I to do with all this repulsive business?

BRACK. Nothing. But you will have to answer the question: Why did you give Eliert Løvborg the pistol? And what conclusion will people draw from the fact that you did give it to him?

HEDDA. [*Bowing her head.*] That is true. I didn't think of that.

BRACK. Well, fortunately, there is no danger as long as I keep silent.

HEDDA. [*Looks up at him.*] That means you have me in your power, Judge! You have me at your beck and call from now on.

BRACK. [*Whispers softly*] Dearest Hedda—believe me—I shall not abuse my advantage.

HEDDA. I am in your power, all the same. Subject to your commands and wishes. No longer free—not free! . . . [*Rises impetuously.*] No, I won't endure that thought. Never!

BRACK. [*Looks at her half mockingly.*] People manage to get used to the inevitable.

HEDDA. [*Returns his look.*] Yes, perhaps. [*She crosses to the writing-table. Suppressing an involuntary smile and imitating Tesman's intonations*] Well? How's it going, George, eh?

TESMAN. Heaven knows, dear. In any case, it will take months to do.

HEDDA. [*As before.*] Think of that! [*She runs her fingers softly through Mrs Elvsted's hair.*] Doesn't it seem strange to you, Thea? Here you are working with Tesman—as you used to work with Eilert Løvborg?

THEA. If I could only inspire your husband in the same way!

HEDDA. Oh, no doubt that will come—in time.

TESMAN. You know, Hedda—I'm really beginning to feel something of the sort! Why don't you go and talk to Judge Brack again?

HEDDA. Is there nothing at all—I can do to help?

TESMAN. No, thank you. Not a thing. [*Turning his head.*] You'll have to keep Hedda company from now on, my dear Judge.

BRACK. [*With a glance at Hedda.*] It will give me the greatest of pleasure!

HEDDA. Thanks. But this evening I feel a little tired. I will go and lie down on the sofa for a little while.

TESMAN. Yes, do that dear—eh?

[*Hedda goes into the inner room and closes the portières after her. A short pause. Suddenly she is heard playing a wild dance tune on the piano.*

THEA. [*Starts up from her chair.*] Oh—what's that?

TESMAN. [*Runs to the centre opening.*] Dearest Hedda, don't play dance music tonight! Think of Aunt Rina! And of poor Eilert!

HEDDA. [*Sticks her head out between the curtains.*] And of Aunt Julia. And of all the rest of them. Never mind. From now on, I promise to be quiet.   [*She closes the curtains again.*

TESMAN. [*At the writing-table.*] I don't think it is good for her to see us at this distressing work; I have an idea, Mrs Elvsted. You can move over to Aunt Julia's and then I'll come over in the evenings and we'll work there. Eh?

THEA. Perhaps that would be the best thing to do.

HEDDA. [*From the inner room.*] I can hear what you are saying, Tesman. What am I to do with all those long evenings—here— by myself?

TESMAN. [*Turning over the papers.*] Oh, I am sure Judge Brack will be kind enough to drop in and see you.

BRACK. [*In the armchair, calls out gaily*] Every single evening, with the very greatest of pleasure, Mrs Tesman! I'm sure we'll have a very jolly time together, we two.

HEDDA. [*In a loud clear voice.*] Yes, that's what you hope, Judge, isn't it?—Now that you are cock-of-the-walk——

[*A shot is heard within. Tesman, Mrs Elvsted and Brack leap to their feet.*

TESMAN. Now she is playing with those pistols again.

[*He throws back the portières and runs in, followed by Mrs Elvsted. Hedda lies stretched out on the sofa, dead. Confusion and cries. Berta, alarmed, comes in from the right.*

TESMAN. [*Cries out, to Brack.*] Shot herself! Shot herself in the temple! Think of that!

BRACK. [*Sinks into the armchair, half fainting.*] Good God!—but— people don't *do* such things!

CURTAIN

THE MASTER BUILDER

THE MASTER BUILDER

ACT I

A plainly furnished workroom in the house of Masterbuilder Solness. In the left wall folding doors lead to the hall. To the right is the door to the inner rooms. In the back wall an open door leads to the draughtsmen's office. Downstage left a desk with books, papers and writing materials. Above the door a stove. In the right-hand corner a sofa with a table and a couple of chairs. On the table a water pitcher and glass. Downstage right a smaller table with a rocking chair and an armchair. The worklights are lit in the draughtsmen's office and there are lighted lamps on the corner table and the desk.

In the draughtsmen's office Knud Brovik and his son Ragnar are seated working over plans and calculations. Kaia Fosli stands at the desk in the front room writing in a ledger. Knud Brovik is a thin old man with white hair and beard. He wears a somewhat threadbare but well-brushed black coat. He wears glasses and a white, rather discoloured neckcloth. Ragnar Brovik is a well-dressed, light-haired man in his thirties, with a slight stoop. Kaia Fosli is a slight young girl just over twenty, carefully dressed and delicate looking. She wears a green eyeshade. All three go on working for some time in silence.

BROVIK. [*Rises suddenly from the drawing-table as though in distress; he breathes heavily and laboriously as he comes forward into the doorway.*] It's no use! I can't bear it much longer!

KAIA. [*Goes towards him.*] Dear uncle—you feel very ill this evening, don't you?

BROVIK. I get worse every day.

RAGNAR. [*Has risen and comes forward.*] Why don't you go home, Father—try and get some sleep.

BROVIK. [*Impatiently.*] Go to bed, I suppose!

KAIA. Then, take a little walk——

RAGNAR. Yes, do. I'll go with you.

BROVIK. [*Insistently.*] No, I won't go till he gets back. I must have

79

it out with him [*with suppressed bitterness*] with the Boss. I must have it settled, once and for all.

KAIA. [*Anxiously.*] Oh, no, uncle—please wait——

RAGNAR. Better wait, Father.

BROVIK. [*Breathes painfully.*] I haven't much time for waiting.

KAIA. [*Listening.*] Sh! I hear him on the stairs!

[*All three go back to work. A short pause.*

[*Halvard Solness comes in from the hall. He is a middle-aged man but strong and vigorous, with close-cropped curly hair, a dark moustache and thick dark eyebrows. His grey-green jacket is buttoned and has a turned-up collar and broad lapels. He wears a soft grey felt hat and carries a couple of portfolios under his arm.*

SOLNESS. [*By the door, points towards the draughtsmen's office and asks in a whisper.*] Have they gone?

KAIA. [*Softly, shaking her head.*] No. [*She takes off the eyeshade.*

[*Solness crosses the room, throws his hat on a chair, puts the portfolios on the table by the sofa and comes back towards the desk. Kaia continues to write in the ledger, but seems nervous and uneasy.*

SOLNESS. [*Out loud.*] What are you entering there, Miss Fosli?

KAIA. [*With a start.*] It's just something that . . .

SOLNESS. Let me see, Miss Fosli . . . [*He bends over her, pretending to look in the ledger and whispers*] Kaia!

KAIA. [*Softly, still writing.*] Yes?

SOLNESS. Why do you always take that shade off when I come in?

KAIA. Because I look so ugly with it on.

SOLNESS. [*With a smile.*] And you don't want to look ugly, Kaia?

KAIA. [*Half glancing at him.*] No—not when you are here.

SOLNESS. [*Gently strokes her hair.*] Poor, poor little Kaia!

KAIA. [*Bending her head.*] Sh! They'll hear you!

[*Solness strolls across to the right, turns and pauses at the draughtsmen's office.*

SOLNESS. Did anyone call while I was out?

RAGNAR. Yes—those young people who want to build at Løvstrand——

SOLNESS. [*In a growling tone.*] Oh, those two! Well, they'll just have to wait—I'm not quite clear about the plans yet.

RAGNAR. They're very eager to see some drawings as soon as possible——

SOLNESS. [*As before.*] Yes, yes—I know! They're all the same!

BROVIK. They're so looking forward to having a home of their own. . . .

SOLNESS. I know—the same old story! So they grab the first thing that comes along—a mere roof over their heads—nothing to call a home! No thank you! If that's all they want let them go to somebody else. Tell them that the next time they come!

BROVIK. [*Pushes his glasses up on his forehead and looks at him in amazement.*] How do you mean—'somebody else'? Would you give up the commission?

SOLNESS. [*Impatiently.*] Well, why not? I'm not interested in building that sort of trash! Anyhow—I know nothing about these people.

BROVIK. Oh, they're reliable enough. Ragnar knows them quite well—he sees quite a lot of them—they're thoroughly respectable young people.

SOLNESS. Respectable! Respectable! That's not the point! Why can you never understand me? You don't see what I mean! [*Angrily.*] I don't care to deal with a lot of strangers. Let them apply to whom they like as far as I'm concerned.

BROVIK. [*Rising.*] You really mean that?

SOLNESS. [*Sulkily*] Why shouldn't I mean it? [*He walks about the room.*

[*Brovik exchanges a look with Ragnar, who makes a gesture of warning; he then comes into the front room.*

BROVIK. I'd like to have a talk with you, if I may.

SOLNESS. Of course.

BROVIK. [*To Kaia.*] Kaia—go in there for a few minutes.

KAIA. [*Uneasily.*] But, say, uncle——

BROVIK. Do as I say, child—and close the door after you.

[*Kaia goes reluctantly into the draughtsmen's office, and glancing anxiously and imploringly at Solness, shuts the door.*

BROVIK. [*Lowers his voice.*] I don't want the poor children to know how ill I am.

SOLNESS. It's true—you haven't looked well lately.

BROVIK. I get weaker every day.

SOLNESS. Why don't you sit down?

BROVIK. Thanks—may I?

SOLNESS. [*Placing the armchair.*] Here—sit here. Well?

BROVIK. [*Has seated himself with difficulty.*] Well, you see—it's about Ragnar. I'm worried about Ragnar—what's to become of him?

SOLNESS. Why should you be worried about him? He can work here for me as long as he likes.

BROVIK. But that's just what he doesn't like; he feels he can't stay here any longer.

SOLNESS. Why not? He does pretty well here it seems to me. But, of course, if he wants more money——

BROVIK. No, no! That has nothing to do with it. [*Impatiently.*] But he thinks it's time he did some work on his own account.

SOLNESS. Do you think Ragnar is capable enough for that?

BROVIK. That's just the point—I've begun to have doubts about the boy. After all, you've never given him a single word of encouragement. And yet—he must have talent—I can't help feeling that.

SOLNESS. But what does he know? He's had absolutely no experience—he's a good draughtsman—but is that enough?

BROVIK. [*Looks at him with concealed hatred and speaks in a hoarse voice.*] Experience! You hadn't had much experience either when you came to work for me; but you managed to make a name for yourself! [*Breathes with difficulty.*] You pushed your way up—outstripping me and all the others!

SOLNESS. Well, you see, I was lucky.

BROVIK. Yes! You were lucky—that's true enough! All the more reason for you to be generous! I want to see Ragnar do some work on his own before I die. And then—I'd like to see them married, too.

SOLNESS. [*Sharply.*] Married? Is Kaia so very keen on that?

BROVIK. Not Kaia so much; but Ragnar speaks of it every day. [*Imploringly.*] You must give him a chance! Help him to get some independent work! Let me see the boy do something on his own——

SOLNESS. [*Peevishly.*] What do you expect me to do? Drag commissions down from the moon for him?

BROVIK. He has the chance of a commission now—quite a big piece of work.

SOLNESS. [*Uneasily, startled.*] Has he?

BROVIK. Yes, if you'd give your consent——

SOLNESS. What sort of work?

BROVIK. [*With slight hesitation.*] They might commission him to build that house at Løvstrand.

SOLNESS. That! I'm building that myself!

BROVIK. But it doesn't really interest you——

SOLNESS. [*Flaring up.*] Not interest me! How dare you say that?

BROVIK. You said so yourself just now.

SOLNESS. Never mind what I said. So they'd let Ragnar build their house, would they?

BROVIK. Well, you see, he's a friend of theirs—and, just for fun, he's made some drawings—worked out some plans and estimates——

SOLNESS. And are they pleased with these drawings of his?

BROVIK. If you'd look them over—give them your approval——

SOLNESS. Then they'd give Ragnar the commission?

BROVIK. They seemed delighted with his ideas—they found them different—new and original, they said.

SOLNESS. New and original, eh? Not the old-fashioned stuff I go in for, I suppose! [*With suppressed irritation.*] So that's why they came while I was out; they wanted to see Ragnar!

BROVIK. No, no! They came to see you—they wanted to talk it over with you—find out if you would consider retiring from——

SOLNESS. [*Angrily.*] I—retire!

BROVIK. If you approved of Ragnar's drawings——

SOLNESS. I retire in favour of your son!

BROVIK. Withdraw from the agreement, they meant——

SOLNESS. It comes to the same thing! [*Laughs angrily.*] So that's it, is it? Halvard Solness is to think about retiring now! He must make room for younger men—for the youngest of all, perhaps. He must make room—room—room!

BROVIK. God knows there's plenty of room for more than one single man——!

SOLNESS. I'm not so sure of that. But I tell you one thing—I shall never retire! I'll give way to no one! Never of my own free will. I'll never consent to that!

BROVIK. [*Rises with difficulty.*] I see. Don't you realize that I'm a dying man? Am I never to see any work of Ragnar's doing? Would you deny me the joy of seeing my faith in Ragnar justified?

SOLNESS. [*Turns away and mutters.*] Don't say any more just now——

BROVIK. You must answer this one question! Am I to face death in such bitter poverty?

SOLNESS. [*After a short struggle with himself he says in a low but firm voice.*] You must face death as best you can.

BROVIK. Very well—so be it.   [*Goes upstage.*

SOLNESS. [*Following him, half in desperation.*] Don't you understand—
I can do nothing about it! I'm made that way—I can't change
my nature!

BROVIK. No—I don't suppose you can. [*Reels and supports himself
against the table.*] May I have a glass of water?

SOLNESS. Of course. [*Fills a glass and hands it to him.*] Here you are.

BROVIK. Thanks. [*Drinks and puts the glass down again.*]

SOLNESS. [*Goes and opens the door of the draughtsmen's office.*] Ragnar—
You'd better take your father home.

> [*Ragnar rises quickly. He and Kaia come into the front room.*

RAGNAR. What's the matter, Father?

BROVIK. Give me your arm—— Now, let us go.

RAGNAR. Very well. Put your things on too, Kaia.

SOLNESS. No. Miss Fosli must stay a moment—there's a letter I
want written.

BROVIK. [*Looks at Solness.*] Good night. Sleep well—if you can.

SOLNESS. Good night.

> [*Brovik and Ragnar go out by the hall door. Kaia goes to the desk.
> Solness stands with bent head, to the right, by the armchair.*

KAIA. Is there a letter?

SOLNESS. [*Curtly.*] No, of course not. [*Looks at her sternly.*] Kaia!

KAIA. [*Anxiously, in a low voice.*] Yes?

SOLNESS. [*With an imperious gesture.*] Come here! At once!

KAIA. [*Hesitantly.*] Yes.

SOLNESS. [*As before.*] Nearer!

KAIA. [*Obeying.*] What do you want of me?

SOLNESS. [*Looks at her for a moment.*] Is all this your doing?

KAIA. No, no! You mustn't think that!

SOLNESS. But it's true that you want to get married—isn't it?

KAIA. [*Softly.*] Ragnar and I have been engaged for four or five
years—and so——

SOLNESS. And so you think it's about time you got married—is
that it?

KAIA. Ragnar and Uncle are so insistent—I suppose I shall have to
give in.

SOLNESS. [*More gently.*] But, Kaia—surely you must care for Ragnar
a little bit, too?

KAIA. I cared a great deal for him once—before I came here to you.

SOLNESS. And, now?

KAIA. [*Passionately, clasping her hands and holding them out towards him.*]

Now there's only one person in the world I care about—you know that! I shall never love anyone else!

SOLNESS. Yes—that's what you say! And yet you'd go away—leave me here to struggle on alone.

KAIA. But couldn't I stay here with you—even if Ragnar——?

SOLNESS. [*Dismissing the idea.*] No! That's out of the question! If Ragnar goes off and starts work on his own—he'll need you himself.

KAIA. [*Wringing her hands.*] Oh, I don't see how I *can* leave you! It's utterly impossible!

SOLNESS. Then get these foolish ideas out of Ragnar's head! By all means marry him if you like . . . [*In a different tone.*] I mean . . . for his own sake, try and persuade him not to give up his position here. For then—I'll be able to keep you here too, my dear little Kaia.

KAIA. Yes—yes—how wonderful that would be . . . if we could only manage it.

SOLNESS. [*Takes her head in his hands and whispers*] I can't do without you—I must have you near me, Kaia—every single day——

KAIA. [*With nervous exaltation.*] Oh, God!

SOLNESS. [*Kisses her hair.*] Kaia! . . . Kaia!

KAIA. [*Sinks down at his feet.*] You're so good to me! So incredibly good to me!

SOLNESS. [*Vehemently.*] Get up! For God's sake get up! I hear someone coming!

[*He helps her to her feet. She staggers over to the desk.*
[*Mrs Solness enters by the door on the right. She is thin and seems wasted with grief, but shows traces of bygone beauty. Dressed in good taste, wholly in black. Speaks somewhat slowly, in a plaintive voice.*

MRS SOLNESS. [*In the doorway.*] Halvard!

SOLNESS. [*Turns.*] Oh . . . Is that you, my dear?

MRS S. [*With a glance at Kaia.*] I hope I'm not disturbing you. . . .

SOLNESS. Of course not—Miss Fosli has just a short letter to write——

MRS S. Yes—so I see.

SOLNESS. What did you want, Aline?

MRS S. I just wanted to tell you Dr Herdal is in the drawing-room—won't you come in and join us, Halvard?

SOLNESS. [*Gives her a suspicious glance.*] Hm . . . Has the doctor anything special to say to me?

MRS S. Nothing special, Halvard. He really came to call on me, but he thought he'd like to say how do you do to you at the same time.

SOLNESS. [*Laughs to himself.*] Yes, I dare say. . . . Well, just ask him to wait.

MRS S. Then you'll come in presently?

SOLNESS. Perhaps. . . . Presently . . . presently, my dear—in a little while.

MRS S. [*With another glance at Kaia.*] You won't forget, Halvard?
                    [*She withdraws, closing the door behind her.*

KAIA. [*Softly.*] Oh dear! I'm afraid Mrs Solness was annoyed with me. . . .

SOLNESS. Nonsense! Well—no more than usual, at any rate. Still, I think you'd better go now, Kaia.

KAIA. Yes . . . I'd better go. . . .

SOLNESS. [*Severely.*] And mind you get this matter settled for me—do you hear?

KAIA. Oh, if it was only a question of *me*——

SOLNESS. I will have it settled, I say! By tomorrow at latest!

KAIA. [*Terrified.*] If the worst comes to the worst—I'd gladly break off my engagement. . . .

SOLNESS. [*Angrily.*] Break off your engagement! You must be mad!

KAIA. [*Distractedly.*] I *must* stay here with you. It's impossible for me to leave you . . . utterly impossible!

SOLNESS. [*In a sudden outburst.*] But what about Ragnar, then? It's Ragnar that I . . .

KAIA. [*Looks at him with eyes full of terror.*] You mean . . . it's only because of Ragnar that you——?

SOLNESS. [*Controlling himself.*] No—no! Of course not! You don't understand me. . . . Don't you see—it's you that I want, Kaia. You above everything. And because of that, you must persuade Ragnar to stay on here. There . . . there . . . now, run along home.

KAIA. Yes. Well—good night.

SOLNESS. Good night. [*As she starts to go.*] Oh, by the way—did Ragnar leave those drawings of his here?

KAIA. I don't think he took them with him——

SOLNESS. Find them for me, will you? I might have a look at them, after all.

KAIA. [*Happily.*] Oh! *Would* you?

SOLNESS. Just for your sake, little Kaia. . . . Hurry up now! Find them for me. Quickly! . . . Do you hear?

[*Kaia hurries into the draughtsmen's office, searches anxiously in the table drawer, finds a portfolio and brings it in with her.*

KAIA. Here they are. . . .

SOLNESS. Good. Just put them on the table.

KAIA. [*Puts down the portfolio.*] Good night. . . . You *will* think kindly of me?

SOLNESS. You know I always do that. . . . Good night, dear little Kaia. [*Glances to the door right.*] Go now. . . . Go!

[*Mrs Solness and Dr Herdal enter by the door on the right. He is a stoutish elderly man, with a round, good-humoured face.*

MRS S. [*Still in the doorway.*] Halvard, I really can't keep the doctor any longer.

SOLNESS. Bring him in here, then.

MRS S. [*To Kaia, who is turning down the desk lamp.*] Have you finished the letter, Miss Fosli?

KAIA. [*Confused.*] The letter——?

SOLNESS. Yes. It was just a short one.

MRS S. It must have been very short.

SOLNESS. You may go now, Miss Fosli. And be sure to be here in good time in the morning.

KAIA. I will, Mr Solness. Good night, Mrs Solness.   [*Exits to hall.*

MRS S. How very lucky you were to find that young girl, Halvard.

SOLNESS. Yes. She's useful in many ways.

MRS S. So it seems.

DR HERDAL. Is she good at book-keeping, too?

SOLNESS. Well—she's had a good deal of experience these last two years—and she's so good-natured and willing—anxious to help in every way.

MRS S. That must be very gratifying.

SOLNESS. It is—especially when you're not accustomed to that sort of thing.

MRS S. [*In a tone of gentle remonstrance.*] How can you say that, Halvard?

SOLNESS. I'm sorry, my dear Aline. I beg your pardon.

MRS S. Don't mention it. So—doctor, you'll come back later and join us for a cup of tea?

HERDAL. I have just one more patient to see—then I'll be back.

MRS S. Thank you, doctor.   [*She goes out by the door on the right.*

SOLNESS. Are you in a hurry, doctor?

HERDAL. No, not at all.

SOLNESS. May I talk to you for a little while?

HERDAL. With the greatest of pleasure.

SOLNESS. Good . . . then, let's sit down. [*He motions the doctor to take the rocking-chair and sits down himself in the armchair. He gives the doctor a searching look.*] Tell me—did you notice anything about Aline?

HERDAL. Just now—while she was here?

SOLNESS. Yes. In her attitude towards me. Did you notice anything?

HERDAL. [*Smiling.*] Well—one could hardly help noticing that your wife——

SOLNESS. Yes?

HERDAL. That your wife doesn't seem to care much for this Miss Fosli.

SOLNESS. Oh, is that all! Yes—I've noticed that myself.

HERDAL. And I suppose that's not really very surprising, is it?

SOLNESS. What?

HERDAL. That she should resent your seeing so much of another woman.

SOLNESS. Perhaps you're right—and Aline too. But I'm afraid that can't be helped.

HERDAL. Couldn't you get a man for the job?

SOLNESS. You mean an ordinary clerk? No, that wouldn't do at all.

HERDAL. But, what if your wife—you know how nervous and delicate she is—what if this situation is too much of a strain for her?

SOLNESS. Even so—there's nothing I can do about it. I must keep Kaia Fosli; no one else can take her place.

HERDAL. No one else?

SOLNESS. [*Curtly.*] No, no one!

HERDAL. Might I ask you a rather personal question, Mr Solness?

SOLNESS. By all means.

HERDAL. One must admit that in some things women have an uncomfortably keen intuition——

SOLNESS. That's true, but——?

HERDAL. And, if your wife so thoroughly resents this Kaia Fosli——

SOLNESS. Well?

HERDAL. Is there really not the faintest reason for this instinctive dislike?

SOLNESS. [*Looks at him and rises.*] Aha!

HERDAL. Now don't be angry—be frank with me; isn't there?

SOLNESS. [*With curt decision.*] No.

HERDAL. None whatever, eh?

SOLNESS. Only her own suspicious nature.

HERDAL. I gather there have been quite a number of women in your life, Mr Solness.

SOLNESS. That may be true——

HERDAL. And no doubt you were deeply attached to some of them, weren't you?

SOLNESS. I don't deny it.

HERDAL. But in this case—there's nothing of that sort?

SOLNESS. Nothing at all—on my side.

HERDAL. But—on hers?

SOLNESS. I don't think you have the right to ask that question, doctor.

HERDAL. Well—we were discussing your wife's intuition, you know——

SOLNESS. Yes . . . so we were. For that matter—Aline's intuition, as you call it, may not be so far wrong after all.

HERDAL. There! You see!

SOLNESS. [*Sits down.*] Dr Herdal—I'd like to tell you a strange story —that is, if you'd care to hear it——

HERDAL. I like listening to strange stories.

SOLNESS. Very well. Perhaps you remember that I took Knud Brovik and his son into my employ—when the old man's business failed——

HERDAL. Yes—I remember vaguely——

SOLNESS. They're useful fellows, you see—both highly gifted, each in his own way. But then, of course, young Ragnar got himself engaged—and decided he wanted to get married and start to build on his own account. They're all the same, these young people——

HERDAL. [*Laughing.*] They do have a bad habit of wanting to get married!

SOLNESS. But that didn't happen to suit me—I needed Ragnar myself—and the old man too; he's a first-class engineer; good at calculating bearing-strains, cubic contents—all that technical stuff, you know——

HERDAL. No doubt that's indispensable.

SOLNESS. Yes, it is; but Ragnar was determined to work on his own; nothing would dissuade him.

HERDAL. Then what made him stay on with you?

SOLNESS. I'll tell you how that happened. One day Kaia Fosli came here to the office. She came to see them on some errand or other —she had never been here before. When I saw how infatuated Ragnar was with her, it occurred to me that if I were to give her a job here, I might get him to stay on too——

HERDAL. That was logical enough—

SOLNESS. Yes, but wait a minute! I never said a word about it at the time. I just stood looking at her, and wished with all my might that I could persuade her to work here. I simply said a few friendly words to her, and then she went away.

HERDAL. Well?

SOLNESS. Well, the next day, towards evening—after old Brovik and Ragnar had gone home—she came here again, and behaved as if we'd come to some agreement.

HERDAL. Agreement? What about?

SOLNESS. About the very thing I'd had in mind the day before— though I had actually never said a word about it.

HERDAL. That was strange——

SOLNESS. Yes, wasn't it? It was as though she'd read my thoughts. She asked what her duties were to be—when I wanted her to start work—and so on——

HERDAL. I suppose she thought she'd like a job here, so she could be near Ragnar.

SOLNESS. That's what I thought at first; but that wasn't it. No sooner had she started to work here, than she began to drift away from him.

HERDAL. Over to you, you mean?

SOLNESS. Exactly. She seemed to be constantly aware of me. Whenever I look at her—even when her back's turned—I can tell that she feels it; she trembles nervously whenever I come near her——

HERDAL. That's easily explained——

SOLNESS. Perhaps. But how did she know what I was thinking that first evening? Why did she behave as if I had asked her to come here, when actually I had only thought about it? I had wished it —had willed it, if you like but silently; inwardly. How did she know? Can you explain that, Dr Herdal?

HERDAL. No, I must confess I can't.

SOLNESS. No—you can't, can you? That's why I've never mentioned it—— But it's become a damn nuisance to me in the long
run; every day I have to keep up this pretence—and it's not fair
to her, poor girl. [*Vehemently.*] But there's nothing I can do about
it. If she leaves me—then Ragnar will leave too.

HERDAL. Haven't you explained this to your wife?

SOLNESS. No.

HERDAL. Well—why on earth don't you?

SOLNESS. [*Looks at him intently and says in a low voice.*] Because—well
—because I find a sort of salutary self-torture in allowing Aline
to do me this injustice.

HERDAL. [*Shakes his head.*] I'm afraid I don't understand you, Mr
Solness.

SOLNESS. Yes—don't you see? It's like paying off part of a huge,
immeasurable debt.

HERDAL. To your wife?

SOLNESS. Yes. It seems to relieve my mind. I feel I can breathe
more freely for a while.

HERDAL. I don't understand you in the least.

SOLNESS. Very well—then let's not talk about it. [*He saunters across
the room, comes back and stops beside the table. He looks at the doctor
with a sly smile.*] Well, doctor? I suppose you think you've
drawn me out very cleverly?

HERDAL. [*With some irritation.*] Drawn you out? Again I haven't
the faintest idea what you mean, Mr Solness.

SOLNESS. Oh, come! Why deny it? Do you suppose I haven't
noticed it?

HERDAL. Noticed what?

SOLNESS. [*Slowly, in a low voice.*] The way you've been observing
me of late.

HERDAL. Observing you? I? Why should I do that?

SOLNESS. Because you think that I'm—— Damn it! Because you
think the same of me that Aline does!

HERDAL. And what does *she* think of you?

SOLNESS. [*Recovering his self-control.*] Aline has begun to think that
I'm—well—let's call it ill.

HERDAL. You? Ill? She's never mentioned such a thing to me.
What does she think is the matter with you?

SOLNESS. [*Leans over the back of the chair and says in a whisper*] Aline
is convinced that I am mad. That's what she thinks.

HERDAL. [*Rising.*] But, my dear Mr Solness——!

SOLNESS. I tell you it *is* so! And she's convinced you of it too! Don't think I haven't noticed it. I'm not fooled so easily, Dr Herdal!

HERDAL. [*Looks at him in amazement.*] I give you my word, Mr Solness, such a thought has never crossed my mind.

SOLNESS. [*With an incredulous smile.*] It hasn't—eh?

HERDAL. Never! Nor your wife's mind either—I could swear to that.

SOLNESS. I wouldn't do that if I were you. Who knows? Perhaps, in a way, she may be right.

HERDAL. Well, really—— I must say!

SOLNESS. [*Interrupting with a sweep of his hand.*] Well, well—my dear doctor—we won't discuss it any further. We must simply agree to differ. [*Changes to a tone of quiet amusement.*] But I suppose, doctor——

HERDAL. What?

SOLNESS. Since you don't believe that I'm ill—or crazy—or mad—or whatever you want to call it——

HERDAL. Well?

SOLNESS. I suppose you consider me a very happy man?

HERDAL. Would I be mistaken in that?

SOLNESS. [*Laughs.*] No, no! Of course not! God forbid! To be Halvard Solness—Solness the great Master Builder! What could be more delightful!

HERDAL. You've been an amazingly lucky man—I should think you'd admit that!

SOLNESS. I have indeed—I can't complain on that score.

HERDAL. Ever since the old house burned down—that was your first bit of luck.

SOLNESS. [*Seriously.*] It was Aline's old home—don't forget that.

HERDAL. Yes. It must have been a great grief to her.

SOLNESS. She never got over it—though that was twelve or thirteen years ago.

HERDAL. No—the consequences were too tragic.

SOLNESS. It was all too much for her.

HERDAL. Still—that fire is what started your career; you built your success on those ruins; you were just a poor boy from a country village, and now you're at the head of your profession. You must admit, luck was on your side, Mr Solness.

SOLNESS. [*Looks at him in embarrassment.*] Yes, that's just why I'm so horribly afraid.

HERDAL. You afraid? Why? Because you've had the luck on your side?

SOLNESS. Yes, it fills me with terror. Some day that luck will turn, you see.

HERDAL. Nonsense! What should make the luck turn?

SOLNESS. [*Firmly. With assurance.*] The younger generation.

HERDAL. The younger generation? Oh, come now! You're not an old man yet! Your position here is more assured than ever.

SOLNESS. The luck will turn. I know it. I feel the day approaching. Some young man will suddenly shout 'Get out of my way!'; then all the others will crowd after him, clamouring, threatning: 'Make room! Make room! Make room!' You'll see, doctor— one of these days the younger generation will come knocking at my door——

HERDAL. [*Laughing.*] Well, what if they do?

SOLNESS. What if they do? That will be the end of Master Builder Solness.

> [*There is a knock at the door on the left.*

[*With a start.*] What is that? Didn't you hear?

HERDAL. Someone knocked at the door.

SOLNESS. [*Loudly.*] Come in!

[*Hilda Wangel enters from the hall. She is of medium height, supple, and delicate of build. Somewhat sunburnt. She wears hiking clothes, carries a knapsack on her back, a plaid in a strap and an alpenstock.*

HILDA. [*Goes straight up to Solness, her eyes sparkling with happiness.*] Good evening!

SOLNESS. [*Looks at her doubtfully.*] Good evening——

HILDA. [*Laughs.*] Don't tell me you don't recognize me!

SOLNESS. I'm sorry—but, just for the moment——

HERDAL. [*Approaching.*] But *I* recognize you, my dear young lady.

HILDA. [*Pleased.*] Oh! I remember you! You're the one who——

HERDAL. Of course! [*To Solness.*] We met up in the mountains last summer. [*To Hilda.*] What became of the other ladies?

HILDA. They went on to the West Coast——

HERDAL. Didn't they approve of all the fun we had?

HILDA. Probably not!

HERDAL. [*Shaking his finger at her.*] You must admit—you did flirt with us a bit!

HILDA. What did you expect? I couldn't compete with all that knitting!

HERDAL. [*Laughs.*] No! Knitting's not much in your line!

SOLNESS. Have you just arrived in town?

HILDA. Just this moment.

HERDAL. All alone, Miss Wangel?

HILDA. All alone!

SOLNESS. Wangel? Is your name Wangel?

HILDA. [*Looks at him with amused surprise.*] Of course it is!

SOLNESS. Are you by any chance Dr Wangel's daughter—from Lysanger?

HILDA. [*As before.*] Of course! Whose daughter did you think I was?

SOLNESS. Oh, then I suppose we met up there; that summer I built the tower on the old church.

HILDA. [*More seriously.*] Of course that's when we met!

SOLNESS. Well—that's a long time ago.

HILDA. [*Looks at him intensely.*] It's exactly the ten years.

SOLNESS. You must have been a mere child then.

HILDA. [*Carelessly.*] I was about twelve or thirteen——

HERDAL. Is this your first trip to town, Miss Wangel?

HILDA. Yes, it is.

SOLNESS. And have you no friends here?

HILDA. Just you—and your wife, of course.

SOLNESS. Oh, so you know her too?

HILDA. Very slightly—we met quite briefly, at the sanatorium.

SOLNESS. In Lysanger?

HILDA. Yes. She asked me to come and see her if ever I came to town. [*Smiles.*] Not that that was necessary, of course.

SOLNESS. Funny she should never have mentioned it.

> [*Hilda puts her stick down by the stove, takes off her knapsack and lays it and the plaid on the sofa. Dr Herdal offers to help her. Solness stands and gazes at her.*

HILDA. Well—is it all right for me to stay the night here?

SOLNESS. I expect that can be managed——

HILDA. You see—I didn't bring any clothes with me—just what I have on. I have a change of underwear in my knapsack—but that'll have to go to the wash—it's very dirty.

SOLNESS. We'll take care of that—I'll just call my wife.

HERDAL. Meanwhile, I'll visit my patient.

SOLNESS. Yes, do. And you'll come back later?

HERDAL. [*With a playful glance at Hilda.*] Don't worry—I'll be back! [*Laughs.*] You were right after all, Mr Solness——

SOLNESS. How do you mean?

HERDAL. The younger generation did come knocking at your door!

SOLNESS. [*Cheerfully.*] In quite a different way though!

HERDAL. Oh, in a very different way! That's undeniable!

[*Dr Herdal goes out by the hall door. Solness opens the door on the right and calls through to the other room.*

SOLNESS. Aline! Would you be kind enough to come in here a minute? There's a Miss Wangel here—a friend of yours.

MRS S. [*Appears in the doorway.*] Who did you say it was? [*Sees Hilda.*] Oh, it's you, Miss Wangel. [*Goes to her and shakes hands.*] So you did come to town, after all.

SOLNESS. Miss Wangel just arrived. She wants to know if she may stay the night here.

MRS S. Here with us? Of course—with pleasure.

SOLNESS. Just till she can get her clothes in order, you know.

MRS S. I'll help you as best I can—it's no more than my duty. Your trunk will be here presently, I suppose?

HILDA. Oh, I have no trunk!

MRS S. Well—everything will work out for the best I dare say. If you'll just stay and talk to my husband for a while, I'll see about getting a room comfortable for you.

SOLNESS. Why not put her in one of the nurseries? They're all ready as it is——

MRS S. Yes—we have plenty of room there—— [*To Hilda.*] Sit down now and rest a little.   [*She goes out right.*

[*Hilda with her hands behind her back strolls about the room looking at various things. Solness stands down front beside the table and follows her with his eyes.*

HILDA. [*Stops and looks at him.*] Are there so many nurseries here?

SOLNESS. There are three nurseries in the house.

HILDA. You must have a great many children!

SOLNESS. No, we have no children. So you'll have to be the child here for the time being.

HILDA. Yes—for tonight. I shan't cry! I intend to sleep like a log!

SOLNESS. You must be very tired.

HILDA. Not a bit! No, it's not that; but it's such fun just to lie in bed and dream——

SOLNESS. Do you usually dream at night?

HILDA. Almost always.

SOLNESS. What do you dream about most?

HILDA. I won't tell you! Some other time, perhaps.
[*She again strolls about the room, stops at the desk and examines some of the books and papers.*

SOLNESS. Are you looking for something?

HILDA. No—I was just interested in all these things. [*Turns towards him.*] Perhaps I shouldn't touch them?

SOLNESS. Go right ahead!

HILDA. Do you write in this great ledger?

SOLNESS. No. That's for the accountant.

HILDA. A woman?

SOLNESS. [*Smiles.*] Yes; of course.

HILDA. Does she work here every day?

SOLNESS. Yes.

HILDA. Is she married?

SOLNESS. No; she's single.

HILDA. Indeed!

SOLNESS. But she expects to marry soon.

HILDA. Well—that'll be nice for her.

SOLNESS. Yes—but not so nice for me—for then I'll have no one to help me.

HILDA. You're sure to find someone else just as good.

SOLNESS. How would you like to stay here—and write in the ledger?

HILDA. Not I, thank you! Nothing like that for me! [*She again strolls across the room and sits down in the rocking-chair. Solness joins her at the table.*] There are better things than that to be done around here! [*Looks at him with a smile.*] Don't you think so too?

SOLNESS. Unquestionably! I suppose you'll start by visiting all the shops and decking yourself out in the height of fashion.

HILDA. [*Amused.*] No—I think I'll leave the shops alone!

SOLNESS. Why?

HILDA. Well—you see—I'm all out of money!

SOLNESS. No trunk and no money—eh?

HILDA. Neither the one nor the other! But what does that matter now!

SOLNESS. You know—I really like you for that!

HILDA. Only for that?

SOLNESS. For that among other things—— [*Sits in the armchair.*] Is your father still alive?

HILDA. Yes—Father's alive.

SOLNESS. Do you plan to study at the university here?

HILDA. No, that hadn't occurred to me.

SOLNESS. But I suppose you'll be here for some time?

HILDA. It depends how things turn out. [*She sits awhile looking at him, half seriously, half smiling. Then she takes off her hat and puts it on the table in front of her.*] Master Builder?

SOLNESS. Yes?

HILDA. Have you a very bad memory?

SOLNESS. Bad memory? No—not that I know of——

HILDA. Well—aren't you going to talk to me about what happened up there?

SOLNESS. [*Startled for a moment.*] At Lysanger? [*Indifferently.*] I don't see much to talk about in that?

HILDA. [*Looks at him reproachfully.*] How can you sit there and say such things!

SOLNESS. Well—suppose you talk to *me* about it.

HILDA. When the tower was finished—don't you remember all the excitement in the town?

SOLNESS. Yes—I shall never forget that day.

HILDA. [*Smiles.*] Oh, you won't, won't you? That's kind of you!

SOLNESS. Kind?

HILDA. There was a band in the churchyard and hundreds and hundreds of people—we schoolgirls were dressed all in white—and we all carried flags——

SOLNESS. Oh, yes! Those flags! I certainly remember them——

HILDA. And then you climbed up the scaffolding—right to the very top. You had a great wreath in your hand, and you hung it high up on the weather vane——

SOLNESS. [*Curtly interrupting.*] I used to do that in those days—it's an old custom, you know.

HILDA. It was wonderfully thrilling to stand below and look up at you. What if he were to fall over—he, the Master Builder himself!

SOLNESS. [*As though trying to divert her from the subject.*] That might easily have happened too; one of those little devils dressed in white carried on so and kept screaming up at me——

HILDA. [*Sparkling with pleasure.*]—'Hurrah for Master Builder Solness!'

SOLNESS. —and then she kept brandishing her flag and waving it so wildly—the sight of it made me feel quite dizzy.

HILDA. [*Seriously. In a low voice.*] That particular little devil—that was I.

SOLNESS. [*Staring at her intently.*] Of course—I see that now. It must have been you.

HILDA. It was so wonderfully thrilling! It didn't seem possible to me that any Master Builder in the whole world could build such a tremendously high tower. And then to see you up there yourself—right at the very top—as large as life! And to know that you weren't in the least bit dizzy—that was what made one so—dizzy to think of!

SOLNESS. How could you be so sure that I was not——

HILDA. You dizzy? Of course not! I knew that with my whole being! Besides—if you had been—you could never have stood up there and sung.

SOLNESS. [*Looks at her in amazement.*] Sung? Did *I* sing?

HILDA. Of course you did!

SOLNESS. [*Shakes his head.*] I've never sung a note in my life.

HILDA. Well—you sang then! It sounded like harps in the air.

SOLNESS. [*Thoughtfully.*] There's something very strange about all this.

HILDA. [*Is silent a while, looking at him; then says in a low voice*] But of course the *real* thing—happened afterwards.

SOLNESS. What 'real' thing?

HILDA. [*Sparkling with vivacity.*] I surely needn't remind you of *that*?

SOLNESS. Please—*do* remind me a little of *that* too!

HILDA. Don't you remember, a great dinner was given for you at the club——

SOLNESS. Yes. That must have been the same afternoon—for I left the next morning.

HILDA. And from the club, you came on to our house——

SOLNESS. I believe you're right, Miss Wangel! It's amazing! You seem to remember every little detail——

HILDA. 'Little details'—is that what you call them? I suppose it was a 'little detail' too that I happened to be alone in the room when you came in?

SOLNESS. Oh? Were you alone?

HILDA. [*Ignoring this.*] You didn't call me a 'little devil' then.

SOLNESS. No. I suppose not——

HILDA. You told me I looked lovely in my white dress. You said I looked like a little princess.

SOLNESS. I expect you did, Miss Wangel. And I remember feeling so free and buoyant that day——

HILDA. And then you said that when I grew up I was to be *your* princess——

SOLNESS. [*Laughing a little.*] Well—well! I said that too, did I?

HILDA. Yes, you did. And when I asked how long I'd have to wait, you said you'd come back again in ten years—and carry me off like a troll—to Spain, or some such place. And you promised to buy me a kingdom there.

SOLNESS. [*As before.*] There's nothing like a good dinner to make you feel generous! But—did I really say all that?

HILDA. [*Laughing to herself.*] Yes, you did. You even told me what the kingdom was to be called.

SOLNESS. Well—What?

HILDA. It was to be called the Kingdom of Orangia, you said.

SOLNESS. A very appetizing name!

HILDA. I didn't like it a bit! It sounded almost as if you were making fun of me.

SOLNESS. Of course I *couldn't* have been doing that.

HILDA. Well, I should hope not—considering what you did next.

SOLNESS. What in God's name did I do next?

HILDA. Don't tell me you've forgotten that too! I know better; you couldn't *help* remembering it.

SOLNESS. Won't you give me just a little hint? Well?

HILDA. [*Looks at him intently.*] You came and kissed me, Master Builder.

SOLNESS. [*Rising, open-mouthed.*] I did!

HILDA. Yes, you did. You took me in your arms and bent my head back and kissed me—many times.

SOLNESS. Now really—my dear Miss Wangel——!

HILDA. You surely don't intend to deny it?

SOLNESS. I most certainly *do* deny it!

HILDA. [*Looks at him scornfully.*] Oh, indeed!

[*She goes slowly up to the stove and remains standing motionless, her face averted from him, her hands behind her back. Short pause.*

SOLNESS. [*Moves up behind her cautiously.*] Miss Wangel——! [*Hilda is silent and doesn't move.*] Now don't stand there like a statue. You must have dreamt these things—— [*Lays his hand on her arm.*] Now look here! [*Hilda moves her arm impatiently. A thought strikes him.*] Or perhaps—wait a minute! There's some mystery behind all this—I must have thought about it. I must have willed it, wished it, longed to do it, and then—— Perhaps that would explain it. [*Hilda is still silent.*] Oh, very well then—damn it!—then I *did* do it, I suppose!

HILDA. [*Turns her head a little but without looking at him.*] Then you admit it now?

SOLNESS. Anything you like.

HILDA. You took me in your arms?

SOLNESS. Yes——

HILDA. Bent my head back?

SOLNESS. Very far back——

HILDA. And kissed me?

SOLNESS. Yes, I did.

HILDA. Many times?

SOLNESS. As many times as you like.

HILDA. [*Turns towards him quickly. Once more her eyes are sparkling with happiness.*] There, you see! I got it out of you at last!

SOLNESS. [*With a slight smile.*] Yes. How could I possibly have forgotten a thing like that.

HILDA. [*Again a little sulkily, retreats from him.*] Oh, you've probably kissed so many people in your day!

SOLNESS. No—you mustn't think that of me!

[*Hilda sits down in the armchair. Solness stands leaning against the rocking-chair and watches her intently.*

SOLNESS. Miss Wangel!

HILDA. Well?

SOLNESS. And then what happened? I mean—what came of all this between us two?

HILDA. Nothing came of it—you know that perfectly well—just then all the others came in, and then—isch!

SOLNESS. Of course—all the others came in. To think of my forgetting that too.

HILDA. I don't believe you've really forgotten anything. You're just a bit ashamed, that's all. You couldn't possibly forget a thing of that sort.

SOLNESS. No—one wouldn't think so.

HILDA. [*Again sparkling with life.*] I suppose, now, you'll tell me you've forgotten what date it was?

SOLNESS. What date?

HILDA. Yes—on what day of what month did you hang the wreath on the tower? Well? Tell me at once!

SOLNESS. I'm afraid I've forgotten the actual date—I remember it was ten years ago, some time in the autumn.

HILDA. [*Nods her head slowly several times.*] Yes, it *was* ten years ago—on the 19th of September.

SOLNESS. Yes, it must have been around that time. Fancy your remembering that too! But, wait a minute—isn't it——? Yes! It's the 19th of September today.

HILDA. Yes it is. And the ten years are up. And you didn't come as you had promised me.

SOLNESS. Promised? Threatened, I suppose you mean.

HILDA. Why? It didn't seem like a threat to me.

SOLNESS. Well, then—making a little fun of you, perhaps.

HILDA. Was that all you wanted? To make fun of me?

SOLNESS. I was just teasing you, I suppose—I don't remember anything about it—but it couldn't have been anything else; after all, at that time you were only a child.

HILDA. Don't be so sure! Perhaps I wasn't quite such a child either. Not quite such a callow little brat as you imagine.

SOLNESS. [*With a searching look.*] Did you really, in all seriousness, expect me to come back again?

HILDA. [*Conceals a half-teasing smile.*] Of course I did!

SOLNESS. You really expected me to come back to your home and carry you off with me?

HILDA. Just like a troll—yes!

SOLNESS. And make a princess of you?

HILDA. That's what you promised.

SOLNESS. And give you a kingdom as well?

HILDA. [*Gazing at the ceiling.*] Why not? Oh, perhaps not an ordinary, *everyday* sort of kingdom——

SOLNESS. But something else just as good?

HILDA. Oh, at *least* as good! [*Looks at him a moment.*] I thought to myself—if he can build the highest church tower in the world, he must surely be able to raise some sort of a kingdom as well——

SOLNESS. [*Shakes his head.*] I can't quite make you out, Miss Wangel.

HILDA. Can't you? It all seems so simple to me.

SOLNESS. No; I can't make out whether you mean all you say—or whether you're just joking.

HILDA. [*Smiles.*] Making fun of you, perhaps—I too?

SOLNESS. Precisely—making fun of us both. [*Looks at her.*] How long have you known that I was married?

HILDA. I've always known that. Why? What makes you ask?

SOLNESS. [*Lightly.*] Oh, nothing—it just occurred to me. [*Looks at her seriously and says in a low voice*] Why have you come here?

HILDA. I want my kingdom—the time is up!

SOLNESS. [*Laughs involuntarily.*] What an amazing girl you are!

HILDA. [*Gaily.*] Out with my kingdom, Master Builder. [*Raps the table with her fingers.*] My kingdom on the table!

SOLNESS. [*Pushing the rocking-chair nearer and sitting down.*] No, but seriously—why have you come? What do you really want to do here?

HILDA. Well, to begin with—I want to go round and look at all the things you've built.

SOLNESS. That'll give you plenty of exercise!

HILDA. Yes—I know you've built a tremendous lot!

SOLNESS. I have. Especially these last few years——

HILDA. Many church towers too? Immensely high ones?

SOLNESS. No, I don't build church towers any more. Nor churches either.

HILDA. Then what do you build now?

SOLNESS. Homes for human beings.

HILDA. [*Thoughtfully.*] Couldn't you build some sort of a—some sort of a church tower over those homes as well?

SOLNESS. [*With a start.*] What do you mean by that?

HILDA. I mean—something that soars—that points straight up into the free air—with the vane at a dizzy height!

SOLNESS. [*Pondering.*] How extraordinary that you should say that. That's what I've always longed to do.

HILDA. [*Impatiently.*] Well—why don't you *do* it then?

SOLNESS. [*Shakes his head.*] I don't think people would approve of it.

HILDA. Wouldn't they? How can they be so stupid!

SOLNESS. [*In a lighter tone.*] I'm building a home for myself, however —just over there——

HILDA. For yourself?

SOLNESS. Yes—it's almost finished—and there's a tower on that.

HILDA. A high tower?

SOLNESS. Yes.

HILDA. Very high?

SOLNESS. Much too high for a home—people are sure to say!

HILDA. I'll go out and see that tower first thing in the morning, Master Builder.

SOLNESS. [*Sits resting his cheek on his hand and gazes at her.*] What's your name, Miss Wangel—your first name, I mean?

HILDA. My name's Hilda, of course.

SOLNESS. [*As before.*] Hilda, eh?

HILDA. You must have known that! You called me Hilda yourself, that day when you—misbehaved.

SOLNESS. Did I really?

HILDA. Yes. Only then you said 'little Hilda'—I didn't like that.

SOLNESS. So you didn't like that, Miss Hilda.

HILDA. Not at a time like that! *Princess* Hilda, however, would sound very well, I think.

SOLNESS. Princess Hilda of—what was to be the name of the kingdom?

HILDA. I'll have nothing more to do with that stupid kingdom! I'm determined to have quite a different one.

SOLNESS. [*Leaning back in the chair, still gazing at her.*] Isn't it strange! The more I think of it, the more it seems to me that all these years I've been tormented by——

HILDA. By what?

SOLNESS. By some half forgotten experience that I kept trying to recapture. But I never could remember clearly what it was.

HILDA. You should have tied a knot in your handkerchief, Master Builder.

SOLNESS. Then I should have only tormented myself wondering what the knot was about.

HILDA. Yes! There are trolls of that sort in the world too!

SOLNESS. [*Rises slowly.*] What a good thing it is that you've come to me now.

HILDA. [*Looks deep into his eyes.*] Is it a good thing?

SOLNESS. Yes—don't you see? I've been so lonely here—gazing at everything so helplessly. [*In a lower voice*] I must tell you, Hilda —I've begun to be so afraid—so terribly afraid of the younger generation.

HILDA. [*With a little snort of contempt.*] The younger generation! Surely that's nothing to be afraid of!

SOLNESS. Oh yes, it is! That's why I've locked and barred myself in. [*Mysteriously.*] I tell you one of these days the younger generation will thunder at my door—they'll break through and overwhelm me!

HILDA. In that case, I think that you yourself should go out and open the door to the younger generation.

SOLNESS. Open the door?

HILDA. Of course! Let them come in to you—in friendship.

SOLNESS. No, no! Don't you see? The younger generation comes bringing retribution. It heralds the turn of fortune; it marches triumphantly, under a new banner.

HILDA. [*Rises, looks at him, and says with quivering lips*] Can I be of use to you, Master Builder?

SOLNESS. You can indeed! For you too march under a new banner, it seems to me. Yes! Youth matched against youth!

[*Dr Herdal comes in by the hall door.*

HERDAL. Well! So you and Miss Wangel are still here.

SOLNESS. Yes—we found so much to talk about——

HILDA. Old things as well as new.

HERDAL. Did you really?

HILDA. It's been the greatest fun! Mr Solness has the most remarkable memory. He remembers things so vividly—down to the tiniest detail!

[*Mrs Solness enters by the door right.*

MRS S. Your room is ready now, Miss Wangel.

HILDA. How very kind you are.

SOLNESS. [*To Mrs S.*] The nursery?

MRS S. Yes, the middle one. Well—shall we go in to supper?

SOLNESS. [*Nodding to Hilda.*] Hilda shall sleep in the nursery, she shall!

MRS S. [*Looks at him.*] Hilda?

SOLNESS. Yes, Miss Wangel's name is Hilda. I knew her when she was a little girl.

MRS S. Did you really, Halvard? Come, let us go in. Supper is on the table.

[*She takes Dr Herdal's arm and goes out with him to the right. Hilda has meanwhile been collecting her belongings.*

HILDA. [*Softly and rapidly to Solness.*] Was that true what you said just now? Can I be of use to you?

SOLNESS. [*Takes her things from her.*] You are the one being I have needed most.

HILDA. [*Looks at him with happy eyes full of wonder and clasps her hands.*] But then—oh, how wonderful the world is!

SOLNESS. [*Eagerly.*] How do you mean?

HILDA. Why then—I *have* my kingdom!

SOLNESS. [*Involuntarily.*] Hilda!

HILDA. [*Again with quivering lips.*] Almost—I was going to say.

[*She goes out to the right, Solness following her.*]

CURTAIN

A small, prettily furnished drawing-room in Solness's house. In the back, a glass door leading out to the veranda and garden. The right-hand corner is cut off transversely by a large bay window, in which are flower stands. The left-hand corner is similarly cut off by a transverse wall, in which is a small door papered like the wall. On each side, an ordinary door. In front, on the right, a console table with a large mirror over it. Well-filled stands of plants and flowers. In front, on the left, a sofa with a table and chairs. Farther back, a bookcase. Well forward in the room, in front of the bay window, a small table and some chairs. It is early in the day.
Solness sits by the little table with Ragnar Brovik's portfolio open in front of him. He is turning the drawings over and closely examining some of them. Mrs Solness moves about noiselessly with a small watering-pot, attending to her flowers. She is dressed in black as before. Her hat, cloak, and gloves lie on a chair near the mirror. Unobserved by her, Solness now and then follows her with his eyes. Neither of them speaks.
Kaia Fosli enters quietly by the door on the left.

SOLNESS. [*Turns his head and says with casual indifference.*] Oh—it's you.

KAIA. I just wanted to let you know that I was here——

SOLNESS. Very well. Did Ragnar come too?

KAIA. No, not yet. He had to wait for the doctor. But he's coming presently to find out——

SOLNESS. How is the old man feeling?

KAIA. Not at all well. He begs you to excuse him—he'll have to stay in bed today.

SOLNESS. Of course. Let him rest. But you'd better get to your work now——

KAIA. Yes. [*Pauses at the door.*] Would you like to speak to Ragnar when he comes?

SOLNESS. No—I've nothing special to say to him.

[*Kaia goes out again to the left. Solness remains seated, turning over the drawings.*

MRS S. [*Over beside the plants.*] I expect he'll die now as well.

SOLNESS. [*Looks up at her.*] As well as who?

106

MRS S. [*Not answering him.*] Yes—old Brovik is going to die too. You'll see, Halvard.

SOLNESS. My dear Aline, don't you think you should go out for a little walk?

MRS S. Yes, I suppose I should.

[*She continues to attend to the flowers.*

SOLNESS. [*Bending over the drawings.*] Is she still asleep?

MRS S. [*Looking at him.*] Miss Wangel? So it's Miss Wangel you're thinking about.

SOLNESS. [*Indifferently.*] I just happened to remember her.

MRS S. Miss Wangel was up long ago.

SOLNESS. Really. Was she?

MRS S. When I went in to see her, she was putting her things in order.   [*She goes to the mirror and slowly begins to put on her hat.*

SOLNESS. [*After a short pause.*] Well—we've found a use for one of our nurseries after all, Aline.

MRS S. So we have.

SOLNESS. It seems to me that's better than having them all empty.

MRS S. Yes, you're right—that emptiness is dreadful.

SOLNESS. [*Closes the portfolio, rises and goes to her.*] You'll see, Aline— from now on things are going to be much better—more cheerful. Life will be easier—especially for you.

MRS S. [*Looks at him.*] From now on?

SOLNESS. Yes, you'll see, Aline——

MRS S. Because *she* has come here? Is that what you mean?

SOLNESS. [*Checking himself.*] I mean—after we've moved into the new house.

MRS S. [*Takes her coat.*] Really, Halvard? Do you think things will be better then?

SOLNESS. Of course they will, Aline. I'm sure you must think so too.

MRS S. I think nothing at all about the new house.

SOLNESS. [*Downcast.*] It's hard for me to hear you talk like that, considering it's mostly for your sake that I built it.

[*He offers to help her on with her coat.*

MRS S. [*Evading him.*] I'm afraid you do far too much for my sake.

SOLNESS. [*With a certain vehemence.*] You mustn't say such things, Aline; I can't bear it!

MRS S. Then I won't say them, Halvard.

SOLNESS. But I stick to what I said—you'll see—things'll be much easier for you over there.

MRS S. Heavens! Easier for me!

SOLNESS. [*Eagerly.*] Yes, I tell you, you *must* see that! There'll be so many things to remind you of your old home.

MRS S. Father's and Mother's home—that was burned to the ground.

SOLNESS. [*In a low voice.*] Yes, poor Aline! I know what a great grief that was to you.

MRS S. [*Breaking out in lamentation.*] You can build as much as you like, Halvard—you'll never be able to build another real home for me.

SOLNESS. [*Crosses the room.*] Then for God's sake don't let's talk about it any more!

MRS S. We don't as a rule talk about it—you always carefully avoid the subject.

SOLNESS. [*Stops suddenly and looks at her.*] Avoid? Why should I avoid it?

MRS S. Don't think I don't understand you, Halvard. I know you want to spare me—you try to find excuses for me—as much as you possibly can.

SOLNESS. [*Looks at her in astonishment.*] For *you*, Aline? *I* find excuses for *you*!

MRS S. Yes, Halvard—for me; I know that only too well.

SOLNESS. [*Involuntarily; to himself.*] That too!

MRS S. As for the old house—it was meant to be, I suppose. But it's what came after the fire—the dreadful thing that followed! That's what I can never——!

SOLNESS. [*Vehemently.*] You must stop thinking about *that*, Aline!

MRS S. How can I help thinking about it! And for once I must speak about it too! I can't bear it any longer—I'll never be able to forgive myself!

SOLNESS. [*Exclaiming.*] Yourself——!

MRS S. Yes. I should have been strong, Halvard. I had my duties both to you and to the little ones. I shouldn't have let the horror overwhelm me—nor the grief at the loss of my old home. [*Wrings her hands.*] Oh, Halvard, if I'd only had the strength!

SOLNESS. [*Softly, much moved, comes towards her.*] Aline—promise me that you will never think these thoughts again—promise me that!

MRS S. Promise! One can promise anything!

SOLNESS. [*Clenches his hands and crosses the room.*] Oh, this is all hopeless—hopeless! Can we never have any brightness in our home? Never a ray of sunlight?

MRS S. This is not a *home*, Halvard.

SOLNESS. No. You're right. [*Gloomily.*] And I don't suppose it'll be any better in the new house either.

MRS S. No. It won't be any better. It'll be just as empty and desolate there as it is here.

SOLNESS. [*Vehemently.*] Then why in God's name did we build it?—can you tell me that?

MRS S. That's a question only you can answer, Halvard.

SOLNESS. [*With a suspicious glance at her.*] What do you mean by *that*, Aline?

MRS S. What do I mean?

SOLNESS. Yes—damn it! You said it so strangely. What are you trying to imply, Aline?

MRS S. Halvard—I assure you——

SOLNESS. [*Comes closer.*] I know what I know, Aline. I'm neither blind nor deaf—just remember that!

MRS S. What are you talking about, Halvard? What is it?

SOLNESS. [*Stands in front of her.*] You know perfectly well you manage to find a furtive hidden meaning in the most innocent word I happen to say!

MRS S. *I* do, Halvard! How can you say that!

SOLNESS. [*Laughs.*] It's natural enough, I suppose—when you're dealing with a sick man——

MRS S. [*Anxiously.*] Sick! Are you ill, Halvard?

SOLNESS. [*Violently.*] A half-mad man, then—a lunatic, if you prefer to call it that!

MRS S. [*Feels blindly for a chair and sits down.*] Halvard—for God's sake!

SOLNESS. But you're both wrong, do you hear? Both you and the doctor! I'm in no such state! [*He walks up and down the room. Mrs Solness follows him anxiously with her eyes. Finally, he goes up to her and says calmly*] As a matter of fact there's absolutely nothing wrong with me.

MRS S. No. There isn't, is there? But then, what is it that troubles you so?

SOLNESS. It's this terrible burden of debt—I sometimes feel I can't bear it any longer!

MRS S. Debt? But you owe no one anything, Halvard.

SOLNESS. [*Softly. With emotion.*] I owe a boundless debt to you—to you—to *you*, Aline.

MRS S. [*Rises slowly.*] What are you hiding from me, Halvard? Tell me the truth.

SOLNESS. I'm not hiding anything from you. I've never harmed you—never deliberately, never intentionally, that is—and yet I feel crushed by a terrible sense of guilt.

MRS S. Towards me?

SOLNESS. Yes—mostly towards you.

MRS S. Then you must be—ill—after all, Halvard.

SOLNESS. [*Gloomily.*] Yes. I suppose I must be—or not far from it. [*He looks towards the door on the right, which is opened at this moment.*] Ah! Now it gets lighter!

        [*Hilda comes in. She has made some alteration to her dress.*

HILDA. Good morning, Master Builder!

SOLNESS. [*Nods.*] Did you sleep well?

HILDA. Splendidly! Like a child in a cradle! I lay there and stretched myself like—like a princess!

SOLNESS. [*Smiles a little.*] You were quite comfortable then?

HILDA. I was indeed!

SOLNESS. Did you have any dreams?

HILDA. Yes—but horrid ones!

SOLNESS. Really?

HILDA. Yes. I dreamt I was falling over a high steep precipice. Do you ever dream that sort of thing?

SOLNESS. Yes, now and then.

HILDA. It's wonderfully thrilling, though; you feel yourself falling farther and farther—down and down——

SOLNESS. I know! It makes your blood run cold.

HILDA. Do you draw your legs up under you when you're falling?

SOLNESS. As high as I possibly can.

HILDA. So do I!

MRS S. [*Takes her gloves.*] I'd better go into town now, Halvard. [*To Hilda.*] I'll try and get some of the things you need, Miss Wangel.

HILDA. [*Starts to throw her arms round her neck.*] Dear, darling Mrs Solness! You're really much too kind to me—incredibly kind!

MRS S. [*Deprecatingly, freeing herself.*] Not at all—it's no more than my duty. I'm only too glad to do it.

HILDA. [*Offended, pouts.*] There's really no reason why I shouldn't go myself—now that I look so respectable. What do you think?

MRS S. To tell you the truth, I'm afraid people might stare at you a little.

HILDA. [*Contemptuously.*] Is *that* all? That'd be fun!

SOLNESS. [*With suppressed ill humour.*] Yes, but then people might think *you* were mad too.

HILDA. Mad? Why? Is the place so full of mad people?

SOLNESS. [*Points to his own forehead.*] Here is *one*, at any rate——

HILDA. You—Master Builder!

MRS S. Now really, my dear Halvard!

SOLNESS. You surely must have noticed it.

HILDA. No, I can't say I have. [*Thinks a moment and laughs a little.*] Though there was *one* thing——

SOLNESS. Do you hear that, Aline?

MRS S. What thing, Miss Wangel?

HILDA. I won't tell you.

SOLNESS. Oh, yes—do!

HILDA. No thanks—I'm not quite as mad as *that*!

MRS S. When you are alone Miss Wangel's sure to tell you, Halvard.

SOLNESS. Oh—you think so?

MRS S. Of course. After all, she's such an old friend of yours—you've known her ever since she was a child, you tell me.

[*She goes out by the door on the left.*

HILDA. [*After a short pause.*] Your wife doesn't seem to like me very much.

SOLNESS. Why do you say that?

HILDA. Wasn't it pretty obvious?

SOLNESS. [*Evasively.*] It's just her manner—Aline's become very shy these past few years——

HILDA. Oh—has she really?

SOLNESS. But underneath she's an immensely kind, gentle, good-hearted creature—you'll see, when you know her better——

HILDA. Perhaps. But I wish she wouldn't talk so much about her duty.

SOLNESS. Her duty?

HILDA. Yes. Why did she have to say she'd get those things for me because it was her *duty*? I hate that ugly, horrid word!

SOLNESS. Why?

HILDA. I don't know—it sounds so cold and harsh and prickly: duty, duty, duty! It *is* prickly! Don't you think so too?

SOLNESS. I've never thought about it.

HILDA. Well, it *is*! And if she's as kind as you say she is—why does she use a word like that?

SOLNESS. Well—what on earth should she have said?

HILDA. She could have said she'd *love* to do it, because she'd taken such a tremendous fancy to me. She could have said something like that—something warm and friendly—don't you see?

SOLNESS. [*Looks at her.*] That's what you'd have liked, is it?

HILDA. Yes, of course. [*She wanders about the room, stops at the book-cases and examines the books.*] What a lot of books you have!

SOLNESS. Yes—I seem to have collected a good many——

HILDA. Do you read them all too?

SOLNESS. When I was young I used to try to. Do you read much?

HILDA. No, never! I've given it up—it all seems so irrelevant.

SOLNESS. That's just how I feel.

[*Hilda wanders about a little, stops at the small table, opens the portfolio and turns over the contents.*

HILDA. Are these your drawings?

SOLNESS. No; they were done by a young man who's my assistant here.

HILDA. Then he's been studying with you, I suppose.

SOLNESS. He's learned something from me, I dare say.

HILDA. Then he must be very clever. [*Looks at a drawing.*] Isn't he?

SOLNESS. He could be worse. He serves my purpose——

HILDA. I expect he's frightfully clever!

SOLNESS. Why? Do you see that in the drawings?

HILDA. What? These things! No! But if he's a pupil of yours——

SOLNESS. I've had lots of pupils in my time—but they haven't amounted to much.

HILDA. I can't think how you can be so stupid, Master Builder!

SOLNESS. Stupid? Why do you think me stupid?

HILDA. You must be—or you wouldn't waste your time teaching all these people——

SOLNESS. Why not?

HILDA. What for? You're the only one who should be allowed to build. You should build everything yourself, Master Builder—you alone!

SOLNESS. [*Involuntarily.*] Hilda!

HILDA. Well?

SOLNESS. Whatever put that idea into your head?

HILDA. Why? Am I so wrong?

SOLNESS. No—it's not that—— But, do you know something, Hilda?

HILDA. What?

SOLNESS. I myself am obsessed by that very thought. I sit here alone, in silence, brooding over it incessantly.

HILDA. That's quite natural, it seems to me.

SOLNESS. [*Gives her a somewhat searching look.*] You'd probably already noticed it——

HILDA. No—I can't say I had.

SOLNESS. But, a few minutes ago—when you admitted to thinking me a little—queer—in just one thing, you said——

HILDA. Oh! I was thinking of something quite different.

SOLNESS. What was it?

HILDA. I won't tell you.

SOLNESS. [*Crossing the room.*] Just as you like. [*He stops at the bow window.*] Come here, Hilda. I want to show you something.

HILDA. [*Goes towards him.*] What?

SOLNESS. Do you see—over there in the garden——?

HILDA. Yes?

SOLNESS. Just beyond the stone quarry——

HILDA. Oh—the new house, you mean?

SOLNESS. Yes—the one they're working on; it's nearly finished.

HILDA. It seems to have a very high tower——

SOLNESS. The scaffolding is still up.

HILDA. Is that your new house?

SOLNESS. Yes.

HILDA. The one you'll soon be moving into?

SOLNESS. Yes.

HILDA. [*Looks at him.*] Are there nurseries in that house too?

SOLNESS. Three—just as there are here.

HILDA. And no children.

SOLNESS. No—and there never will be.

HILDA. [*With a half-smile.*] Well? Wasn't I right?

SOLNESS. How?

HILDA. Aren't you a little—mad, after all?

SOLNESS. So that's what you were thinking of.

HILDA. Yes—all those empty nurseries I slept in.

SOLNESS. [*Lowers his voice.*] We *have* had children—Aline and I——

HILDA. [*Breathlessly.*] Have you?

SOLNESS. Two little boys. They were the same age——

HILDA. Twins, then.

SOLNESS. Yes, twins. It's eleven or twelve years ago——

HILDA. [*Cautiously.*] And are they both——? Did you lose them? Both of them?

SOLNESS. [*With quiet emotion.*] They only lived two weeks—not even that. Oh, Hilda—it's so good that you've come to me; now at last I have someone I can talk to!

HILDA. Can't you talk to—*her* too?

SOLNESS. Not about this. Not as I want to—as I need to [*Gloomily.*] And there are so many *other* things I can never talk to her about!

HILDA. [*In a subdued voice.*] So *that* was all you meant, when you said you needed me!

SOLNESS. Chiefly, yes. Yesterday at least—today, I'm no longer sure—— [*Breaking off.*] Sit down, Hilda—sit there, so you can look out into the garden. [*Hilda seats herself in the corner of the sofa. Solness draws up a chair.*] Would you like to hear about it?

HILDA. Very much.

SOLNESS. [*Sits down.*] Good—then I'll tell you the whole story.

HILDA. I can see the garden from here—and I can see you, Master Builder—so tell me all about it. Begin!

SOLNESS. [*Points through the window.*] There used to be an old house where the new house stands—Aline and I spent the first years of our marriage there; it had belonged to her mother—and we inherited it, and the huge garden as well.

HILDA. Was there a tower on the old house, too?

SOLNESS. No—nothing like that! It looked like a large, ugly, gloomy wooden box from the outside; but inside it was comfortable enough.

HILDA. What happened? Did you tear it down?

SOLNESS. No. It burnt down.

HILDA. All of it?

SOLNESS. Yes.

HILDA. Was it a great loss to you?

SOLNESS. That depends on how you look at it. As a builder—that fire was the making of me——

HILDA. Was it? Then——

SOLNESS. It was just after the birth of the two little boys——

HILDA. The poor little twins, yes.

SOLNESS. They were so sturdy and healthy—and they were growing so fast—you could see a difference from day to day——

HILDA. Yes. Babies do grow quickly at first.

SOLNESS. It was such a pretty sight to see Aline lying there with the two of them in her arms. But then came the night of the fire——

HILDA. [*With excitement.*] What happened? Tell me! Was anyone burnt?

SOLNESS. No, not that. Everyone got out of the house safely——

HILDA. Well—what then?

SOLNESS. Well, you see—it was a terrible shock to Aline; all the shouts—the confusion—the flames—the sudden fear—she and the little boys were sound asleep; they got them out just in time; they had to drag them out of bed, and carry them just as they were, out into that bitter night——

HILDA. Was that why they——?

SOLNESS. No; they recovered from that. But later, Aline developed a fever, and it affected her milk; she would insist on nursing them herself—it was her duty, she said. And our two little boys, they—they—oh!

HILDA. They didn't get over that?

SOLNESS. No, they didn't get over that. That is how we lost them.

HILDA. How terrible for you.

SOLNESS. Hard enough for me; but ten times harder for Aline. [*Clenching his hands in suppressed fury.*] Why are such things allowed to happen in this world! [*Shortly and firmly.*] From the day I lost them, I had no joy in building churches.

HILDA. Didn't you even like building the church tower in our town?

SOLNESS. No, I didn't like it. I remember how glad I was when that tower was finished.

HILDA. *I* remember that too.

SOLNESS. I shall never build anything of that sort again. Neither churches nor church towers.

HILDA. [*Nods slowly.*] Only houses for people to live in.

SOLNESS. Homes for human beings, Hilda.

HILDA. But homes with high towers—and spires soaring above them!

SOLNESS. If possible. [*In a lighter tone.*] Well—as I told you—that fire was the making of me—as a builder, that is.

HILDA. Why don't you call yourself architect, like the others?

SOLNESS. My education wasn't thorough enough for that. What I know, I've mostly found out for myself.

HILDA. But you climbed to the top just the same!

SOLNESS. Thanks to the fire, yes. Most of the old garden I cut up small into building lots; I was free to try out my ideas—to build exactly as I chose. Then—nothing could stop me; success came with a rush.

HILDA. [*Looks at him keenly.*] What a happy man you must be, Master Builder.

SOLNESS. [*Gloomily.*] Happy! You sound like all the others!

HILDA. I should think you *must* be happy. If you could only stop thinking about the two little boys.

SOLNESS. [*Slowly.*] They're not so easy to forget, Hilda.

HILDA. [*Somewhat uncertainly.*] Not even after all these years?

SOLNESS. [*Stares at her without answering.*] So you think me a happy man——

HILDA. Well, *aren't* you? I mean—apart from that?

SOLNESS. [*Still looking at her.*] When I told you all that about the fire——

HILDA. Yes?

SOLNESS. Weren't you struck by one particular thing?

HILDA. [*After thinking in vain for a moment.*] No. What do you mean?

SOLNESS. Weren't you struck by the fact that it was solely because of that fire that I had the chance to build these homes for human beings? These comfortable, warm, cheerful homes where a mother and a father and a whole troop of children could enjoy life in peace and happiness—sharing the big things and the little things— and, best of all, *belonging* to each other, Hilda?

HILDA. [*Ardently.*] Well—isn't that a great happiness for you, to be able to build these beautiful homes?

SOLNESS. What about the price, Hilda? The terrible price I had to pay for that opportunity?

HILDA. But can't you *ever* get over that?

SOLNESS. No. In order to build these homes for others, I had to give up—give up for ever—a real home of my own.

HILDA. [*Cautiously.*] But was that *really* necessary? 'For ever', you say.

SOLNESS. Yes. That was the price of this happiness. This so-called 'happiness' was not to be bought any cheaper.

HILDA. [*As before.*] But, couldn't you still——?

SOLNESS. No. Never. That's another consequence of the fire—and of Aline's illness afterwards.

HILDA. [*Looks at him with an indefinable expression.*] And yet you build all these nurseries!

SOLNESS. [*Seriously.*] Haven't you ever been attracted by the impossible, Hilda? Hasn't it ever called out to you—cast its spell over you?

HILDA. [*Thinking.*] The impossible! [*With sudden animation.*] Of course! Do you feel that too?

SOLNESS. Yes.

HILDA. Then there must be a bit of a troll in you too.

SOLNESS. Why troll?

HILDA. What would *you* call that sort of thing?

SOLNESS. [*Rises.*] It may be so—— [*Vehemently.*] But how can I help becoming a troll—when things always work out as they do for me!

HILDA. How do you mean?

SOLNESS. [*In a low voice, with inward emotion.*] Listen to this carefully, Hilda. All that I have been able to achieve—everything I've built and created—all the beauty, security, comfort—magnificence too, if you like—— [*Clenches his hands.*] Oh, it's too terrible to think of——!

HILDA. What *is* it that's so terrible?

SOLNESS. All of this had to be paid for—not in money—but in human happiness. And I don't mean just *my* happiness either—but that of other people. Think of that, Hilda! That is the price my position as an artist has cost me—and others. And I have to look on, and watch the others paying that price for me day after day; over and over again for ever!

HILDA. [*Rises and looks at him steadily.*] I suppose now you're thinking of—*her*?

SOLNESS. Mostly of Aline, yes. She too had a vocation in life, just as I had. [*His voice quivers.*] But Aline's vocation had to be sacrificed, so that mine could force its way up to a sort of great victory. Her vocation had to be stunted, crushed—smashed to pieces! You see—Aline, too, had a talent for building.

HILDA. She? For building?

SOLNESS. [*Shakes his head.*] Oh, I don't mean houses and towers and spires—not *my* kind of building——

HILDA. What then?

SOLNESS. Aline had a gift for building up the souls of little children, Hilda. She could teach them to become beautiful and strong in mind and body; she could help them to grow up into fine, honourable human beings. That was her talent. But it's all been wasted—it's of no use to anyone now. It's like a smouldering heap of ruins.

HILDA. Well—even if this were true——

SOLNESS. It is! It is true—I know it!

HILDA. But it's surely not your fault!

SOLNESS. [*Fixes his eyes on her.*] I wonder. That is the great, the terrible question. It torments me day and night!

HILDA. But *why*?

SOLNESS. Well, you see—perhaps it *was* my fault in a way.

HILDA. You mean—the fire?

SOLNESS. Everything! The whole business! On the other hand—I may have had nothing to do with it.

HILDA. [*Looks at him with a troubled expression.*] If you talk like that, Master Builder, I'll begin to think you are—ill, after all.

SOLNESS. I dare say I'll never be quite sane on that subject.

[*Ragnar Brovik cautiously opens the little door in the left-hand corner. Hilda steps forward.*]

RAGNAR. [*As he sees Hilda.*] Oh, excuse me, Mr Solness——

SOLNESS. No, no! Don't go! Let's get it over with.

RAGNAR. I wish we could.

SOLNESS. Your father is no better, I hear.

RAGNAR. He's failing very rapidly now. That's why I must beg you to write a few encouraging words on one of my drawings; just something for Father to see before he——

SOLNESS. [*Vehemently.*] I don't want to hear any more about those drawings of yours!

RAGNAR. Have you looked at them?

SOLNESS. Yes, I have.

RAGNAR. And they're no good? And I suppose *I'm* no good either.

SOLNESS. [*Evasively.*] You stay on here with me, Ragnar. You can have everything your own way. You can marry Kaia—you'll have no worries—you may even be happy. too. But don't think of building on your own account.

RAGNAR. I'd better go home and tell Father what you say—I promised him I would. Is this what you want me to tell him, before he dies?

SOLNESS. [*With a groan.*] As far as I'm concerned—tell him what you like! Why tell him anything? [*With a sudden outburst.*] There's nothing I can do about it, Ragnar.

RAGNAR. May I have the drawings to take with me?

SOLNESS. Yes take them—take them by all means! They're there on the table.

RAGNAR. [*Goes to the table.*] Thanks.

HILDA. [*Puts her hand on the portfolio.*] No—leave them here!

SOLNESS. What for?

HILDA. Because I want to look at them too.

SOLNESS. But, I thought you had——! [*To Ragnar.*] Well—just leave them, then.

RAGNAR. Very well.

SOLNESS. And now—hurry back to your father.

RAGNAR. Yes; I suppose I must.

SOLNESS. [*As if in desperation.*] And, Ragnar—don't ask me to do things that are beyond my power! Do you hear, Ragnar, you mustn't!

RAGNAR. No, no. I beg your pardon.

[*He bows and goes out by the corner door. Hilda goes over and sits down on a chair near the mirror.*

HILDA. [*Looking at Solness angrily.*] That was a very ugly thing to do.

SOLNESS. You think so too?

HILDA. Yes, it was disgusting! It was hard, and cruel, and wicked!

SOLNESS. You don't understand the facts.

HILDA. I don't care! You oughtn't to be like that!

SOLNESS. You said yourself just now that I alone should be allowed to build.

HILDA. I may say such things—it's not for you to say them.

SOLNESS. Who has a better right? I've paid a high enough price for my position.

HILDA. That precious domestic comfort of yours—I suppose you mean!

SOLNESS. And what about my peace of mind, Hilda?

HILDA. [*Rising.*] Peace of mind! Yes, I see! I understand—poor Master Builder! You think that you——

SOLNESS. [*With a quiet laugh.*] Sit down again, Hilda. I want to tell you something funny.

HILDA. [*Sits down; with intent interest.*] Well?

SOLNESS. I know it sounds ludicrous! But the whole question revolves round a little crack in the chimney.

HILDA. A crack in the chimney?

SOLNESS. Yes—that's how it started.

> [*He moves a chair nearer Hilda and sits.*]

HILDA. [*Impatiently, taps her knee.*] Well—now for the crack in the chimney, Master Builder!

SOLNESS. A long time before the fire, I'd noticed that little crack in the flue. Whenever I went up to the attic, I looked to see if it was still there.

HILDA. And it *was*?

SOLNESS. Yes; for no one else knew about it.

HILDA. And you said nothing?

SOLNESS. No. Not a word.

HILDA. And you didn't think of repairing it?

SOLNESS. I thought of it—but never got down to it. Each time I decided to get to work, it was exactly as if a hand held me back. Not today, I thought—tomorrow; and I did nothing about it.

HILDA. What made you put it off like that?

SOLNESS. I became obsessed with an idea. [*Slowly, and in a low voice.*] Through that little black crack in the chimney, I might perhaps force my way upward as a builder.

HILDA. [*Looking straight in front of her.*] That must have been thrilling!

SOLNESS. It was almost irresistible—quite irresistible. It all seemed so simple at the time. I wanted it to happen on a winter morning, just before noon. Aline and I were to be out driving in the sleigh. At home, the servants were to have built great fires in all the stoves——

HILDA. Of course it was to have been very cold that day——

SOLNESS. Bitterly cold, yes. And they would naturally want Aline to be nice and warm when she came in——

HILDA. I suppose she's very chilly by nature——

SOLNESS. Yes, she is. And on the way home we were to have seen the smoke——

HILDA. Only the smoke?

SOLNESS. At first, yes. But by the time we got to the garden gate, the old wooden box was to be a roaring mass of flames. That's the way I wanted it to be.

HILDA. Oh why—*why* couldn't it have happened so!

SOLNESS. You may well say that, Hilda.

HILDA. But, Master Builder—are you quite sure the fire *was* caused by that crack in the chimney?

SOLNESS. On the contrary—I'm quite sure the crack in the chimney had nothing to do with it.

HILDA. What!

SOLNESS. It was proved quite definitely that the fire broke out in a clothes closet, in an entirely different part of the house.

HILDA. Then what's all this nonsense about a crack in the chimney!

SOLNESS. May I go on talking to you a little longer, Hilda?

HILDA. Yes—if you'll try and talk sense!

SOLNESS. I'll try. [*He moves his chair nearer. In a confidential tone.*] Don't you believe, Hilda, that there exist certain special, chosen people, who have been endowed with the power and faculty of *wishing* a thing, *desiring* a thing, *willing* a thing, so persistently, so —inexorably—that they make it happen? Don't you believe that?

HILDA. [*With an indefinable expression in her eyes.*] If that is true, we'll find out some day, whether *I* am one of the chosen.

SOLNESS. It's not by our own power alone that we can accomplish such things; we must have the Helpers and Servers with us in order to succeed; and they never come of their own accord—we have to summon them; to call on them; inwardly—persistently.

HILDA. What *are* these Helpers and Servers?

SOLNESS. We'll discuss that some other time; let's go on talking about the fire now.

HILDA. Don't you think that fire would have happened—even if you hadn't wished for it?

SOLNESS. If old Knud Brovik had owned that house, it would never have burnt down so conveniently for him—I'm convinced of that. He doesn't know *how* to call for the Helpers—nor for the Servers either. [*Rises in unrest.*] So you see, Hilda, perhaps I *am* to blame for the death of the two little boys; and perhaps it's my fault too, that Aline never became what she could and should have been; what she most longed to be.

HILDA. No! It's the fault of the Helpers and Servers!

SOLNESS. But who *called* for the Helpers and Servers? I did! And they came, and obeyed my will. [*In increasing excitement.*] And these good people call that 'having luck on your side'! Do you know what that kind of luck feels like? It's as though I had an open wound here on my breast; and the Helpers and Servers flay pieces of skin off other people in order to heal my wound. But it goes on burning and throbbing—it never heals—never!

HILDA. [*Looks at him attentively.*] You *are* ill, Master Builder. I'm inclined to think you're *very* ill.

SOLNESS. Why not say mad? That's what you mean.

HILDA. No, I don't mean mentally.

SOLNESS. What *do* you mean then? Tell me!

HILDA. I wonder if you weren't born with a sickly conscience.

SOLNESS. A sickly conscience? What in the world is that?

HILDA. I mean that your conscience is too delicate and feeble; it won't face the hard things; it refuses to carry any burden that seems heavy!

SOLNESS. [*Growls.*] And what sort of a conscience *should* one have?

HILDA. I would prefer your conscience to be—thoroughly robust.

SOLNESS. Robust? I see. Is *your* conscience robust, may I ask?

HILDA. Yes, I think so. I've never noticed that it wasn't.

SOLNESS. I dare say it's never been put to the test.

HILDA. [*With a quivering of the lips.*] I don't know about that. It wasn't any too easy for me to leave Father—I'm so awfully fond of him——

SOLNESS. Oh, well! For a month or two——!

HILDA. I feel I shall never go home again.

SOLNESS. Never? Then why did you leave him?

HILDA. [*Half seriously, half banteringly.*] Have you forgotten again that the ten years are up?

SOLNESS. Nonsense! Was anything wrong at home?

HILDA. [*Seriously.*] No. But something within me urged and goaded me to come here—it was as though something beckoned to me and lured me on.

SOLNESS. [*Eagerly.*] That's it! That's *it*, Hilda! There's a troll in you, just as there is in me; and it's the troll in us that summons the powers outside us; and then, whether we like it or not, we're forced to give in.

HILDA. You know—I believe you're right, Master Builder.

SOLNESS. [*Walks about the room.*] Oh, what a lot of invisible devils there are in this world, Hilda!

HILDA. Devils, too?

SOLNESS. [*Stops.*] Good devils and bad devils. Blond devils and dark devils! If only we could be sure which kind had hold of us—then things would be simple enough!   [*He paces about.*

HILDA. [*Follows him with her eyes.*] Yes! Or if we had a vigorous, radiantly healthy conscience—and had the courage to follow our own will!

SOLNESS. [*Stops beside the table.*] I'm afraid most people are as weak as I am, in that respect.

HILDA. I shouldn't wonder.

SOLNESS. [*Leaning against the table.*] In the Sagas—have you read any of the old Sagas?

HILDA. Yes! When I used to read books——

SOLNESS. The Sagas tell about the Vikings who sailed to foreign lands, and plundered, and burned, and killed all the men——

HILDA. And captured the women——

SOLNESS. Carried them off with them——

HILDA. Took them home in their ships——

SOLNESS. And behaved to them—like the very worst of trolls!

HILDA. [*Looks straight before her with a half-veiled expression.*] I think that must have been thrilling!

SOLNESS. [*With a short, deep, laugh.*] To carry off women?

HILDA. To *be* carried off.

SOLNESS. [*Looks at her a moment.*] Indeed.

HILDA. [*As if breaking the thread of the conversation.*] But what made you speak of these Vikings, Master Builder?

SOLNESS. What robust consciences *they* must have had! They went home again and could eat and drink, and were as happy as children. And as for the women! They must have liked those ruffians—they quite often refused to leave them! Can you understand that, Hilda?

HILDA. Of course! I understand those women perfectly.

SOLNESS. Oho! Perhaps you'd do the same yourself?

HILDA. Why not?

SOLNESS. Live of your own free will with a ruffian?

HILDA. Yes. If I loved him.

SOLNESS. But how *could* you love a man like that?

HILDA. Good Heavens, Master Builder! You know you don't *choose* whom you're going to love!

SOLNESS. [*Looks meditatively at her.*] No. I suppose the troll in you takes care of that.

HILDA. [*Half laughing.*] Yes—and all those devils that you know so well! The blond ones, and the dark ones too!

SOLNESS. [*Quietly and warmly.*] I hope the devils will choose well for you, Hilda.

HILDA. They've already chosen for me—once and for all.

SOLNESS. [*Looks at her earnestly.*] Hilda, you're like a wild bird of the woods.

HILDA. Far from it! I don't hide away under the bushes.

SOLNESS. No. Perhaps you're more like a bird of prey.

HILDA. Perhaps. [*Very vehemently.*] And why not a bird of prey? Why shouldn't I, too, go hunting? And carry off the prey I want—if I can get my claws into it—and conquer it.

SOLNESS. Hilda—do you know what you are?

HILDA. I suppose I'm some sort of strange bird——

SOLNESS. No. You're like the dawning day. When I look at you— I feel as though I were watching the sunrise.

HILDA. Tell me, Master Builder—are you sure, you've never called *me* to you? Inwardly, you know?

SOLNESS. [*Softly and slowly.*] I'm almost sure I must have.

HILDA. What did you want of me?

SOLNESS. You are Youth, Hilda.

HILDA. Youth? That Youth you're so afraid of?

SOLNESS. [*Nods slowly.*] And that in my heart I yearn towards so deeply——

[*Hilda rises, goes to the little table, and fetches Ragnar's portfolio.*

HILDA. [*Holds out the portfolio to him.*] What about these drawings, Master Builder——?

SOLNESS. [*Shortly; waving them away.*] Put those things away! I've seen enough of them!

HILDA. But you're going to write on them for him, you know.

SOLNESS. Write on them! Never!

HILDA. But the poor old man's dying! It would make them both so happy! And he might get the commission too.

SOLNESS. That's just exactly what he would get! He's made sure of that!

HILDA. Well—if that's true—it surely couldn't hurt you to tell a little lie for once?

SOLNESS. A lie? [*Raging.*] Hilda—take those damn drawings away!

HILDA. [*Draws the portfolio towards her.*] All right, all right! Don't bite me! You talk of trolls—it seems to me you're behaving like a troll yourself! [*Looks round the room.*] Where's the pen and ink?

SOLNESS. There isn't any here.

HILDA. [*Goes towards the door.*] That young lady must have some in the office——

SOLNESS. Stay where you are, Hilda! You want me to lie, you say. I suppose, for the old man's sake, I might do that; I broke him—destroyed him——

HILDA. Him, too?

SOLNESS. I needed room for myself. But this Ragnar must never be allowed to get ahead——

HILDA. Poor thing—there's not much hope of that—you say he has no talent.

SOLNESS. [*Comes closer to her and whispers.*] If Ragnar Brovik gets his chance, he'll break me—destroy me, as I did his father.

HILDA. Destroy you! You mean—he has the power for *that*?

SOLNESS. He has indeed! *He* is the younger generation waiting to thunder at my door—to make an end of Halvard Solness!

HILDA. [*Looks at him with quiet reproach.*] And you would bar him out! For shame, Master Builder!

SOLNESS. My struggle has cost me agony enough! And I'm afraid the Helpers and Servers won't obey me any longer.

HILDA. Then you'll just have to get on without them.

SOLNESS. It's hopeless. Hilda. Sooner or later the luck will turn. Retribution is inexorable.

HILDA. [*In distress, putting her hands over her ears.*] Don't talk like that! Do you want to kill me? Do you want to rob me of what means more to me than life!

SOLNESS. What is that?

HILDA. The need to see you great. To see you with a wreath in your hand—high, high up, upon a church tower! [*Calm again.*] Now—get out your pencil, Master Builder—you must have a pencil in your pocket——

SOLNESS. [*Takes one from his pocket.*] Yes—here's one——

HILDA. [*Lays the portfolio on the table.*] Good. We'll just sit down here, Master Builder——

[*Solness seats himself at the table. Hilda stands behind him, leaning over the back of the chair.*

HILDA. —and we'll write on the drawings; something very nice—very kind—for this horrid Ruar—whatever his name is!

SOLNESS. [*Writes a few words, turns his head and looks at her.*] Tell me one thing, Hilda.

HILDA. Yes?

SOLNESS. If you were really waiting for me all these ten years——

HILDA. Well?

SOLNESS. Why didn't you write to me? Then I could have answered you.

HILDA. [*Hastily.*] No, no, no! That's just what I didn't want!

SOLNESS. Why not?

HILDA. I was afraid that might ruin everything. But we were writing on the drawings, Master Builder.

SOLNESS. So we were.

HILDA. [*Bends forward and looks over his shoulder as he writes.*] Kindly and generously. Oh, how I hate—how I hate this Roald——!

SOLNESS. [*Writing.*] Have you never really loved anyone, Hilda?

HILDA. [*Harshly.*] What? What did you say?

SOLNESS. Have you never loved anyone, I asked.

HILDA. Anyone else, I suppose you mean.

SOLNESS. [*Looks up at her.*] Anyone else, yes. Have you never? In all these ten years? Never?

HILDA. Oh, yes; now and then. When I was furious with you for not coming.

SOLNESS. Then you *have* cared for other people too?

HILDA. Maybe a little—for a week or so. Good Heavens, Master Builder! You must know all about things like that!

SOLNESS. What have you come for, Hilda?

HILDA. Don't waste time talking! The poor old man might go and die in the meantime!

SOLNESS. Answer me, Hilda. What do you want of me?

HILDA. I want my kingdom.

SOLNESS. Hm. . .

    [*He gives a rapid glance toward the door on the left, and then goes on writing on the drawings. At that moment Mrs Solness enters; she has some packages in her hand.*]

MRS S. I've brought a few of the things myself, Miss Wangel. The large parcels will be sent later on.

HILDA. You're really much too kind to me!

MRS S. My simple duty—nothing else.

SOLNESS. [*Reads over what he has written.*] Aline?

MRS S. Yes, Halvard?

SOLNESS. Did you happen to notice whether she—whether the book-keeper was out there?

MRS S. Of course she was there. She was at her desk—as she always is when *I* go through the room.

SOLNESS. [*Puts the drawings in the portfolio. Rises.*] Then I'll just give her these, and tell her that——

HILDA. [*Takes the portfolio from him.*] Oh, let me have that pleasure! [*Goes to the door, but turns.*] What's her name?

SOLNESS. Miss Fosli.

HILDA. No, no! That sounds so formal! Her first name, I mean!

SOLNESS. Kaia—I believe.

HILDA. [*Opens the door and calls out.*] Kaia! Hurry! Come in here! The Master Builder wants to talk to you.

[*Kaia appears at the door.*

KAIA. [*Looks at him in alarm.*] You want me——?

HILDA. [*Handing her the portfolio.*] Take these home, Kaia. The Master Builder has written on them now.

KAIA. At last!

SOLNESS. Give them to the old man as soon as possible——

KAIA. I'll go home with them at once——

SOLNESS. Yes, do. Now Ragnar will have his chance to build.

KAIA. May he come and thank you——?

SOLNESS. [*Harshly.*] I want no thanks! Tell him that from me.

KAIA. Yes—I will.

SOLNESS. And tell him too that I shall no longer need his services —nor yours either.

KAIA. [*Softly—tremulously.*] Nor mine—either?

SOLNESS. You'll have other things to think of now—a great deal to attend to—that's as it should be. Take the drawings home now, Miss Fosli. At once! Do you hear!

KAIA. [*As before.*] Yes, Mr Solness.   [*She goes out.*

MRS S. Heavens! What deceitful eyes she has!

SOLNESS. She? That poor little creature?

MRS S. Oh, I can see what I can see, Halvard. So you're really dismissing them?

SOLNESS. Yes.

MRS S. Her, as well?

SOLNESS. Wasn't that what you wanted?

MRS S. But how will you get on without her? No doubt you have someone in reserve, Halvard.

HILDA. [*Playfully.*] As for me—*I'd* be no good at a desk!

SOLNESS. Never mind, never mind, Aline. Everything will be all right. You just think about getting ready to move into your new home—as quickly as possible. This evening we'll hang up the wreath—[*turns to Hilda*] at the very top of the tower. What do you say to *that*, Miss Hilda?

HILDA. It'll be wonderful to see you up there again—high up!

SOLNESS. Me!

MRS S. Whatever put that into your head, Miss Wangel! My husband—who always gets so dizzy!

HILDA. Dizzy! He!

MRS S. Oh, yes. I assure you.

HILDA. But I saw him myself at the top of a high church tower!

MRS S. Yes—I've heard rumours about that. But it's quite impossible.

SOLNESS. [*Vehemently.*] Impossible! Impossible! But I stood there all the same!

MRS S. How can you say that, Halvard. You know you don't even dare go out on the second-storey balcony here. You've always been like that!

SOLNESS. You may see something different this evening.

MRS S. [*In alarm.*] No, no! God forbid that I should ever see that! I'll send word to the doctor at once. He must prevent you.

SOLNESS. But, Aline——!

MRS S. For you are ill, Halvard—this proves it. Oh, God! Oh, God!
[*She goes hastily out to the right.*

HILDA. [*Looks at him intently.*] Is it so, or is it not?

SOLNESS. That I get dizzy?

HILDA. That my Master Builder *dare* not, *cannot* climb as high as he builds?

SOLNESS. Is that how you look at it?

HILDA. Yes.

SOLNESS. Is there no part of me that's safe from you, Hilda?

HILDA. [*Looks towards the window.*] Up there then—right up there!

SOLNESS. [*Comes to her.*] You could live in the topmost room of the tower, Hilda—you could live there like a princess.

HILDA. [*Indefinably; half in jest half in earnest.*] That's what you promised——

SOLNESS. Did I really?

HILDA. You said I was to be a princess—that you'd give me a kingdom—and then you went and——

SOLNESS. [*Cautiously.*] Are you sure it wasn't all a dream—just something you imagined?

HILDA. [*Sharply.*] You mean that you didn't do it?

SOLNESS. I scarcely know myself. [*More softly.*] But I *do* know one thing now—and that is——

HILDA. What? Tell me at once!

SOLNESS. That I *ought* to have done it!

HILDA. [*Exclaims, with animation.*] *You* could never be dizzy!

SOLNESS. Then this evening we will hang up the wreath, Princess Hilda.

HILDA. [*With a bitter curve of her lips.*] Over your new home—yes!

SOLNESS. Over the new house—that will never be a home for me.
                              [*He goes out through the garden door.*

HILDA. [*Looks straight in front of her with a far-away expression, and whispers to herself. The only words audible are*]—frightfully thrilling!

CURTAIN

ACT III

The large broad veranda of Solness's house. Part of the house, with outer door leading to the veranda, is seen to the left. A railing along the veranda to the right. At the back, from the end of the veranda, a flight of steps leads down to the garden below. Tall old trees in the garden spread their branches over the veranda and towards the house. Far to the right, in among the trees, a glimpse is caught of the lower part of a new villa, with scaffolding round so much as is seen of the tower. In the background the garden is bounded by an old wooden fence. Outside the fence, a street with low tumbledown cottages.

Evening sky with sunlit clouds.

On the veranda, a garden bench stands along the wall of the house, and in front of the bench a long table. On the other side of the table, an armchair and some stools. All the furniture is of wickerwork.

Mrs Solness, wrapped in a large white crêpe shawl, sits resting in the armchair and gazes over to the right. Shortly after Hilda Wangel comes up the flight of steps from the garden. She is dressed as in the last act and wears a hat. She has in her bodice a little nosegay of small common flowers.

MRS S. [*Turning her head a little.*] So you've been round the garden, Miss Wangel?

HILDA. Yes. I've been exploring it——

MRS S. And found some flowers too I see.

HILDA. There are such heaps of them—in among the bushes.

MRS S. Fancy! Are there really? Still? You see—I scarcely ever go there.

HILDA. [*Comes nearer.*] Really? Don't you? I should have thought you'd take a run down there every day.

MRS S. [*With a faint smile*] I don't 'run' anywhere. Not any more, Miss Wangel.

HILDA. But you must go down there sometimes—there are such lovely things to see there.

MRS S. It's all become so alien to me. I'm almost afraid to see it again.

HILDA. Your own garden!

MRS S. I don't feel that it *is* mine any longer.

130

HILDA. How do you mean?

MRS S. No—it's no longer mine, Miss Wangel. It was different when mother and father were alive. But they've done such dreadful things to the garden; they've divided it up and built houses for a lot of strangers—people I don't know; and they sit at their windows and stare at me.

HILDA. [*Brightly.*] Mrs Solness?

MRS S. Yes?

HILDA. Do you mind if I stay here with you for a while?

MRS S. Of course not. I'd be delighted—if you'd care to.

HILDA. [*Moves a stool over by the armchair and sits down.*] Ah! How nice it is to sit and sun oneself like a cat!

MRS S. [*Lays her hand gently on the back of Hilda's head.*] It's kind of you to want to sit here with me. I thought you were on your way to join my husband.

HILDA. Why should I want to join him?

MRS S. I thought perhaps you were helping him with something.

HILDA. No. Anyway—he's not at home just now. He's down there with the workmen. He looked so ferocious, I didn't dare talk to him!

MRS S. He's so kind and gentle underneath all that——

HILDA. He! Kind and gentle!

MRS S. You don't really know him yet, Miss Wangel.

HILDA. [*Gives her an affectionate look.*] Are you glad to be moving into the new house?

MRS S. I suppose I should be glad—for it's what Halvard wants——

HILDA. Oh, not just because of that!

MRS S. Oh yes, Miss Wangel. After all it's my duty to try and please him. Still—there are times when it's very hard to force one's mind to obedience.

HILDA. That must be very hard indeed.

MRS S. Yes, it is. Especially when one has as many faults as I have——

HILDA. Or when one has suffered as much as you have——

MRS S. What do you know about that?

HILDA. Your husband told me.

MRS S. He seldom talks about such things to me. Yes—I've been through a great deal in my life, Miss Wangel.

HILDA. [*Nods sympathetically.*] Poor Mrs Solness! First the old house burnt down——

MRS S. [*With a sigh.*] Yes. I lost everything I had.

HILDA. And what followed was even worse——

MRS S. [*With a questioning look.*] Worse?

HILDA. That must have been the worst of all.

MRS S. How do you mean?

HILDA. You lost the two little boys.

MRS S. Oh, the little boys—yes. Well, you see—that was a thing apart. That was the will of the Almighty. One must bow before His will—yes, and be thankful too.

HILDA. Are you able to do that?

MRS S. Not always, I'm afraid. Although I know that it's my duty —still, I often fail in it.

HILDA. I think that's very natural.

MRS S. I have to keep reminding myself that it was a just punish-ment for me——

HILDA. Punishment? Why?

MRS S. Because I hadn't the strength to bear misfortune.

HILDA. But—I don't understand——

MRS S. No, no Miss Wangel. Don't talk to me any more about the two little boys. We must be glad for them; they are at peace and happy now. No—it's the small losses in life that break one's heart. It's losing all the little things—things that might seem insignificant to other people.

HILDA. [*Lays her arms on Mrs Solness's knee and looks up at her affectionately.*] Dear Mrs Solness—what sort of things do you mean?

MRS S. As I say—just little things. The old family portraits were all burnt on the walls. The old silk dresses were burnt—they had been in the family for countless generations. All mother's and grandmother's lace—and all the jewels—they were burnt too. And then—all the dolls.

HILDA. The dolls?

MRS S. [*Her voice choked with tears.*] I had nine lovely dolls.

HILDA. And they were burnt too?

MRS S. All of them. Oh, it was hard—so hard for me.

HILDA. Were they dolls you'd played with as a little girl? Had you stored them away all those years?

MRS S. They were not stored away. The dolls and I went on living together.

HILDA. You mean, after you were grown up?

MRS S. Yes, long after that.

HILDA. And even after you were married too?

MRS S. Oh, yes. As long as he knew nothing about it, it was—— But they were all burnt up, poor things. No one thought of saving them. Oh, it's so tragic to think of. You mustn't laugh at me, Miss Wangel.

HILDA. I'm not laughing in the least.

MRS S. In a way, you see, there was life in them, too. I carried them under my heart. Like little unborn children.

[Dr Herdal comes out of the house and sees Mrs Solness and Hilda.

HERDAL. Are you sitting out here catching cold, Mrs Solness?

MRS S. It's so pleasant and warm here today.

HERDAL. But is anything the matter? I had a note from you.

MRS S. *[Rises.]* Yes. There's something I must talk to you about.

HERDAL. Very well. Then perhaps we had better go in. *[To Hilda.]* I see you're still dressed for mountain climbing, Miss Wangel.

HILDA. In full regalia! But I don't intend to go breaking my neck today. We two will sit quietly here and look on.

HERDAL. What are we to look on at?

MRS S. *[Softly to Hilda, in a frightened tone.]* Hush, hush! For God's sake! He's coming. Do try to get that idea out of his head. And let us be friends, Miss Wangel. Don't you think we can?

HILDA. *[Throws her arms impetuously round Mrs Solness's neck.]* Oh— if we only could!

MRS S. *[Gently disengaging herself.]* There, there! He's coming, doctor. Let me have a word with you.

HERDAL. Is it about him?

MRS S. Yes—of course it's about him. Do come in.

[She and the doctor enter the house. Next moment Solness comes up from the garden by the flight of steps. A serious look comes over Hilda's face.

SOLNESS. *[Glances at the house door that is closed cautiously from within.]* Have you noticed, Hilda? As soon as I come, she goes.

HILDA. I've noticed that as soon as you come you make her go.

SOLNESS. Perhaps. But I can't help it. *[Looks at her observantly.]* Are you cold, Hilda? You look as if you were cold.

HILDA. It's because I've just come up out of a tomb.

SOLNESS. What does *that* mean?

HILDA. I feel as if I'd been frozen through and through, Master Builder.

SOLNESS. [*Slowly.*] I think I understand——

HILDA. Why did you come up here?

SOLNESS. I saw you from down below.

HILDA. Then you must have seen her too.

SOLNESS. I knew she'd go away at once if I came.

HILDA. Does it make you unhappy—her avoiding you like that?

SOLNESS. In a way it's almost a relief.

HILDA. Not to have her always before your eyes?

SOLNESS. Yes.

HILDA. Not to be constantly reminded of her grief at the loss of the two little boys?

SOLNESS. Yes. Mostly that.

[*Hilda crosses the veranda with her hands behind her back, and stands by the railing gazing out across the garden.*

SOLNESS. [*After a short pause.*] Did you have a long talk with her? [*Hilda doesn't answer but stands there motionless.*] Did you have a long talk, I asked. [*Hilda makes no reply.*] What did she talk about, Hilda? [*Hilda still stands silent.*] Poor Aline! I suppose it was about the little boys. [*Hilda shudders and nods rapidly several times.*] She'll never get over it. Never in this world. [*He goes towards her.*] Now you're standing there again like a statue; just as you did last night.

HILDA. [*Turns and looks at him with great serious eyes.*] I must go away.

SOLNESS. [*Sharply.*] Go away!

HILDA. Yes.

SOLNESS. No! I won't let you!

HILDA. What can I do here now?

SOLNESS. Just *be* here, Hilda!

HILDA. [*Looks him up and down.*] Yes, I dare say! You know it wouldn't stop at that.

SOLNESS. [*Recklessly.*] So much the better!

HILDA. [*Vehemently.*] I can't do any harm to one whom I *know*. I can't take anything that belongs to her.

SOLNESS. Who ever said you *would*?

HILDA. A stranger, yes! That's quite a different thing. Someone I'd never laid eyes on. But someone I've come close to——! No, no! Never that! No!

SOLNESS. But I've suggested nothing of that sort.

HILDA. Oh, Master Builder—you know well enough what would happen if I stayed. So I must go away.

SOLNESS. What'll become of *me* if you go away? What shall I have to live for then?

HILDA. [*With an inscrutable look in her eyes.*] There's no need to worry about *you*. You have your duties to her. Live for those duties.

SOLNESS. It's too late, Hilda. All these powers, these—these——

HILDA. Devils?

SOLNESS. Yes, devils! And the troll within me too; they have drained the life-blood out of her. [*Laughs bitterly.*] They did it for my happiness. And now I'm chained alive to this dead woman. I! I who cannot bear to live without joy in life!

HILDA. [*Goes round the table and sits down on the bench, her elbows on the table and her head in her hands. Sits and stares at him a moment.*] What will you build next, Master Builder?

SOLNESS. [*Shakes his head.*] I don't think I'll build much more, Hilda.

HILDA. No cheerful, happy homes—for a mother and a father and a whole troop of children?

SOLNESS. I wonder—will there be any use for such homes from now on?

HILDA. Poor Master Builder! And for ten whole years you've dedicated your life to that alone!

SOLNESS. You're right there, Hilda.

HILDA. [*In a sudden outburst.*] Oh, how absurd it all is! How senseless!

SOLNESS. All—what?

HILDA. This business of not daring to grasp your own happiness— your own life! And all because someone you *know*, happens to stand in the way.

SOLNESS. Someone you've no right to cast aside.

HILDA. I wonder. I wonder if that's *really* true. Perhaps, after all, one *has* the right——? And yet—somehow—— Oh! To be able to sleep it all away! [*She stretches out her arms flat across the table and rests her head on them, closing her eyes.*

SOLNESS. [*Turns the armchair round and sits down at the table.*] Did you have a happy home up there with your father, Hilda?

HILDA. [*Without moving, as though half asleep.*] All I had was a cage.

SOLNESS. And you really don't want to go back there?

HILDA. [*As before.*] Wild birds can't live in cages.

SOLNESS. They must be free to hunt in the open air——

HILDA. [*As before.*] Birds of prey were meant for hunting.

SOLNESS. [*Lets his eyes dwell on her.*] Oh! To have the Viking spirit in life, Hilda!

HILDA. [*In her usual voice, opens her eyes but still doesn't move.*] And the other thing? Say what that was!

SOLNESS. A robust conscience.

[*Hilda sits erect on the bench, once more full of animation. Her eyes are happy and sparkling.*

HILDA. [*Nods to him.*] I know what you're going to build next, Master Builder!

SOLNESS. Then you know more than I do, Hilda.

HILDA. Yes. Master Builders are so stupid.

SOLNESS. Well? What's it to be?

HILDA. [*Nods again.*] The castle.

SOLNESS. What castle?

HILDA. *My* castle, of course.

SOLNESS. So you want a castle now?

HILDA. You owe me a kingdom, don't you?

SOLNESS. That's what you *say.*

HILDA. All right. So you owe me this kingdom; and you can't have a kingdom without a castle I should hope!

SOLNESS. [*More and more animated.*] No. They usually go together.

HILDA. Very well. Then build it for me at once!

SOLNESS. [*Laughs.*] Must you have it this very instant?

HILDA. Of course! For the ten years are up—and I'm not going to wait any longer. So—out with my castle, Master Builder!

SOLNESS. It's no joke to owe you anything, Hilda!

HILDA. You should have thought of that before—it's too late now. So—[*raps on the table*] my castle on the table! It's my castle, and I want it at once!

SOLNESS. [*More seriously, leaning towards her with his arms on the table.*] How do you see this castle of yours, Hilda?

HILDA. [*Her expression becomes more and more veiled. She seems to be peering into her innermost being.*] My castle must stand on a high hill —high, high up. It must have a clear view on all sides—so that I can see far, far around.

SOLNESS. I suppose it's to have a high tower?

HILDA. A tremendously high tower. And at the very top of the tower there must be a balcony. And I shall stand out on it——

SOLNESS. [*Involuntarily clutches at his forehead.*] How can you bear to stand at such a dizzy height——!

HILDA. Ah, but I shall! I shall stand up there and look down at all the others—at those who are building churches. And homes for a mother and a father and a whole troop of children. And you shall come and look down at them too.

SOLNESS. [*Softly.*] Will the Master Builder be allowed to come up to the princess?

HILDA. If the Master Builder will.

SOLNESS. [*More softly still.*] Then I think he will come.

HILDA. [*Nods.*] Yes. The Master Builder will come.

SOLNESS. But he'll never build any more—poor Master Builder!

HILDA. [*With animation.*] Ah, but he will! We two will build together. We'll build the loveliest—the very loveliest thing in all the world.

SOLNESS. [*Intently.*] Hilda—tell me what that is!

HILDA. [*Smiles at him, shakes her head a little and talks as though to a child.*] Master builders are such very—very stupid people.

SOLNESS. Yes, I know they are. But tell me what it is—this loveliest thing in all the world that we two are to build together?

HILDA. [*Is silent for a moment, then says with an indefinable expression in her eyes*] Castles in the air.

SOLNESS. Castles in the air?

HILDA. [*Nodding.*] Castles in the air, yes. Do you know what sort of a thing a castle in the air is?

SOLNESS. It's the loveliest thing in the world, you say.

HILDA. [*Rises abruptly, and makes a gesture of repulsion with her hand.*] The loveliest thing in the world! Castles in the air—they're so easy to take refuge in. And they're easy to build too—especially for builders who have a—dizzy conscience.

SOLNESS. [*Rises.*] From now on, we two will build together, Hilda.

HILDA. [*With a half doubting smile.*] A real castle in the air?

SOLNESS. Yes. One on a firm foundation.

[*Ragnar Brovik comes out of the house. He carries a large green wreath, decked with flowers and ribands.*

HILDA. [*In a burst of happiness.*] The wreath! Oh, it'll be splendid!

SOLNESS. [*In surprise.*] Why have *you* brought the wreath, Ragnar?

RAGNAR. I promised the foreman I would.

SOLNESS. [*With relief.*] Then your father must be better?

RAGNAR. No.

SOLNESS. Wasn't he pleased with what I wrote?

RAGNAR. It came too late.

SOLNESS. Too late?

RAGNAR. He was unconscious by the time she brought it. He'd had a stroke.

SOLNESS. Then you must go home to him. You must stay with him, Ragnar.

RAGNAR. He doesn't need me any more.

SOLNESS. But, surely, you ought to *be* there!

RAGNAR. She's there with him—sitting by his bed.

SOLNESS. [*Rather uncertainly.*] Kaia?

RAGNAR. [*With a dark look.*] Yes, Kaia.

SOLNESS. Go home to them both, Ragnar. Give me the wreath.

RAGNAR. [*Suppressing a mocking smile.*] You don't mean that you're going to——

SOLNESS. I'll take it down to the men. [*Takes the wreath from him.*] You go on home. We don't need you here today.

RAGNAR. No—I dare say you don't need me. But today I'm going to stay.

SOLNESS. Very well. As you like.

HILDA. [*By the railing.*] I'm going to stand here and watch you, Master Builder.

SOLNESS. *Watch* me?

HILDA. It'll be wonderfully thrilling!

SOLNESS. [*In a low tone.*] We'll discuss that later, Hilda.

> [*He takes the wreath and goes down the steps into the garden.*

HILDA. [*She watches him go, then turns to Ragnar.*] I should think you might at least have thanked him!

RAGNAR. Thanked him! Do you expect me to thank him?

HILDA. Yes, of course you should!

RAGNAR. It seems to me it's *you* I ought to thank.

HILDA. How can you say such a thing?

RAGNAR. [*Without answering her.*] But I warn you, Miss Wangel. You don't really know him yet.

HILDA. [*Passionately.*] No one knows him as *I* do——!

RAGNAR. [*With a bitter laugh.*] Thank him, indeed! When he's held me back year after year! When he's made my own father doubt me—made me doubt myself—and all because he wanted to——!

HILDA. [*As though sensing something.*] What? Tell me at once!

RAGNAR. Because he wanted to keep her with him.

HILDA. [*With a start towards him.*] That girl at the desk?

RAGNAR. Yes.

HILDA. [*Clenching her hands, threateningly.*] That's not true! You're telling lies about him!

RAGNAR. I didn't believe it either until today—when she told me herself.

HILDA. [*As though beside herself.*] What did she say? Tell me! At once! At once!

RAGNAR. She said—that he had taken possession of her whole being—her whole being, she said. That all her thoughts were for him alone. She said she could never leave him. That she must stay here where he is——

HILDA. [*With flashing eyes.*] She won't be allowed to!

RAGNAR. [*As if feeling his way.*] Who won't allow her?

HILDA. [*Rapidly.*] *He* won't permit it either!

RAGNAR. No—of course not. I understand everything now. From now on she'd only be in the way.

HILDA. You don't understand anything or you wouldn't talk like that. *I*'ll tell you why he wanted her to stay here.

RAGNAR. Well—why?

HILDA. Because he wanted *you* to stay.

RAGNAR. Did he tell you that himself?

HILDA. No, but it's true! It *must* be true! [*Wildly.*] I will—*I will* have it so!

RAGNAR. But the moment *you* came—he let her go.

HILDA. It was *you* that he let go! Why should he care about a strange girl like her!

RAGNAR. [*After a moment's thought.*] Could he have been afraid of me all these years?

HILDA. *He* afraid! I wouldn't be so conceited if I were you.

RAGNAR. He must have realized long ago that I had something in me. Besides—a coward—that's just what he is, you see.

HILDA. Yes! I'm likely to believe that!

RAGNAR. Well—in some ways he is a coward—the great Master Builder! Oh, he's not afraid of destroying other people's happiness—father's and mine, for instance—but just ask him to climb up a miserable bit of scaffolding, and see what he says!

HILDA. You should have seen him at the top of a high tower as I once saw him.

RAGNAR. You saw *that*?

HILDA. Yes—indeed I did! He fastened the wreath to the church vane—and he looked so proud and free!

RAGNAR. He's supposed to have done that once—just once in his life, they say. It's become a sort of legend among us younger men. But no power on earth would induce him to do it again.

HILDA. He'll do it again today!

RAGNAR. [*Scornfully.*] Yes—I dare say!

HILDA. We shall see it!

RAGNAR. We'll neither of us ever see that.

HILDA. [*With passionate vehemence.*] I will see it! I *will* and I *must* see it!

RAGNAR. But he won't do it. He simply *dare* not do it. It's like an illness—don't you see?

[*Mrs Solness comes out on to the veranda.*

MRS S. [*Looking round.*] Isn't he here? Where did he go?

RAGNAR. Mr Solness is down with the men.

HILDA. He took the wreath with him.

MRS S. [*Terrified.*] Took the wreath! Oh God! Brovik—go down to him. Try and get him to come up here.

RAGNAR. Shall I say you want him, Mrs Solness?

MRS S. Yes, do—dear Brovik. No, no! Better not say *I* want him— tell him some people have just come and are asking to see him.

RAGNAR. Very well. I'll tell him, Mrs Solness.

[*He goes down the steps to the garden.*

MRS S. Oh, I'm so anxious about him, Miss Wangel.

HILDA. What is there to be so afraid of?

MRS S. Surely you can understand? What if he really meant it? What if he were really to try and climb the scaffolding?

HILDA. Do you think he will?

MRS S. He's so unpredictable—it's impossible to tell. He might do anything!

HILDA. Then—perhaps you too think that he's——?

MRS S. I no longer know *what* to think of him, Miss Wangel. The doctor's just told me various things that—well—putting them together with several things I've heard him say——

HERDAL. [*Comes out of the house.*] Hasn't he come up yet?

MRS S. He'll be here soon, I think. They've just gone for him.

HERDAL. [*Comes towards her.*] You're wanted inside, Mrs Solness——

MRS S. No, no. I'll stay out here and wait for Halvard.

HERDAL. But some ladies have come to call——

MRS S. Good heavens—how tiresome! Just at this moment!

HERDAL. They insist on watching the ceremony.

like a dead woman—of her own will

MRS S. Then I suppose I'd better go in—after all, it's my duty——

HILDA. Why not ask them to go away?

MRS S. Oh, I can't very well do that. As long as they're here it's my duty to see them. But you stay out here, Miss Wangel, and talk to him when he comes.

HERDAL. Keep him up here as long as possible.

MRS S. Yes, do—dear Miss Wangel. Be firm with him. Make him give up that mad idea.

HILDA. Wouldn't it be best for you to do that?

MRS S. Yes—heaven knows—that *is* my duty. But one has duties in so many directions that I——

HERDAL. [*Looks towards the garden.*] Here he comes!

MRS S. Oh dear! And I have to go in!

HERDAL. [*To Hilda.*] Don't say anything to him about my being here.

HILDA. I dare say I'll be able to find something else to talk to him about.

MRS S. And be sure and keep him here, Miss Wangel. I believe you can do it best.

[*Mrs Solness and Dr Herdal go into the house. Hilda remains standing on the veranda.*

SOLNESS. [*Comes up the steps from the garden.*] I hear someone wants to see me.

HILDA. It's only I, Master Builder.

SOLNESS. Oh, it's you, Hilda. I was afraid it might be Aline and the doctor.

HILDA. You're very easily frightened, I hear.

SOLNESS. Do you think so?

HILDA. Yes. I'm told you're afraid—afraid of climbing about—on scaffoldings, they say.

SOLNESS. Well—that's quite a special thing.

HILDA. Then you are afraid of it?

SOLNESS. Yes, I am.

HILDA. Afraid of falling down and killing yourself?

SOLNESS. No—not of that.

HILDA. Of what, then?

SOLNESS. I'm afraid of retribution, Hilda.

HILDA. Retribution? [*Shakes her head.*] I don't understand that.

SOLNESS. Hilda—sit down a minute. I want to tell you something.

HILDA. I'm listening, Master Builder!

[*She sits on a stool by the railing and looks at him expectantly.*

SOLNESS. [*Flings his hat on the table.*] You know that I began by building churches——

HILDA. [*Nods.*] Yes. I know that very well!

SOLNESS. You see—I came from a pious home in a little country village. I suppose that's why I thought the finest thing I could devote my life to, was the building of churches.

HILDA. Yes. I see.

SOLNESS. And I think I may say that I built those humble little churches with such honest fervour that—that——

HILDA. Well?

SOLNESS. Well—that I think he should have been pleased with me.

HILDA. *He?* What *he?*

SOLNESS. He for whom they were built, of course. To whose honour and glory they were dedicated.

HILDA. And do you think he *wasn't* pleased with you?

SOLNESS. *He* pleased with *me?* How can you say that, Hilda? Didn't he give the troll in me full power? Didn't he give me mastery over all these—these——

HILDA. Devils?

SOLNESS. Yes—devils! Of both kinds! No. I soon found out that he wasn't pleased with me. [*Mysteriously.*] That was really why he let the old house burn down.

HILDA. Was that the reason?

SOLNESS. Yes, don't you see? He wanted me to become a great master in my own sphere, so that I could go on building ever more glorious churches for him. At first I didn't realize what he was up to—and then, suddenly, I saw it clearly.

HILDA. When was that?

SOLNESS. It was when I built the church tower at Lysanger.

HILDA. I thought so.

SOLNESS. I was up there alone in strange surroundings . . . I had plenty of time to think and meditate. And I suddenly understood why he had taken my little children from me. He didn't want me to become attached to anything; I was to be allowed no love or happiness, you understand. I was to be nothing but a Master Builder, and I was to devote my life solely to building for him. But I soon put a stop to that!

HILDA. What did you do then?

SOLNESS. First I searched my own heart—put myself to the test——

HILDA. And then?

SOLNESS. Then I did the impossible. I no less than he.

HILDA. The impossible?

SOLNESS. I had never before been able to climb to a great height. But that day I did it.

HILDA. Yes, you did!

SOLNESS. And as I stood up there, high over everything, I said to him: Listen to me, Almighty One! From now on I will be a free Master Builder; free in my sphere, just as you are in yours. I will never more build churches for you; only homes for human beings.

HILDA. [*With great shining eyes.*] That was the song that I heard in the air!

SOLNESS. Yes. But he won in the end.

HILDA. How do you mean?

SOLNESS. This building homes for human beings isn't worth a rap, Hilda!

HILDA. Is that how you feel now?

SOLNESS. Yes. Because now I see it. People have no use for these homes of theirs. Not to be happy in—no. And if I had such a home, I probably wouldn't have any use for it either. What does it all amount to—now that I look back on it? What have I ever built? What have I ever sacrificed for the chance of building? Nothing! Nothing! It all amounts to nothing!

HILDA. Then—will you never build anything any more, Master Builder?

SOLNESS. On the contrary—now I'm just going to begin!

HILDA. What will you build? What? Tell me at once!

SOLNESS. I believe there's just one possible dwelling-place for human happiness—that's what I'm going to build now.

HILDA. Master Builder—you mean our castles in the air?

SOLNESS. Castles in the air, yes.

HILDA. I'm afraid you'd grow dizzy before you got half way up.

SOLNESS. Not if I were to climb hand in hand with you, Hilda.

HILDA. With me alone? Will there be no others?

SOLNESS. What others?

HILDA. [*With suppressed resentment.*] That—Kaia—at the desk, for instance. Poor thing—don't you want to take her with you too?

SOLNESS. Aha! So *that* was what Aline was talking to you about.

HILDA. Is it so, or is it not?

SOLNESS. I won't answer that question! You must believe in me wholly and completely!

HILDA. For ten years I have believed in you so utterly—so utterly!

SOLNESS. You must go on believing in me!

HILDA. Then let me see you again free and high up!

SOLNESS. [*Sadly.*] I can't be like that every day, Hilda.

HILDA. You must be! I want you to be! [*Imploringly.*] Just this once more, Master Builder! Do the impossible again!

SOLNESS. [*Looks deep into her eyes.*] If I try it, Hilda, I shall stand up there and talk to him as I did before.

HILDA. [*With growing excitement.*] What will you say to him?

SOLNESS. I shall say to him: Listen to me, Almighty Lord—you may judge me as you will. But from now on I shall build only the loveliest thing in all the world——

HILDA. [*Carried away.*] Yes, yes, yes!

SOLNESS. I shall build it with a princess whom I love——

HILDA. Yes, tell him that! Tell him that!

SOLNESS. And then I'll say to him: Now I shall go down and throw my arms round her and kiss her——

HILDA. —many times! Say that!

SOLNESS. —many, many times, I'll say.

HILDA. —and then?

SOLNESS. Then I shall wave my hat—come down to earth again—and do as I told him.

HILDA. [*With outstretched arms.*] Now I see you again as I did when there was song in the air!

SOLNESS. [*Looks at her with bowed head.*] Hilda—how have you become what you are?

HILDA. How have you made me what I am?

SOLNESS. [*Quickly and firmly.*] The princess shall have her castle.

HILDA. [*Joyfully, clapping her hands.*] Master Builder! My lovely, lovely castle! *Our* castle in the air!

SOLNESS. On a firm foundation.

[*A crowd of people have gathered in the street, dimly seen through the trees. The sound of a brass band is heard from beyond the new house. Mrs Solness, wearing a fur-piece round her neck, Dr Herdal carrying her white shawl over his arm, and several ladies, come out on the veranda. At the same moment Ragnar comes up from the garden.*]

MRS S. [*To Ragnar.*] Are we to have music, too?

RAGNAR. Yes; it's the band from the builders' union. [*To Solness.*] I was to tell you—the foreman is ready to go up with the wreath.

SOLNESS. [*Takes up his hat.*] Very well; I'll go down to him.

MRS S. [*Anxiously.*] Need you go down there, Halvard?

SOLNESS. [*Shortly.*] I must be below with the men.

MRS S. But you'll stay down below—won't you, Halvard? You'll stay down with the men?

SOLNESS. Isn't that where I usually stay? On ordinary occasions?

[*He goes down the steps to the garden.*

MRS S. [*At the parapet, calls after him.*] And do tell the foreman to be careful! Promise me that, Halvard!

HERDAL. [*To Mrs Solness.*] You see how right I was? He's forgotten all about that nonsense.

MRS S. Oh, what a relief! Twice workmen have fallen and been killed on the spot. [*Turns to Hilda.*] Thank you, Miss Wangel, for being so firm with him. I'm sure I could never have managed him.

HERDAL. [*Teasingly.*] Just leave it to Miss Wangel! She can be firm with a man, when she puts her mind to it!

[*Mrs Solness and the doctor join the ladies who stand on the steps looking out over the garden. Hilda remains standing in the foreground by the railing. Ragnar goes over to her.*

RAGNAR. [*With suppressed laughter; in a whisper.*] Miss Wangel—do you see all those young people down there in the street?

HILDA. Yes.

RAGNAR. Those are my fellow students. They're here to watch the Master!

HILDA. What do they want to watch him for?

RAGNAR. They like to see him obliged to stay below; they know he'd never dare climb, even to the top of his own house.

HILDA. So that's why they're here, is it?

RAGNAR. Yes—all these years he's kept us down. We like to see him forced to stay down below himself.

HILDA. Well—you won't see that this time.

RAGNAR. Really? Where will we see him then?

HILDA. High up! High up at the top of the tower! That's where you'll see him!

RAGNAR. Do you expect me to believe that?

HILDA. It is his will to climb to the top—so at the top you shall see him.

RAGNAR. His *will*! Yes, I dare say—but he simply can't do it. He'd get dizzy before he was half way up. He'd have to crawl down again on his hands and knees!

HERDAL. [*Pointing towards the new house.*] Look! There goes the foreman up the ladder!

MRS S. He has the wreath to carry too. Oh, I do hope he'll be careful!

RAGNAR. [*With a shout of incredulity.*] But—it's——

HILDA. [*Jubilant.*] It's the Master Builder himself!

MRS S. [*With a cry of terror.*] Yes, it's Halvard! Oh, God! Halvard! Halvard!

HERDAL. Sh! Don't shout to him!

MRS S. [*Beside herself.*] I must go to him—I must get him to come down!

HERDAL. [*Holding on to her.*] Stand still—all of you! Not a sound!

HILDA. [*Motionless, follows Solness with her eyes.*] He climbs and he climbs. Higher and higher. Higher and higher! Look! Just look!

RAGNAR. [*Scarcely breathing.*] He *must* turn back now. He can't do anything else.

HILDA. He climbs and he climbs. He'll soon be at the top now.

MRS S. I shall die of terror. I can't bear to look at him!

HERDAL. Don't watch him then.

HILDA. There he stands on the topmost planks—right at the very top!

HERDAL. No one must move—Do you hear!

HILDA. [*Exultant; with quiet intensity.*] At last! At last! I see him great and free again!

RAGNAR. [*Almost speechless.*] But this is——

HILDA. All these ten years I've seen him so! How proud he looks! Wonderfully thrilling all the same. Look at him! Now he's hanging the wreath on the vane!

RAGNAR. But—this is utterly impossible!

HILDA. It *is* the impossible that he's doing now. [*With that indefinable expression in her eyes.*] Do you see anyone else up there with him?

RAGNAR. There is no one else.

HILDA. Yes—there's someone he's striving with.

RAGNAR. No—you're mistaken——

HILDA. Don't you hear a song in the air either?

RAGNAR. It must be the wind in the tree tops.

HILDA. I hear a song. A mighty song! [*Shouts with wild joyful ecstasy.*] Look! Look! Now he's waving his hat! He's waving to us down here! Oh, wave—wave back to him—for now it is finished! [*Snatches the white shawl from the doctor, waves it and shouts up to Solness.*] Hurrah for Master Builder Solness!

HERDAL. Stop it! Stop it—for God's sake!

> [*The ladies on the veranda wave their handkerchiefs, and shouts of 'Hurrah!' come from the streets below. There is a sudden silence—then the crowd bursts into a shriek of horror. A human body, with a few planks and fragments of wood, is seen dimly, crashing down behind the trees.*

MRS S. AND THE LADIES. [*Simultaneously.*] He's falling! He's falling!

> [*Mrs Solness sways and falls back in a faint. The ladies support her amidst cries and confusion. The crowd in the street breaks through the fence and storms into the garden. Dr Herdal rushes down there too. A short pause.*

HILDA. [*Stares fixedly upward and says as though petrified*] My Master Builder.

RAGNAR. [*Trembling, leans against the railing.*] He must have been killed outright—smashed to pieces.

ONE OF THE LADIES. [*As Mrs Solness is being helped into the house.*] Run for the doctor——

RAGNAR. I can't move——

LADY. Then call down to him!

RAGNAR. [*Makes an effort to call out.*] Is there any hope? Is he still alive?

A VOICE FROM BELOW. The Master Builder is dead.

ANOTHER VOICE. [*Nearer.*] His whole head is crushed in—he fell right into the stone quarry.

HILDA. [*Turns to Ragnar and says quietly.*] I can't see him up there any more.

RAGNAR. What a ghastly thing. So—after all—he couldn't do it.

HILDA. [*As though under a spell, with quiet triumph.*] But he climbed to the very top. And I heard harps in the air. [*Waves the shawl and cries out with wild intensity.*] My Master Builder!

CURTAIN

JOHN GABRIEL BORKMAN

JOHN GABRIEL BORKMAN

ACT I

*Mrs Borkman's drawing-room. The door is at the back right of centre stage;
there are windows to the left of the door along a slanting back wall and
there is an arched opening which leads to the conservatory right of the
door. An armchair stands right centre and a settee with a table behind it
are left centre parallel with the windows; on this table is a lighted lamp.
There is another table left of the conservatory entrance; there is a stove
down right and a chair stands right of it in the downstage right corner.
There are long net or lace curtains at the windows as well as long heavy
curtains. It is evening outside the windows but the heavy curtains are not
drawn. There is a wall bell left of the stove.*

*When the curtain rises, Gunhild Borkman, grey-haired and distinguished
in a haughty kind of way, is sitting on the settee crocheting; there is a
workbasket beside her. Bells from a passing sledge are heard. She listens
and whispers to herself.*

MRS BORKMAN. Erhart! At last!

    *[She gets up and peeps through the curtains. Her face falls and she
returns to her work on the settee.*

                       [The Maid enters with a visiting card on a tray.

That's not Mr Erhart, is it?

MAID. No, ma'am, it's a lady.

MRS BORKMAN. Mrs Wilton?

MAID. No, ma'am, I've never seen her before.

MRS BORKMAN. Let me see. [*She takes the card, looks at it and gets up
hastily.*] Are you sure this is for me?

MAID. She asked for you, ma'am.

MRS BORKMAN. She said she wanted to see Mrs Borkman?

MAID. Yes, ma'am.

MRS BORKMAN. Very well. Show her in.

    *[The Maid exits. She returns immediately with Miss Ella Rentheim,
Mrs Borkman's sister. Ella Rentheim is beautiful but her face*

shows signs of great suffering. Her hair is white. Mrs Borkman
rises. There is silence for a while as the sisters gaze intently at each
other.]

ELLA. [*Moving left of the armchair.*] You're surprised to see me,
Gunhild?

MRS BORKMAN. Haven't you come to the wrong place? The bailiff
lives in the wing.

ELLA. I haven't come to see the bailiff today. I've come to see you.

MRS BORKMAN. I see. Sit down.

ELLA. Thank you, but I think I'll stand.

MRS BORKMAN. Just as you like. Won't you take off your coat?

ELLA. I'll loosen it. It's rather warm in here.

MRS BORKMAN. Is it? I always feel cold.   [*She sits again on the settee.*
    [*Up stairs the pacing of Mr Borkman, back and forth, can be heard.*

ELLA. It's nearly eight years since we last met, isn't it?

MRS BORKMAN. Since we last spoke to each other, yes.

ELLA. You've probably seen me when I've paid my annual visit to
the bailiff.

MRS BORKMAN. [*Nodding.*] Once or twice.

ELLA. I've caught a glimpse of you, once or twice, watching me
from the window.

MRS BORKMAN. You must have remarkably good eyesight to see
me through those thick curtains. The last time we spoke to each
other—it was here in this room——

ELLA. [*Moving a little towards her sister.*] Yes, yes, I know, Gunhild.

MRS BORKMAN. —the week before he—before they let him out.

ELLA. Don't talk about that, please.

MRS BORKMAN. It was the week before he was—released.

ELLA. I know—I shall never forget it. I don't want to talk about
it—I hate to think about it even.

MRS BORKMAN. How can we *not* think about it? When something
as dreadful as that happens to you, how can you ever hope to get
it out of your mind? Why did it have to happen to us? To us, of
all people! Everybody thought so well of us.

ELLA. We weren't the only sufferers, Gunhild.

MRS BORKMAN. Oh, I can't worry my head about other people.
All they lost was a bit of money and a few odd papers. But what
about me? And Erhart? He was a tiny child when it happened.
The disgrace of it! The dishonour! And the ruin!

ELLA. Tell me, Gunhild, how is he?

MRS BORKMAN. Who? Erhart?

ELLA. No, not Erhart. You know whom I mean.

MRS BORKMAN. [*Angrily.*] Do you think I ever ask how he is?

ELLA. You don't have to ask.

MRS BORKMAN. You don't think I have anything to do with him, do you? I never meet him, I never see him.

ELLA. Never see him?

MRS BORKMAN. A jailbird? A man who spent eight years in prison. [*Hiding her face in her hands.*] The shame of it! The humiliation! Do you remember what the name of John Gabriel Borkman used to stand for? No, I'll never look at him again, never.

ELLA. I knew you were hard, Gunhild, but . . .

MRS BORKMAN. Where he's concerned, yes, I'm hard.

ELLA. He's your husband, after all.

MRS BORKMAN. Didn't he tell them in court that I was the cause of his ruin? That it was I who squandered his money away?

ELLA. Well, wasn't there just a grain of truth in what he said?

MRS BORKMAN. If there was, it's because he encouraged me. He told me he had to live in style; it was essential in his position.

ELLA. I know all that, but it was your business to keep an eye on the purse strings, and that's what you didn't do.

MRS BORKMAN. How was I to know that the money he gave me to squander wasn't his money? He did a bit of squandering on his own account, too. Ten times as much as I did.

ELLA. Well, he *did* have a position to keep up.

MRS BORKMAN. We must 'live in style', he used to tell me. Well he 'lived in style' all right—with his coach and four and everyone bowing and scraping to him as though he were the king, and calling him by his Christian name, too, as though he were the king. 'John Gabriel', 'John Gabriel the Great'. The whole country knew what a great man 'John Gabriel' was.

ELLA. At that time he *was* a great man.

MRS BORKMAN. That's what everyone thought. Never once did he give me a hint of the real position, never a whisper of where the money was coming from.

ELLA. Nobody else knew either.

MRS BORKMAN. I'm not interested in anybody else. It was his duty to tell me the truth. But he just lied and went on lying.

ELLA. No, no, Gunhild, he was secretive, I admit, but he didn't tell lies.

MRS BORKMAN. Call it what you like, what does it matter? I only know that because of him my whole world fell to pieces.

ELLA. [*To herself as she sits in the armchair.*] Your world, and his, and other people's, too.

> [*Again the pacing of Borkman can be heard above.*

MRS BORKMAN. But it's not the end of the story yet. It can't be. I'll show them.

ELLA. What do you mean?

MRS BORKMAN. I'll redeem my name, I tell you, my name and my honour and my position. And there's someone who's going to help me, someone who's only living for the day he can wipe out every memory of my husband's crimes.

ELLA. Gunhild, Gunhild!

MRS BORKMAN. He will make up to me for the wrong his father did me.

ELLA. You mean, Erhart . . .

MRS BORKMAN. Yes, Erhart; my son, Erhart. He will reinstate us —our name and our fortune. Everything will be restored to us. Perhaps even more.

ELLA. How can he do that?

MRS BORKMAN. It *must* be done and it *will* be done, and Erhart is the man to do it. Tell me the truth, Ella, haven't you been waiting for that to happen too?

ELLA. No, I'm afraid I haven't.

MRS BORKMAN. Then why did you take Erhart to live with you when—when the crash came?

ELLA. Because you were hardly in a position to look after him yourself, Gunhild.

MRS BORKMAN. That's true. And his father had a good excuse. He was behind bars, so . . .

ELLA. [*Indignantly.*] How can you talk like that? You, of all people?

MRS BORKMAN. [*Venomously.*] And how could *you* make yourself a foster-parent to a son of John Gabriel? How could you bring yourself to take charge of a child of mine? You kept him with you for years, you brought him up as though he belonged to you. Why did you do it?

ELLA. I loved him.

MRS BORKMAN. More than I, his mother?

ELLA. Let's not go into that. Erhart was a delicate child.

MRS BORKMAN. Erhart delicate?

ELLA. He was then. And the air on the west coast is much milder than it is here.

MRS BORKMAN. Is it? I didn't know. [*She pauses, then continues.*] Yes, you've been good to Erhart, I don't deny it. But you could afford it. You were one of the lucky ones, Ella. You managed to survive the wreck.

> [*She puts away her crocheting in the workbasket by her side.*

ELLA. There was no managing about it. I didn't know till long afterwards that my money was safe.

MRS BORKMAN. [*Rising.*] Oh well, I haven't much of a head for finance. Let's just say you were fortunate. But tell me this—why did you bring up Erhart for me? What was your reason?

ELLA. My reason?

MRS BORKMAN. You had a reason, hadn't you?

ELLA. I wanted to make things easy for him. I wanted him to be happy.

MRS BORKMAN. [*As she crosses behind the settee and places her workbasket on the table; derisively.*] People in our position have much more important things to think about than happiness.

ELLA. Such as?

MRS BORKMAN. I'm thinking of Erhart. He must make such a success of his career that it must blot out the slur on our name, blot it out for ever.

ELLA. Is that what Erhart wants? Is that what he demands of life?

MRS BORKMAN. [*Taken aback.*] I hope so.

ELLA. Are you sure it's not what you demand of him?

MRS BORKMAN. Erhart and I always make the same demands on ourselves.

ELLA. You're very sure of yourself, Gunhild.

MRS BORKMAN. Yes, thank God.

> [*Borkman's pacing footsteps are heard again.*

ELLA. Then you ought to be a very happy woman despite everything that's happened.

MRS BORKMAN. As far as that goes, I am; but the past keeps coming back and sweeping over me like a storm—and then . . .

> [*Upstairs Borkman paces across the room.*

ELLA. Gunhild, I want you to tell me something. That's why I'm here.

MRS BORKMAN. Yes, what is it?   [*Borkman paces back again.*

ELLA. Erhart doesn't live here with you, does he?

MRS BORKMAN. How can he? He has to stay in town. There's his work.

ELLA. That's what he said when he wrote to me.

MRS BORKMAN. But he's here for a little while every evening.

ELLA. Do you mind if I speak to him? Now?

MRS BORKMAN. He's not here. But I'm expecting him any moment.

ELLA. But, Gunhild, he must be here. I can hear him walking about upstairs.

MRS BORKMAN. [*Looking up.*] In the reception-room?

ELLA. Yes. He's been walking up and down there all the time I've been here.   [*Mrs Borkman returns to the settee and sits down.*

MRS BORKMAN. That's not Erhart.

ELLA. Not Erhart? Who is it then?

MRS BORKMAN. It is—he.

ELLA. [*Slowly.*] Borkman? John Gabriel?

[*Borkman's steps are heard again.*

MRS BORKMAN. He paces the room like that, up and down, down and up; day in, day out; morning, noon and night.

ELLA. I'd heard about it.

MRS BORKMAN. That doesn't surprise me. My neighbours still find lots to gossip about.

ELLA. Erhart mentioned it when he wrote to me. He told me his father lived by himself up there—and you, down here.

MRS BORKMAN. It's been like that ever since he came out of prison. Eight years ago.

ELLA. And I refused to believe it! I said it was impossible.

MRS BORKMAN. Well, you can believe it now. That's how it is and that's how it's going to remain.

ELLA. [*Rising.*] But what a way to live! It must be hell on earth.

MRS BORKMAN. It is. I can't put up with it much longer. To hear him pacing that room up there from the moment I wake up till dead of night! And everything sounds so clear down here, too!

[*The steps above are heard once more.*

ELLA. It's uncanny!

MRS BORKMAN. Like a sick wolf prowling in his cage right over my head. Listen! Backwards and forwards, backwards and forwards, the wolf is on the prowl!

ELLA. [*Moving towards her tentatively.*] But must it be like that? Must he stay up there?

MRS BORKMAN. He's never suggested he'd like to come down here.

ELLA. But have *you* suggested it?

MRS BORKMAN. I! After the way he's treated me! No, thank you! Let the wolf stay where he is.

ELLA. I'm finding it too hot here. I must take my coat off.

MRS BORKMAN. I asked you to earlier on.

> [*Ella Rentheim takes off her hat and coat and places them in the conservatory near the door. Mrs Borkman draws the curtains.*

ELLA. But do you ever meet him? When you're both out, I mean?

MRS BORKMAN. [*Trimming the oil lamp behind the settee; bitterly.*] Where? At parties?

ELLA. [*Moving towards the settee.*] When he goes out for a walk?

MRS BORKMAN. He never goes out of the house.

ELLA. Not even after dark?

MRS BORKMAN. No.

ELLA. He can't bring himself to do that even!

MRS BORKMAN. I suppose not. His hat and coat are in the cupboard in the hall and . . .

ELLA. The cupboard we used to hide in when we were children . . .

MRS BORKMAN. [*Nodding.*] Sometimes, at night, I hear him coming down the stairs, but he stops half way and turns back.

ELLA. How about his old friends? Do they ever come to see him?

MRS BORKMAN. He has no old friends.

ELLA. [*Near the settee.*] He used to have so many.

MRS BORKMAN. He chose the surest way to get rid of them. He was *much* too dear a friend to his friends, was John Gabriel.

ELLA. Perhaps you're right, Gunhild.

> [*She crosses and sits on the left end of the settee.*

MRS BORKMAN. All the same, it was mean, shabby, disgusting, contemptible of them to behave as they did just because they lost a bit of money.

ELLA. So he lives up there alone! All by himself!

MRS BORKMAN. [*Crossing right to attend to the stove.*] Oh, I believe one of his old clerks or secretaries comes out to see him from time to time.

ELLA. Ah, that must be Foldal. They used to be great friends.

MRS BORKMAN. [*Warming her hands.*] So I believe. But I never knew him. I didn't count John Gabriel's clerks among my circle of friends—when I had a circle.

ELLA. But he still comes here to see Borkman?

MRS BORKMAN. Yes. He doesn't seem to be very particular about the people he visits—but he only comes after dark.

ELLA. Foldal lost his money when the bank failed, didn't he?

MRS BORKMAN. I did hear something of the sort. But it was hardly anything.

ELLA. It was everything he possessed.

MRS BORKMAN. Then he possessed very little.

ELLA. Foldal never mentioned it at the trial.

MRS BORKMAN. Erhart has more than made up to him for his losses.

ELLA. Erhart has? How has he managed to do that?

MRS BORKMAN. He's taken Foldal's youngest daughter in hand. He's taught her everything she knows. Thanks to him, she can get a good job now and make her own way in the world. Her father could never have done as much for her.

ELLA. Her father hadn't any money to spend on her education.

MRS BORKMAN. Erhart arranged for her to have music lessons, too. She's got on so well that she frequently comes out here in the evenings and plays for him—up there.

ELLA. He's still fond of music then?

MRS BORKMAN. He must be. He's still got the piano you sent him just before he was let out.

ELLA. Does the poor girl have to trudge all the way from town and back again?

MRS BORKMAN. No, she's staying with a neighbour. Erhart arranged it—a Mrs Wilton.

ELLA. Mrs Wilton?

MRS BORKMAN. Yes. You don't know her, do you?

ELLA. I've heard of her. Mrs Fanny Wilton, isn't it?

MRS BORKMAN. That's right.

ELLA. Erhart has mentioned her in his letters. Is she living out here now?

MRS BORKMAN. Yes, she rented a villa some time ago.

ELLA. [*Hesitating.*] They say her husband divorced her.

MRS BORKMAN. To the best of my knowledge, her husband died several years ago.

ELLA. All the same, he divorced her.

MRS BORKMAN. He deserted her. She was the innocent party.

ELLA. Do you know her well, Gunhild?

MRS BORKMAN. Quite well. She lives near by. She drops in now and again.

ELLA. Do you like her?

MRS BORKMAN. She's very understanding. And she's an excellent judge of character.

ELLA. Oh?

MRS BORKMAN. Take Erhart, for instance. She seems to have seen right into his soul. And because she knows him so well, she adores him. That's as it should be.

ELLA. She must know Erhart better than she knows you.

MRS BORKMAN. [*Moving behind the armchair.*] Well, he used to see quite a lot of her in town, before she moved out here.

ELLA. I wonder why she moved out of town.

MRS BORKMAN. What do you mean?

ELLA. Oh, nothing.

MRS BORKMAN. Yes, you do, Ella.

ELLA. You're right, Gunhild, I do.

MRS BORKMAN. Then tell me straight out.

ELLA. Well, first of all, I want you to know that I consider I have some sort of a claim on Erhart. Or don't you agree?

MRS BORKMAN. I agree that you've spent a lot of money on him, so . . .

ELLA. It has nothing to do with the money. It's because I love him.

MRS BORKMAN. So you've said before. But how can you love my son? You? In view of what's happened?

ELLA. I love him in spite of what's happened! I love him as much as I can love anybody—now.

MRS BORKMAN. Very well, let's agree that you love him. But what . . .

ELLA. I'm worried when I feel he's in danger.

MRS BORKMAN. Erhart in danger? Danger from what? From whom?

ELLA. First of all, from you.

MRS BORKMAN. I?

ELLA. And then from this Mrs Wilton.

MRS BORKMAN. How can you think such things? Of my son too? Erhart has a mission to fulfil, I tell you.

ELLA. [*Casually.*] Oh dear, that mission again!

MRS BORKMAN. [*Rising and crossing to centre.*] Yes, you can sneer.

ELLA. Do you think a young man of Erhart's age, full of red blood and adventure—do you think he's going to sacrifice himself for 'a mission'?

MRS BORKMAN. I know he will.

ELLA. You don't know it and you don't really believe it.

MRS BORKMAN. I tell you I believe it.

ELLA. You want to believe it. If you didn't you'd have nothing left to live for.

MRS BORKMAN. Yes, that's true. And that's what you'd like to see happen, isn't it?

ELLA. Rather that than your so-called redemption at Erhart's expense.

MRS BORKMAN. You want to come between us. You want to separate me from my son.

ELLA. I want to set him free from you, from your will, from your domination.

MRS BORKMAN. You're too late. You had him in your toils for years, till he was fifteen. But he's mine again now.

ELLA. He'll come back to me. [*In a hoarse whisper.*] This isn't the first time we've fought a life-and-death struggle over a man, Gunhild.

MRS BORKMAN. But it was I who won, Ella.

ELLA. Do you still think your victory was worth while?

MRS BORKMAN. No, you're right there.

ELLA. If you win this time it will be another empty victory.

MRS BORKMAN. An empty victory? I'm fighting to keep my son.

ELLA. You're fighting to keep your power over your son.

MRS BORKMAN. And you? What are you fighting for?

ELLA. His love, his soul, his very heart. I want Erhart for myself, I want him completely.

MRS BORKMAN. Never! As long as I live—never!

ELLA. You've done your best to turn him against me already, haven't you?

MRS BORKMAN. Yes, I've taken that liberty. Didn't you detect it in his letters?

ELLA. Yes, you've certainly made yourself felt in his letters.

MRS BORKMAN. [*Moving towards the armchair.*] I've made good use of the last eight years.

ELLA. What have you told him about me? Does it bear repeating?

MRS BORKMAN. Oh, yes. [*She sits in the armchair.*

ELLA. Then repeat it, will you?

MRS BORKMAN. I've told him the truth.

ELLA. And what is that?

MRS BORKMAN. I've impressed on him every hour of the day that he must always bear in mind how indebted we are to you, that we are living here on your charity and that we ought to be grateful to you for being able to live at all.

ELLA. Is that all?

MRS BORKMAN. It's enough. It's humiliating. *I*'ve learned that much.

ELLA. But Erhart knew all that.

MRS BORKMAN. When he came back to me he believed you did it out of your great loving kindness. He doesn't believe that any longer, Ella.

ELLA. What does he believe now?

MRS BORKMAN. The truth. I've asked him why his Aunt Ella never came near us . . .

ELLA. He knew why.

MRS BORKMAN. He knows better now. You'd convinced him it was because you didn't want to embarrass me and—him up there.

ELLA. So it was.

MRS BORKMAN. He's not convinced any longer, Ella.

ELLA. What have you made him believe?

MRS BORKMAN. The truth once more—that you're ashamed of us, that we're beneath your notice. Don't deny it. Didn't you do your utmost to take Erhart away from me? Didn't you?

ELLA. I did that when the scandal blew sky high and the case was the talk of the whole country. Never since.

MRS BORKMAN. It would be all the same if you did. Erhart has a mission. He needs me and I need him. That's why he's dead to you—and you to him.

ELLA. [*Rising.*] We'll see about that. I'm going to stay here now, Gunhild.   [*She moves left, firmly.*

MRS BORKMAN. Stay here? In this house?

ELLA. Yes.

MRS BORKMAN. Here? Tonight?

ELLA. For the rest of my days if necessary.

MRS BORKMAN. [*Collecting herself.*] Very well then, the house is yours . . .

ELLA. Oh, please . . .

MRS BORKMAN. Everything is yours. The chair I'm sitting on is yours, the bed I toss and turn on night after night is yours, the food we eat—we only eat it by the grace of Ella Rentheim.

ELLA. There's nothing we can do about that. Anything Borkman held in his own name would be seized. You know that.

MRS BORKMAN. I know we've got to go on living on your charity.

ELLA. If you want to look at it like that I can't stop you.

MRS BORKMAN. When do you want us to leave here?

ELLA. Leave here?

MRS BORKMAN. [*Very excited.*] You don't think I'd go on living under the same roof as you, do you? I'd rather go to the work-house.

ELLA. Good. Then you can't object if I take Erhart back with me.

MRS BORKMAN. Take my son back with you?

ELLA. Yes. If you agree I'll leave at once.

MRS BORKMAN. [*After a moment's reflection.*] Erhart will make his own choice.

ELLA. You'd let him do that? Would you dare, Gunhild?

MRS BORKMAN. [*Rising and facing her.*] Dare? To let him choose between his mother and you? Yes, I'd dare.

ELLA. Listen! Someone's coming.

MRS BORKMAN. It must be Erhart!

[*A knock is heard. The door opens and Mrs Wilton enters. She is a beautiful woman in the early thirties, in evening dress. She is followed by the Maid, who has not been given time to announce her. The door remains partly open.*

MRS WILTON. My dear Mrs Borkman!

[*She is between the two women.*

MRS BORKMAN. Good evening, Mrs Wilton. [*To the Maid.*] Light the lamp and bring it back.   [*The Maid goes out.*

MRS WILTON. Oh, I'm sorry—you have a visitor.

MRS BORKMAN. Only my sister. She's just arrived.

[*Erhart Borkman pushes open the door and runs in. He is a well-dressed, cheerful-looking young man.*

ERHART. What's this? Aunt Ella here? [*He crosses past Mrs Wilton to Ella's right.*] Hallo, Aunt Ella! What a lovely surprise!

ELLA. [*Her arms round Erhart.*] Erhart! My dear boy! How you've grown! Oh, it's good to see you again.

MRS BORKMAN. What does this mean, Erhart? Have you been hiding out there in the hall?

MRS WILTON. Erhart—Mr Borkman and I came here together.

MRS BORKMAN. Oh? I thought you always came straight here, Erhart?

ERHART. [*Crossing back to the door.*] I called at Mrs Wilton's to collect Frida Foldal.

MRS BORKMAN. Is Miss Foldal here as well?

MRS WILTON. She's outside in the hall.

ERHART. [*Through the open door.*] Go straight upstairs, Frida.

[*He seems put out. He has become cold and his expression is obstinate.*

[*The Maid returns with a lighted lamp which she puts on the table by the conservatory. Mrs Borkman moves down right.*

MRS BORKMAN. [*Too polite.*] If you'd care to stay for the evening, Mrs Wilton . . .

MRS WILTON. It's kind of you, my dear, but I must be getting away. We have another invitation. We're going to the Hinkels.

MRS BORKMAN. We? Whom do you mean?

MRS WILTON. [*Laughing.*] Well, as a matter of fact, I only mean myself. But the ladies of the house instructed me to bring Mr Borkman with me if I should run into him.

MRS BORKMAN. And you *did* run into him, it seems.

MRS WILTON. Yes, wasn't I lucky? He was good enough to call on me—for little Frida.

MRS BORKMAN. But, Erhart, I didn't know you knew the—the Hinkels.

ERHART. [*Moving downstage a little.*] I can hardly say I know them. [*Annoyed.*] You seem to know better than anyone, Mother, whom I know and whom I don't know.

MRS WILTON. But, really, the Hinkels are the friendliest and most hospitable people. You feel at home the moment you go into their house. And it's always full of pretty girls.

MRS BORKMAN. I dare say, but they're not the right sort of company for my son.

MRS WILTON. But, my dear Mrs Borkman, your son is a young man, after all. He . . .

MRS BORKMAN. Thank goodness he is. If he weren't . . .

ERHART. All right, Mother, it goes without saying that I won't be at the Hinkels tonight. I'll stay here with you and Aunt Ella.

MRS BORKMAN. I knew you would, my dear.

ELLA. No, no, Erhart, you mustn't stay at home because of me . . .

ERHART. Yes, yes, Aunt Ella, let's not talk about it any more— unless, of course, it's too late to say 'No'. [*To Mrs Wilton.*] You accepted for me, didn't you?

MRS WILTON. What does that matter? I shall sweep into the *salon* distressed and deserted—can't you see me?—and just say 'No' on your behalf.

ERHART. [*Hesitant.*] Well, if you think they won't mind . . .

MRS WILTON. Saying 'Yes' or 'No' has become quite a habit with me. You can't leave your aunt the very moment you set eyes on her. Shame on you, Monsieur Erhart, that wouldn't be behaving like a good son.

MRS BORKMAN. Son?

MRS WILTON. Well, then, let's say foster-son.

MRS BORKMAN. Thank you for the correction.

MRS WILTON. I sometimes think many people owe more to their foster-mothers than to their real mothers.

MRS BORKMAN. Has that been your experience?

MRS WILTON. I regret to say I hardly knew my own mother, but the right foster-mother might have made me a nicer woman than many people seem to think I am. As for you, Mr Borkman, you will stay at home with mummy and auntie and be a good little boy and have a nice glass of milk. Goodbye, goodbye, dear Mrs Borkman. [*To Ella Rentheim.*] Goodbye.

[*She moves towards the door. Erhart moves up with her on her right. The Ladies bow.*]

ERHART. May I walk part of the way with you?

MRS WILTON. Not a step.

[*Erhart opens the door.*]

I'm used to my own company when I go out for a walk. [*At the door.*] Take care, Mr Borkman, I'm warning you!

ERHART. Warning me? What of?

MRS WILTON. As I make my way down the road distressed and deserted—of course—I shall try to cast a spell on you.

ERHART. [*Laughing.*] What? Again?

MRS WILTON. Take care, young man. As I'm going along I shall concentrate every ounce of my will, and I shall say, 'Mr Erhart Borkman, take your hat at once.'

MRS BORKMAN. And you think he'll take it?

MRS WILTON. [*Laughing.*] Take it? He'll grab it. Then I shall say, 'Now put on your overcoat, and be smart about it. And your goloshes! Whatever you do, don't forget your goloshes! Then follow me. And do exactly what I tell you, exactly what I tell you, exactly what I tell you.'

ERHART. [*Trying to be jocular.*] Oh, but I will.

MRS WILTON. [*Wagging her finger at him.*] Exactly what I tell you, exactly what I tell you. Good night!

[*She laughs, nods to the women and goes. Erhart closes the door.*

MRS BORKMAN. Was she being serious?

ERHART. Of course not, Mother. Couldn't you see she was only joking? Anyway, don't let's bother our heads about Mrs Wilton now. [*He makes Ella sit down with him on the settee on his left.*] Whatever made you come all the way out here, Aunt Ella? In the middle of winter too?

ELLA. I had to come.

ERHART. But why?

ELLA. I had to see a specialist.

MRS BORKMAN. [*Coldly watching them from the corner near the stove.*] Is anything the matter? Are you ill?

ELLA. You know I'm ill.

MRS BORKMAN. I knew you hadn't been in the best of health for some time, but . . .

ERHART. I was always telling you you ought to see a doctor.

ELLA. I hadn't much faith in the local doctors. Besides, it never gave me much trouble then.

ERHART. But is it worse now?

ELLA. I'm afraid it is.

ERHART. But it's not serious, is it?

ELLA. Well, that depends on the way you look at it.

ERHART. In that case, you mustn't dream of going home yet.

ELLA. I'm not.

ERHART. You must stay here. You'll have all the best doctors to choose from.

ELLA. That's what I thought when I came here.

ERHART. We'll find you a place near by, somewhat quiet and cosy.

ELLA. I had a look at my old place this morning.

ERHART. And a nice, comfortable place it was too!

ELLA. All the same, I won't be staying there this time.

ERHART. Why not?

ELLA. I changed my mind when I came here.

ERHART. Changed your mind?

MRS BORKMAN. [*Not looking up.*] Your aunt has decided to live here, Erhart. It's her house, you know.

ERHART. [*Rising.*] Here? With us? Is that true, Aunt Ella?

ELLA. Yes.

MRS BORKMAN. [*Still not looking up.*] Everything here belongs to
your aunt.

ELLA. I'm going to stay here to begin with, anyway. I'll furnish
a little flat for myself in the wing.

ERHART. That's the best thing you could do. There's lots of
room there. [*Suddenly.*] But, I say, you must be tired after your
journey.

ELLA. Yes, I am rather tired.

ERHART. Then why not have an early night?

ELLA. I'm going to.

ERHART. We can have another talk tomorrow or the next day or
whenever you want to. Just the three of us. Wouldn't you like
that, Aunt Ella?

MRS BORKMAN. [*Getting up and bursting out.*] Erhart, you're going to
leave me!

ERHART. [*Startled.*] What are you talking about, Mother?

MRS BORKMAN. You're going to those people—the Hinkels, aren't
you?

ERHART. Well, you don't want me lounging about here keeping
Aunt Ella up half the night, do you? She's a sick woman, Mother.

MRS BORKMAN. So you *are* going to the Hinkels!

ERHART. Why shouldn't I go there? What do you think, Aunt
Ella?

ELLA. I think you're a free man, Erhart, and you must do what you
think best.

MRS BORKMAN. [*Menacingly.*] You're trying to set him against me.

ELLA. I wish I could!

[*Music is heard from above. Erhart crosses to the door.*

ERHART. I can't stand any more of this. Where's my hat? [*To
Ella.*] Do you know that piece she's playing up there?

ELLA. No, what is it?

ERHART. The *Danse Macabre*—the *Dance of Death*. Don't you know
it?

ELLA. Not yet, Erhart.

ERHART. [*To Mrs Borkman.*] Mother, I'm being as patient as I can.
I want to go out tonight.

MRS BORKMAN. You want to get away from me, is that it?

ERHART. I'll be here again soon—tomorrow, possibly.

MRS BORKMAN. You want to get away from me! You want to join
those—those people! No, no, I won't even think about it.

ERHART. They're all enjoying themselves there, Mother. There's life there and music . . .

MRS BORKMAN. [*Pointing upwards.*] There's music here too.

ERHART. That's what's helping to drive me out of here.

ELLA. You wouldn't deny your father a few moments when he can forget his troubles, would you?

ERHART. I wouldn't deny him anything as long as I don't have to listen to it.

MRS BORKMAN. Erhart, now's the time to show your strength. Remember you have a mission in life.

ERHART. Mother, don't start that again—and for God's sake try to understand that I wasn't born to be a missionary. Good night, Aunt Ella. Good night, Mother!   [*Erhart goes out.*

MRS BORKMAN. That was a quick victory, Ella. You've won him back.

ELLA. I wish I could believe you.

MRS BORKMAN. But you won't keep him for long.

ELLA. You mean he'll go back to you?

MRS BORKMAN. To me—or to her.

[*There is a pause. Ella rises.*

ELLA. Then I say her rather than you.

MRS BORKMAN. I understand. And I say the same. She rather than you.

ELLA. Whatever happens to him . . .

MRS BORKMAN. It wouldn't matter very much—I think.

ELLA. [*Going into the conservatory and picking up her coat; as she returns.*] We are twin sisters, Gunhild, but for the first time in our lives, we have the same point of view. Good night!

[*Ella goes out. The music above gets louder.*

MRS BORKMAN. [*Seeming to shrink into herself; in a whisper.*] The wolf is howling again! The sick wolf! [*She falls into the armchair in agony; she whispers.*] Erhart, Erhart, remember your mother! Come back and help your mother! I can't go on any longer . . .

CURTAIN

*The large reception-room in the Rentheim house. There are folding double
doors at an angle back right and a small door angled left in the back
wall. There is a piano, placed so that the player faces the audience, down
right with a settee left of it and facing left. There is a large desk at an
angle left centre with a chair behind it. There is a window down left with
a small chair in front of it. There is a piano stool behind the piano. The
room is lit by a lamp on the desk.*

*When the curtain rises, John Gabriel Borkman is standing left of the
piano, his hands behind his back, listening to Frida Foldal, who is seated
at the piano playing the 'Danse Macabre'. Borkman is a distinguished-
looking man in his late sixties, and Frida is a pretty girl of fifteen; she is
dressed rather cheaply. The music stops and there is a pause.*

BORKMAN. Do you know where I first heard music like that?

FRIDA. No, Mr Borkman.

BORKMAN. Down in the mines.

FRIDA. In the mines?

BORKMAN. I'm a miner's son, you know. Or perhaps you didn't
know.

FRIDA. I didn't know, Mr Borkman.

BORKMAN. Well, I am. And my father used to take me down the
mines, sometimes. The iron ore sings down there.

FRIDA. Sings?

BORKMAN. Yes, as it's hewn out of the rocks. The pickaxe sets it
free and every blow sounds like a bell at midnight ringing in a
new day. The metal sings for sheer joy.

FRIDA. Why does it do that, Mr Borkman?

BORKMAN. Because it's going up into the sunlight to serve man-
kind.   [*He paces up and down.*

FRIDA. [*Looking at her watch and getting up.*] I'm sorry, Mr Borkman,
but I'm afraid it's time for me to go.

BORKMAN. Already?

FRIDA. I must. I'm engaged for this evening.

BORKMAN. Are you playing at a party?

FRIDA. Yes.

BORKMAN. Before an audience?

FRIDA. [*Biting her lip.*] No. I'm playing the dance music.

BORKMAN. [*By the desk.*] The dance music?

FRIDA. Yes, there's going to be a dance after supper.

BORKMAN. Do you enjoy playing at parties?

FRIDA. Oh, yes, I can always make a bit of money that way.
[*She picks up her coat which is on the settee.*

BORKMAN. Is that what you usually think about when you're playing?

FRIDA. No, I'm usually thinking how unfair it is I'm not dancing myself.

BORKMAN. That's what I wanted to find out. Yes, it *is* unfair that you're not allowed to join in, but there's one thing that should more than compensate for that . . .
[*He paces broodingly upstage.*

FRIDA. What is that, Mr Borkman?

BORKMAN. The knowledge that you have ten times as much music in you as all the dancers put together.

FRIDA. Oh, but I'm not so sure that I have.

BORKMAN. You must never be so silly as to lose confidence in yourself.

FRIDA. But, heavens, if the rest of them don't know it . . .

BORKMAN. *You* know it. That's enough. [*He moves behind the desk.*] Where are you playing this evening?

FRIDA. At Mr Hinkel's.

BORKMAN. [*Giving her a quick look.*] Hinkel's?

FRIDA. Yes.

BORKMAN. Does that man dare to throw parties? Can he induce one single person to call on him?

FRIDA. Oh yes, Mrs Wilton says the house is going to be full of people tonight.

BORKMAN. But what kind of people? Do you know that?

FRIDA. No. Oh, yes, I *do* know that Mr Erhart is going to be there.

BORKMAN. Erhart? My son?

FRIDA. Yes.

BORKMAN. How do you know?

FRIDA. He told me so himself, an hour ago.

BORKMAN. Is he out here today?

FRIDA. He's been at Mrs Wilton's all the afternoon.

BORKMAN. Has he been here? I mean, has he been downstairs?

FRIDA. Yes, he looked in to see Mrs Borkman.

BORKMAN. I might have guessed!

FRIDA. Mrs Borkman had a visitor, a lady.

BORKMAN. Who was she?

FRIDA. I don't know. I've never seen her before.

BORKMAN. Oh well, I suppose Mrs Borkman *does* get visitors from time to time.

FRIDA. If I get a chance to speak to Mr Erhart this evening, shall I ask him to come in and see you?

BORKMAN. Certainly not. That's the last thing in the world I want you to do. If people want to call on me they know where to find me. I never ask anyone.

FRIDA. I won't say anything, then. Good night, Mr Borkman.

BORKMAN. [*Pacing up and down.*] Good night!

FRIDA. Do you mind if I go out this way? It's quicker.

BORKMAN. No, no, go whichever way you like. Good night!

FRIDA. Good night, Mr Borkman.

[*Frida exits by the small door. Borkman goes to the piano and is about to close the lid. He changes his mind and starts to pace the room again. He stops and listens, hastily picks up a hand mirror and straightens his tie. A knock is heard. Borkman rests his left hand on the desk and places his right hand inside his coat, Napoleon-wise.*

BORKMAN. [*Standing by the desk.*] Come in!

[*Vilhelm Foldal enters. He is a bent, worn little man with long, thin grey hair and glasses. He is carrying a portfolio and felt hat. He pushes his glasses on to his forehead.*

[*Borkman drops his pose. His disappointment is rather more than his pleasure at seeing Foldal.*] Oh, it's you!

FOLDAL. [*By the settee.*] Good evening, John Gabriel. Yes, it's me.

BORKMAN. It's rather late to pay a call, isn't it?

FOLDAL. Well, it's rather a long way to go, especially when you have to go on foot.

BORKMAN. Then why go on foot? The tram passes your door.

FOLDAL. It's healthier to walk. Besides, I save three-ha'pence. [*He advances towards the desk.*] Well, has Frida been here recently?

BORKMAN. She's only just left. Didn't you run into her outside?

FOLDAL. No. I haven't seen her for ages, not since the day she went to live at Mrs Wilton's.

BORKMAN. [*Sitting down at the desk.*] You may take a seat, Vilhelm.

FOLDAL. [*Crossing to sit on the small chair by the window and sitting gingerly on the edge of a chair.*] Thank you. I can't tell you how I miss my Frida.

BORKMAN. Come, come, you've still got a whole tribe of children at home.

FOLDAL. God knows I have! But Frida was the only one who understood me. [*Sadly.*] The rest of them don't understand me at all.

BORKMAN. No, that's the cross we great men have to bear. The masses, the mob, the man and woman in the street, can never appreciate us.

FOLDAL. It's not only their lack of understanding; I could sit back and hope that appreciation would come in time. It's something even more cruel.

BORKMAN. Nothing could be more cruel.

FOLDAL. Yes, it could, John Gabriel. There was a scene at home tonight, just before I left.

BORKMAN. Was there? Why.

FOLDAL. My family—they despise me.

BORKMAN. [*Indignantly.*] Despise . . . ?

FOLDAL. Oh, I've felt it for some time, but today they went out of their way to make it obvious.

BORKMAN. I've often wondered whether you married the right woman.

FOLDAL. Well, there weren't many to choose from. I can't say I was keen, but I was getting on and everyone needs a mate as he grows older. Apart from that, I was on my beam ends at the time, so . . .

BORKMAN. [*Angrily.*] Was that a dig at me? Are you telling me it was my fault?

FOLDAL. [*Rising.*] Good gracious no, John Gabriel . . .

BORKMAN. Yes, you are, you're raking up the bank crash again.

FOLDAL. But I've never blamed you for that! Good gracious, no!

BORKMAN. Thank goodness for that anyway!

FOLDAL. [*Sitting down again.*] Besides, you mustn't run away with the idea that I'm grumbling about my wife. I know she's got no sense, poor thing, but she's a decent sort in her own way. No, it's the children.

BORKMAN. I can well believe that.

FOLDAL. They've had a better education, so they expect more out of life.

BORKMAN. And the result is—they despise you?

FOLDAL. Well, no one could say I've been much of a success, could they?

BORKMAN. Haven't you ever told them about the play you wrote?

FOLDAL. Of course I have, but it didn't make much of an impression.

BORKMAN. That's because they haven't the sense to understand it, my friend. You may take it from me, your tragedy is unique.

FOLDAL. [*All smiles.*] Yes, there are some good things in it, aren't there, John Gabriel? I only wish someone would put it on! [*He opens his manuscript and starts turning over the pages.*] Let me show you some of the alterations I've made.

BORKMAN. [*Alarmed.*] You haven't brought it with you, have you?

FOLDAL. I have, as a matter of fact. It's such a long time since you've heard it. I thought you might be diverted if I read you an act—or two.

BORKMAN. [*Rising.*] No, no, not now. Let's keep it up our sleeves . . .

FOLDAL. Yes, of course, if you prefer it.

> [*He puts his script back in his portfolio.*
> [*Borkman paces up and down.*

BORKMAN. [*Stopping in front of Foldal.*] What you said just now is true enough—you've been anything but a success in life. But I tell you this, Vilhelm, when my time comes again . . .

FOLDAL. [*Starting to get up.*] Oh, thank you, thank you!

BORKMAN. Don't get up. [*With rising excitement.*] When my time comes again, when they realize that they can get nowhere without me, when they come to me here, in this room, on their bended knees, and entreat me with tears in their eyes to take charge of the bank, the new bank that they created and are incapable of controlling [*he strikes his Napoleonic attitude*] then I shall stand here and receive them! But the whole country, the whole country, I say, will have dinned into its ears the terms which John Gabriel Borkman will lay down before he . . . [*He stops suddenly.*] Why are you looking at me like that? Don't you believe they'll come back to me? That they must, must, must, must come back to me? Don't you believe it?

FOLDAL. God's my witness I do, John Gabriel.

BORKMAN. Well, *I* believe it. I know it as surely as I'm standing here—they'll come back to me. If I weren't convinced of that I'd have put a bullet through my brain long ago.

FOLDAL. Oh, good gracious me, you mustn't . . .

BORKMAN. But they'll come back, I tell you, they'll come back! You wait! They'll be here any day now, any minute. And they'll find me waiting for them.

FOLDAL. I wish they'd hurry up.

BORKMAN. Yes, my friend, it's years now; time passes, life—I dare not think about it! [*He sits again at his desk.*] Do you know what I feel like sometimes?

FOLDAL. What?

BORKMAN. Like a Napoleon wounded in his very first battle.

FOLDAL. [*Patting his portfolio.*] I feel like that too sometimes.

BORKMAN. If you do, it's on a much lower level.

FOLDAL. [*Quietly.*] My little world of drama is very dear to me, John Gabriel.

BORKMAN. [*Violently.*] Yes, but what about me? I'd have made millions. Think of the mines I'd have opened up! The minerals I'd have tapped! The water-power! The new trade routes! The trans-oceanic liners! I'd have organized them all. I, and no one else!

FOLDAL. Yes, I know, you were ready for anything.

BORKMAN. And look at me now! Helpless, like a wounded eagle, watching others swooping on the prey and getting all the pickings, titbit by juicy titbit!

FOLDAL. That's exactly what's happening to me too.

BORKMAN. Just think of it! Success was almost in my grasp. Just a few more days! Every deposit would have been covered; every security, which I had used with so much foresight, would have been back in its place. And not one single person would have lost one single penny of his investments. Giant industrial concerns were on the point of being promoted.

FOLDAL. You were practically there.

BORKMAN. And that was the moment when I was betrayed! That crucial moment! [*Rising.*] Shall I tell you what is the most despicable crime a man can commit?

FOLDAL. What is it?

BORKMAN. [*Moving towards Foldal.*] It's not robbery, it's not perjury, it's not even murder. These are the sort of things men do to people they hate or to people who hate them.

FOLDAL. What is the most despicable crime, John Gabriel?

BORKMAN. [*Stressing his words.*] The most despicable of all crimes is a man's betrayal of his friend's trust.

FOLDAL. [*Rather dubiously.*] Yes, but after all . . .

BORKMAN. [*Angrily.*] I know what you're going to say. I can read it in your face, but you're wrong. Every person whose securities were entrusted to me would have had them restored—down to the last farthing. No. The most despicable crime a man can commit is to make use of his friend's letters, to make public facts that were given him in the strictest confidence and the greatest secrecy like a whisper in a dark, empty, sound-proof, burglar-proof room. The man who can behave like that is rotten through and through with the morals of a super scoundrel. That was my friend and that was the man who ruined me.

FOLDAL. I know whom you mean.

BORKMAN. I hid nothing from him. My life was an open book to him. And then, when the moment was ripe, he turned against me the very weapons I had placed in his hands.

FOLDAL. To this day, I've never understood why—there were all sorts of rumours at the time . . .

BORKMAN. What sort of rumours? Tell me. I don't know a thing. I was clapped straight into jail, don't forget. What were they saying, Vilhelm?

FOLDAL. They said you were in his way, that you'd been offered a seat in the Cabinet.

BORKMAN. I had, but I'd turned it down.

FOLDAL. Then that couldn't have been the reason.

BORKMAN. Oh, no, that wasn't why he betrayed me.

FOLDAL. Then I really can't see why . . .

BORKMAN. I'll tell you, Vilhelm.

FOLDAL. Well?

BORKMAN. There was a woman mixed up in it.

FOLDAL. A woman?

BORKMAN. That's enough now. It's over and done with. [*He moves to the other side of the room.*] As for the Cabinet, neither of us got into it.

FOLDAL. But he did get somewhere; he got to the top.

BORKMAN. And I went to the bottom.

[*He throws himself into the settee.*

FOLDAL. It was a tragedy, a shocking . . .

Act II   JOHN GABRIEL BORKMAN   175

BORKMAN. [*Sarcastically.*] Nearly as shocking as yours if you stop to think about it.

FOLDAL. [*Innocently.*] Oh, quite as shocking.

BORKMAN. [*Smiling.*] And yet, if you look at it from another angle, it has its funny side.

FOLDAL. Funny side? The story of your life?

BORKMAN. Yes, that's the way it seems to be shaping now. Listen to this . . .

FOLDAL. What?

BORKMAN. You didn't meet Frida when you came in just now, did you?

FOLDAL. No.

BORKMAN. At this very moment, while we are sitting here, your little Frida is sitting in the house of the man who ruined me, playing dance music for his guests.

FOLDAL. I didn't know that.

BORKMAN. When she left here she went straight to that man's house.

FOLDAL. [*Apologizing.*] Well, the poor child has to . . .

BORKMAN. And can you guess who she's playing for, among others?

FOLDAL. I don't know.

BORKMAN. My son.

FOLDAL. What?

BORKMAN. What do you say to that, Vilhelm? My son is there now, dancing merrily in the house of the man who destroyed me. Well, is it funny?

FOLDAL. I don't, for one minute, suppose your son knows anything about it.

BORKMAN. Doesn't know anything about it?

FOLDAL. I don't believe he knows how that man . . .

BORKMAN. Don't be shy about using his name. I can stomach it now.

FOLDAL. I'm absolutely certain your son knows nothing about the details of the case.

BORKMAN. Oh, yes, he knows! He knows as surely as we know.

FOLDAL. Then how could he accept an invitation to that house?

BORKMAN. I don't suppose he sees things the way we do. I'd bet my last penny his sympathies are all with them. He probably thinks what the rest of them are thinking—that Hinkel only did his duty as a lawyer when he gave me away.

FOLDAL. But, my dear old friend, who could have made him see things like that?

BORKMAN. [*Rising.*] Who? Who brought him up? His aunt, from the time he was six or seven, and then his mother.

[*He crosses upstage centre.*

FOLDAL. I don't think you're being fair to them, John Gabriel.

BORKMAN. [*Show of temper.*] I've never been unfair to anybody. I say they've both done everything they could to prejudice him against me.

FOLDAL. Oh well, perhaps you're right.

BORKMAN. [*Indignantly.*] Women! They make life a shambles for us! They play the deuce with destiny and bring to an end careers that should have been an unchequered progress to the very stars.

FOLDAL. Not all women!

BORKMAN. Oh? Can you name one single woman who's any good to anybody?

FOLDAL. No, that's what's so awful, I can't.

BORKMAN. And even if there are a few decent women knocking around, what's the good of it if you never meet them?

FOLDAL. There's a lot of good in it, John Gabriel, take my word for it. It's a blessed and elevating thought that somewhere in the world, no matter how far away, a true woman exists.

BORKMAN. For God's sake stop airing that poetic flummery!

[*He sits on the settee again.*

FOLDAL. Are you telling me that my holiest article of faith is poetic flummery?

BORKMAN. Yes, I am. And that's why you've never made your mark in the world. Get that stuff and nonsense out of your system and I might be able to make something of you.

FOLDAL. [*With suppressed anger.*] You couldn't do it.

BORKMAN. I could once I'm back in power again.

FOLDAL. The prospects are rather remote, John Gabriel.

BORKMAN. You're telling me it will never happen, aren't you?

FOLDAL. I don't know what to say.

BORKMAN. [*Rising.*] In that case, you're no good to me.

FOLDAL. [*Rising.*] No good to you?

BORKMAN. If you don't believe my time will come again . . .

FOLDAL. How can I believe it? It's against all logic. You'd have to be reinstated legally . . .

BORKMAN. [*Moves nearer to Foldal.*] Anything else?

FOLDAL. I'm not a lawyer, but I know enough to ...

BORKMAN. Say it's impossible?

FOLDAL. Well, unprecedented.

BORKMAN. Great men create precedents.

FOLDAL. The law doesn't distinguish between great men and little men.

BORKMAN. [*Moving up stage with finality.*] You're no poet, Vilhelm.

FOLDAL. Do you mean that?

BORKMAN. We're wasting each other's time. You'd better not come here again.

FOLDAL. Is that your last word?

BORKMAN. You're no good to me.

FOLDAL. No, no, perhaps not.   [*He picks up his portfolio.*

BORKMAN. You've been lying to me all the time you've been coming here.

FOLDAL. I've never lied to you, John Gabriel.

BORKMAN. Haven't you sat there buoying me up with hope and faith and fortitude? Was that a lie or wasn't it?

FOLDAL. As long as you believed in me it wasn't a lie. As long as you believed in me, I believed in you.

BORKMAN. Then we've been lying to each other. Perhaps we've been lying to ourselves.

FOLDAL. But isn't that the very spirit of friendship, John Gabriel?

BORKMAN. [*Bitterly.*] Yes, that's the truest thing you've ever said. And I've learned it once before. Friendship is a lie!

FOLDAL. So I'm no poet! And you could tell me that—to my face!

BORKMAN. Well, I'm not really a judge of poetry.

FOLDAL. Perhaps you're a better judge than you think.

BORKMAN. I?

FOLDAL. Yes, you. I've had my own doubts now and then. And there's the terrifying doubt that I might have messed up my whole life because of a delusion.

BORKMAN. If you've lost faith in yourself, you're finished.

FOLDAL. That's why it was so comforting to come here. I had faith in myself because you had faith in me. But now—well, you're a stranger to me now.

BORKMAN. And you to me.

FOLDAL. Good night, John Gabriel.

BORKMAN. Good night, Vilhelm.

> [*Foldal goes through the double doors. Borkman stands staring at the door, moves to it with the intention of calling Foldal back, then changes his mind and begins to pace the floor again, hands behind him. He stops and puts out the lamp. There is a pause, then a knock at the door.*

Who's there?

> [*There is no answer. The knock is repeated.*

Who is it? Come in.

> [*He moves to the piano and stands with his back to the door, tense, waiting. Ella Rentheim, with a lighted candle in her hand, comes in the double doors.*

Who are you? What do you want?

> [*Ella closes the door, crosses to the desk and puts the candle on it.*

ELLA. It is I, Borkman.

BORKMAN. [*He stands transfixed; in a whisper.*] Is it—is it Ella? Is it Ella Rentheim?

ELLA. Yes, it's 'your' Ella. That's what you used to call me in the old days. It's such a long time ago now . . .

BORKMAN. Yes, it's you, Ella. I can see you now.

ELLA. You recognize me?

BORKMAN. I do now.

ELLA. I'm older now. Autumn has set in, Borkman. You can see it in my face, can't you?

BORKMAN. You've changed, naturally.

ELLA. I used to have dark curls here on my neck. You loved to twist them round your fingers.

BORKMAN. Of course, that's it! You've changed your hair style!

ELLA. [*Wryly.*] Exactly! I've changed my hair style! That's what makes the difference.

BORKMAN. I didn't know you were in this part of the country.

ELLA. I've only just arrived.

BORKMAN. What made you come here—in the middle of winter too?

ELLA. I'll tell you everything in good time.

BORKMAN. Did you come to see me?

ELLA. You—and others; but it's a long story.

BORKMAN. You're looking tired.

ELLA. I am rather tired.

BORKMAN. Why don't you sit down—on the settee there?

ELLA. Thank you. [*She sits on the settee.*] Yes, I can do with a rest.
[*She pauses.*] It's such a long time since we last met, Borkman.

BORKMAN. [*Moves from behind her to her left.*] A long, long time. And
terrible things have happened in the meantime.

ELLA. In the meantime! It's been a whole lifetime, a wasted lifetime.

BORKMAN. Wasted?

ELLA. Yes, wasted. For both of us.

BORKMAN. [*Coldly.*] I don't consider my life wasted. Not yet.

ELLA. And mine?

BORKMAN. That's your own fault, surely.

ELLA. You're the last person who should say that.

BORKMAN. You could have been perfectly happy without me.

ELLA. Do you really believe that?

BORKMAN. If you'd wanted to—yes.

ELLA. Oh, I know there was someone else who was only too eager
to marry me.

BORKMAN. And you refused him.

ELLA. Yes.

BORKMAN. You refused him again and again. Year after year,
you . . .

ELLA. Year after year, I turned happiness away from my doorstep.
Is that what you're going to tell me?

BORKMAN. I'm telling you you could have been happy with him.
If you had, my tragedy would never have happened.

ELLA. Your tragedy?

BORKMAN. Yes. Everything depended on you.

ELLA. I don't follow you.

BORKMAN. He convinced himself that it was I who was inciting
you to turn him down and to go on turning him down. So he
revenged himself on me. It was so easy too. He was my friend,
my confidant. He'd kept my letters, every one of them. And he
made good use of them too! That was the end of me—until my
time comes again. So you see, Ella, you are really responsible.

ELLA. Well well, Borkman, so it comes to this—if we go into the
matter, really go into it, it's I who must make amends to you.

BORKMAN. [*Wandering restlessly round his desk and back to stage centre.*]
We all see things in a different light. I know everything you've
done for us. You bought back the house and its contents when
they were put up for auction. You allowed me, and your sister,

to live here. You took care of Erhart, educated him, did everything for him . . .

ELLA. I did it as long as I was allowed to do it.

BORKMAN. Allowed by your sister. I never interfered in domestic
affairs. What was I saying? Oh, yes, you've done a lot for me and
your sister; but, after all, you could afford it, Ella, and you could
afford it only because of me.

ELLA. [*Indignantly.*] You're quite wrong, Borkman. I did it because
of my love for Erhart and for you.

BORKMAN. My dear Ella, don't start getting sentimental. I'm only
trying to tell you that if you behaved generously it was because
I made it possible.

ELLA. You made it possible?

BORKMAN. Yes, I. When the decisive moment came, when I didn't
spare either relatives or friends, when I had to use every penny I
could lay my hands on, at that vital moment, I tell you, I did not
take anything that belonged to you although I could have used
your money together with all the millions that had been placed in
my keeping.

ELLA. That's perfectly true, Borkman.

BORKMAN. When they arrested me they found your securities safe
and sound, in the strong room.

ELLA. I've asked myself again and again why you left my money
alone. Why did you do it?

BORKMAN. Why?

ELLA. Yes. Tell me.

BORKMAN. [*Moving away left; scornfully.*] So that I'd have a nice little
nest egg to fall back on in case my plans went wrong. Is that what
you're thinking?

ELLA. Oh, dear me, no! I'm quite certain it never entered your
head that anything could go wrong.

BORKMAN. It didn't. I never dreamed of failure.

ELLA. Then why did you . . . ?

BORKMAN. For the life of me, Ella, I couldn't tell you now what
my reasons were twenty years ago. I only know that when I
used to struggle, all on my own, with the great schemes in my
mind, I felt like some explorer on the eve of a new adventure.
Throughout those long sleepless nights I was perfecting the
great new machine that was going to carry me away into the
Unknown.

ELLA. You? You who never dreamed of failure?

BORKMAN. Men are like that, Ella. We doubt and yet we believe. I suppose that was why I would not take you or your possessions with me on my journey.

ELLA. But why, why? Tell me why?

BORKMAN. [*Looking away*.] We're reluctant to hazard what is dearest to us.

ELLA. But you did hazard what was dearest to you—your whole future, your very life . . .

BORKMAN. Life isn't necessarily the thing that is dearest to us.

ELLA. [*Breathlessly*.] Was that how you felt then?

BORKMAN. It must have been.

ELLA. I was more dear to you than anyone else you knew?

BORKMAN. Yes, yes, I believe you were.

ELLA. And yet, years had passed since you had left me and—and married someone else.

BORKMAN. Left you? You know there were altruistic reasons— well, then, let's say other reasons—that forced me to do what I did. Without his co-operation, I was helpless.

ELLA. Then you left me for—altruistic reasons?

BORKMAN. I tell you I was helpless without his co-operation. And you were the price of his co-operation.

ELLA. And you paid the price. In full. No haggling.

BORKMAN. I had no choice. With me it had to be complete victory or nothing.

ELLA. Tell me, is it true that I was dearer to you than anything else in the whole world?

BORKMAN. It was true then, and it was true afterwards, long, long afterwards.

ELLA. And yet you did a deal with another man for that great love of yours. You sold it to gain control of a bank!

BORKMAN. Necessity knows no law, Ella.

ELLA. [*Rising; passionately*.] You criminal!

BORKMAN. That word has been flung at me before.

ELLA. Oh, I'm not referring to anything you might have done against the law. How you used those bonds or securities or whatever you call them—do you think I care a jot about that? If they had allowed me to stand by your side when you were in the box . . .

BORKMAN. What then, Ella?

ELLA. I'd have put up with everything willingly, gladly, because I was sharing it with you. The scorn, the degradation, I'd have helped you bear everything, everything!

BORKMAN. Would you have done that, Ella? Could you have done it?

ELLA. I would and I could have done it, because I knew nothing then of the terrible crime you had committed.

BORKMAN. What crime? What are you talking about?

ELLA. The crime for which you will never be forgiven.

BORKMAN. Have you gone out of your mind, Ella?

ELLA. [*Coming close to Borkman.*] You're a murderer! You've committed the greatest crime of all.

BORKMAN. Ella, you must be stark, staring mad.

ELLA. You've killed the love in me. It was a living thing and you've killed it. Do you understand what that means? The Bible mentions a mysterious sin for which there is no forgiveness. I never knew what it was, but now I *do* know. The sin for which there is no forgiveness is the murder of the love that lives and thrives in every human heart.

BORKMAN. And you're telling me I've done that?

ELLA. Yes, you've done that. Until this evening I never really understood what had happened to me. When you left me for Gunhild I thought it was just a bit of ordinary philandering on your part and ruthless scheming on hers. I despised you for it and that was all. But now I see it all clearly. You abandoned the woman you loved. Me, me, me! You were willing to trade, for your own ends, the woman who was dearer to you than anyone in the whole world. That's the double murder you committed. The murder of your soul and mine!

BORKMAN. [*Close to Ella.*] You haven't changed, Ella. The same passionate, unbridled outbursts! You'd never be able to see it in any other way. Because you're a woman, one thing is pre-eminent with you——

ELLA. Yes, yes, you're right.

BORKMAN. —your own heart. Nothing else matters.

ELLA. Nothing! Nothing!

BORKMAN. Well then, try to remember that I'm a man. You were the dearest woman in the world to me but, if necessity decrees, then one woman can always be replaced by another.

[*Ella crosses past him to the other side of the room.*

ELLA. Did you find that out after you'd married Gunhild?

BORKMAN. No. But I had an object in life which helped me put up with it. I wanted to have under my control all the sources of power in the country. The riches of the earth and the mountains and the forests and the seas—I wanted to make myself their master, I wanted to govern my own kingdom and bring comfort to the hundreds of thousands who inhabited it.

ELLA. [*Sitting by the window.*] I know. All the evenings we spent together talking over your plans!

BORKMAN. I could always talk to you, Ella.

ELLA. I used to make fun of your ideas. Do you remember when I asked you if you wanted to wake up all the sleeping spirits of the rocks?

BORKMAN. Yes, I remember. 'All the sleeping spirits of the rocks.'

ELLA. But you never saw the joke. You said, 'Yes, yes, Ella, that's what I want to do.'

BORKMAN. [*Coming near to her.*] So it was! But I had to get my foot in the stirrup first. And I could only do it with the help of one man. He would see to it that I was put in charge of the bank if I, on my part . . .

ELLA. If you, on your part, would give up the woman you loved —and who loved you beyond words.

BORKMAN. The man's passion for you was all-consuming. I knew it was the only condition on which he . . .

ELLA. And so you closed your deal with him.

BORKMAN. Yes. I had a lust for power that was bigger than I was. I closed my deal. I had to do it. And he helped me half way up to the heights that were luring me on and on. I went higher and higher, every year, I went still higher . . .

ELLA. And I was blotted out of your life.

BORKMAN. [*Moving away from her.*] And then he hurled me back into the depths. And all because of you, Ella.   [*He sits on the settee.*

ELLA. [*After a short silence.*] Borkman, have you ever thought that there's been a sort of curse on our whole relationship?

BORKMAN. A curse?

ELLA. Yes. Hasn't it ever struck you like that?

BORKMAN. [*Uneasy.*] Yes. But why? Why? Oh, Ella, I can't tell who is right now—you or I.

ELLA. You are the sinner. All the joy of life that used to be in me— you killed it.

BORKMAN. Don't say that. Please, Ella . . .

ELLA. Perhaps I should have said—all my joy in my womanhood. From the day your image began to fade in my mind I have lived my life in the shadows. As the years went by, it became more and more difficult, and in the end absolutely impossible, for me to love any living being—except one person . . .

BORKMAN. Who was that?

ELLA. Erhart, of course.

BORKMAN. Erhart?

ELLA. Erhart—your son, Borkman.

BORKMAN. Has Erhart really meant so much to you?

ELLA. Why do you think I took him to live with me? And kept him as long as I was allowed to? Why?

BORKMAN. I thought it was out of pity—like everything else you did for us.

ELLA. [*Rising.*] Pity! I've been incapable of showing pity since the day you left me. When a poor, half-starved child came begging into my kitchen, shivering with cold and crying for food, I handed him over to the servants. I never wanted to fondle the child or warm him at my fire or get any pleasure from watching him eat and be satisfied. But I wasn't always like that. You have made me what I am. You are responsible for the barrenness that's inside me—yes, and all round me too.

BORKMAN. But there's still Erhart.

ELLA. Yes, there's still your son. Erhart apart, I'm indifferent to the whole world. You've cheated me of the joys of motherhood —and of a mother's tears and sorrows, too. Perhaps that is the greatest loss of all.

BORKMAN. Ella, do you mean that?

ELLA. A mother's tears and sorrows. Perhaps that is what I wanted more than anything. But at that time I was still unable to accept my loss. And that was why I took Erhart. And I won him, won him completely, won his warm, trusting, childish heart until . . .

BORKMAN. Until what?

ELLA. Until his mother—his mother in the eyes of the law, I mean—took him back again.

BORKMAN. [*Rising.*] He'd have had to leave you some time. He had to come to town.

ELLA. It's the loneliness I can't bear, the emptiness. Erhart's very heart belonged to me, and now I have lost it.

BORKMAN. [*Moving up towards the desk.*] I wonder if you have, Ella.
People don't lose their hearts so easily to someone—down there.

ELLA. [*Close to Borkman.*] I've lost Erhart and she has won him
back again. And if she hasn't, someone else has. It's obvious in
the letters he writes me.

BORKMAN. So you came here to take him back with you?

ELLA. If I could do that . . .

BORKMAN. If you've made up your mind to do it, it can be done.
You have stronger claims on him than anyone else.

ELLA. [*Moving quickly away towards the settee.*] Oh, claims, claims!
What's the good of claims? If he doesn't belong to me of his own
free will—then he doesn't belong to me at all. But I must have
him. I must have his love. I must have his very heart. I must
have it now.

BORKMAN. Ella, you must try to remember that Erhart is in the
twenties now. You could hardly expect him to go on giving you
his very heart, as you term it, for much longer now.

ELLA. It wouldn't be for much longer.

BORKMAN. Oh? I'd have thought that if you wanted something
you want it till the day you die.

ELLA. [*Sitting on the settee.*] I do. But that need not be for much
longer.

BORKMAN. What do you mean by that?

ELLA. You know I've been ailing for the last few years.

BORKMAN. Have you?

ELLA. Didn't you know?

BORKMAN. No.

ELLA. Hasn't Erhart ever mentioned it?

BORKMAN. I don't remember.

ELLA. Hasn't he ever mentioned me at all?

BORKMAN. Oh yes, I think he's mentioned you. But, to tell you
the truth, I hardly ever see him. Someone downstairs keeps him
away from me. As far away as possible.

ELLA. Do you know that for certain, Borkman?

BORKMAN. Of course I do. [*Changing his tone.*] So you've been ill,
Ella?

ELLA. I'm afraid so. I took a turn for the worse just recently, so
I came to town to see a specialist.

BORKMAN. Have you seen him yet?

ELLA. This morning.

BORKMAN. What did he say?

ELLA. He confirmed what I'd been suspecting for a long time.

BORKMAN. Yes?

ELLA. I will never get better, Borkman.

BORKMAN. No, no, Ella, you mustn't believe that.

ELLA. The doctors can do nothing for me. The disease must take its course. All they can do is alleviate the pain, but that's something to be thankful for.

BORKMAN. But it'll take a long time yet, believe me.

ELLA. I may last out the winter.

BORKMAN. [*Not thinking.*] Oh well, our winter can be long enough.

ELLA. [*Quietly.*] Long enough for me.

BORKMAN. But what on earth could have brought it on? You've always lived such a healthy life. What can have brought it on?

ELLA. The doctor thought that, at some time or other, I might have gone through some great emotional strain.

BORKMAN. [*Flaring up.*] Ah! I understand! You're telling me it's all my fault.

ELLA. It's too late to go over all that now. I only know that before I leave here I must win Erhart back again. He's part of me now, part of my own heart. It's unbearable to feel that I must die, that I must part for ever from the sun and light and air, and not leave behind me one single person who will think of me and grieve for me and remember me with love as a son remembers and thinks of the mother he has lost.

[*There is a pause. Borkman moves to the piano and fingers the keys.*]

BORKMAN. Take him, Ella, if you can win him.

ELLA. [*Rising and turning to him.*] You give your consent? You do that?

BORKMAN. Yes, and it's not much of a sacrifice either. I can hardly say he belongs to me.

ELLA. Thank you, thank you. Whatever you say, it *is* a sacrifice. And now, there's one more request I want to make. It's something that's very important to me.

BORKMAN. [*Moving down to right of the settee.*] What is it?

ELLA. You'll think it absurd, you may not understand . . .

BORKMAN. [*Sits on the settee and motions Ella to sit on his left.*] Tell me what it is.

ELLA. When I die—and it won't be long now—I shall leave a substantial amount behind me.

BORKMAN. Yes, I suppose you will.

ELLA. Every penny of it is going to Erhart.

BORKMAN. There's no one closer to you than he is.

ELLA. No, there's no one closer to me than he is.

BORKMAN. There's no one in your own family. You're the last.

ELLA. Yes, that's exactly what I mean. When I die, the name of Rentheim dies with me. The thought of it fills me with anguish. To be blotted out—even my name . . .

BORKMAN. [*Angrily.*] Ah, I see what you're getting at!

ELLA. Don't let it happen. Let Erhart take my name when I die.

BORKMAN. [*Harshly.*] I understand you well enough. You want to shield my son from the stigma of his father's name. That's what you want, isn't it?

ELLA. No, never! If you'd ever given me the right to take your name I'd have borne it gladly and defiantly together with you. But I'm about to die. . . . There's a bond in a name much stronger than you believe, Borkman.

BORKMAN. [*Coldly.*] Very well, Ella. I'm independent enough to bear my own name alone.

ELLA. [*Pressing his hands.*] Thank you, thank you! We've settled everything now. I'm satisfied. You've made amends for everything. Now I know that, when I'm gone, Erhart Rentheim will live on after me.

[*The small door is flung open. Mrs Borkman is standing in it. Ella rises. Mrs Borkman moves down centre and faces the two of them.*

MRS BORKMAN. [*Quietly, intensely.*] Never! Never to his dying day will Erhart call himself by that name!

[*Borkman rises and crosses above the settee.*

ELLA. [*Shrinking.*] Gunhild!

BORKMAN. [*Menacingly.*] No one is allowed in this room without permission.

MRS BORKMAN. I gave myself permission.

BORKMAN. What do you want?

MRS BORKMAN. I'm going to fight with every ounce of my strength for your name. I'm going to protect you from the evil that's threatening you.

ELLA. The evil is in you, Gunhild.

MRS BORKMAN. Be that as it may! [*She speaks with raised arm.*] But I tell you this—he will bear his father's name. He will bear it proudly and with honour. And I will always be his mother!

I and only I! My son is mine. And his heart will be mine—mine and no one else's.   [*She goes out and closes the door.*

ELLA. [*Shaken.*] Borkman, Erhart will be ruined if this goes on. You must come to an understanding with her. We must go down to her at once.

BORKMAN. We? I too do you mean?

ELLA. Both of us.

BORKMAN. She's inflexible, Ella, hard as the iron I used to dream of hewing out of the rocks.

ELLA. Come, Borkman, you must try now.

[*Borkman is staring at her uncertainly as—*

THE CURTAIN FALLS

The same setting as Act I. The lamp on the table is still alight.
*When the curtain rises, Mrs Borkman enters; she is very agitated. She looks
out of the window then crosses right and rings the bell; she sits by the
stove. After a moment she rises and rings the bell again more violently.
There is a pause and the Maid enters.*

MRS BORKMAN. Where have you been, girl? I've had to ring twice.
MAID. I heard.
MRS BORKMAN. Then why didn't you answer?
MAID. I had to put something on first, didn't I?
MRS BORKMAN. Go and get dressed at once; then go round for Mr
Erhart.
MAID. You want me to go for Mr Erhart?
MRS BORKMAN. That's what I said. Tell him I want him to come
home immediately. I must speak to him.
MAID. That'll mean waking up the coachman.
MRS BORKMAN. Why?
MAID. He'll have to harness the sledge. It's snowing something
awful.
MRS BORKMAN. Good heavens, girl, it's only just round the corner.
Hurry up and go!
MAID. Just round the corner, is it?
MRS BORKMAN. Of course it is! You know where Mr Hinkel the
lawyer lives, don't you?
MAID. Is that where Mr Erhart is this evening?
MRS BORKMAN. Why, where else should he be?
MAID. I thought he'd be where he usually is.
MRS BORKMAN. And where's that?
MAID. Mrs Wilton's, of course.
MRS BORKMAN. Mrs Wilton's? My son doesn't go there very often.
MAID. [*Muttering.*] Only every day of his life.
MRS BORKMAN. That's just gossip! Go straight to Mr Hinkel and
bring my son back with you.
MAID. Oh, all right then.   [*She is about to go.*
                    [*Ella Rentheim and Borkman appear at the door.*

189

MRS BORKMAN. [*Astonished.*] You? Here? What do you want?

MAID. Oh, Lord help us!

MRS BORKMAN. [*Aside to the Maid.*] Tell him I want him here at once.

MAID. [*Whispering.*] Yes, ma'am.

> [*Ella Rentheim enters followed by Borkman. The Maid steals out behind them and closes the door. Borkman crosses down left. Ella faces Mrs Borkman at the stove.*

MRS BORKMAN. What does he want here?

ELLA. He wants to try to come to an understanding with you, Gunhild.

MRS BORKMAN. He's never tried before.

ELLA. No, but he wants to now.

MRS BORKMAN. The last time we faced each other—it was at the trial when I was asked to explain . . .

BORKMAN. Tonight I'm the one who's going to do the explaining.

MRS BORKMAN. You?

BORKMAN. Not about my failings. Everyone knows about them.

MRS BORKMAN. Everyone.

BORKMAN. [*Moving in to left centre.*] But everyone doesn't know why I did what I did and why I had to do it. Nobody understands that I had to do it because I was true to myself, because I was John Gabriel Borkman. That's what I'm going to make clear.

MRS BORKMAN. You're wasting your time. Temptation is no excuse, any more than a sudden impulse.

BORKMAN. Except in one's own eyes.

MRS BORKMAN. I've heard enough. I've thought over that crime of yours again and again, and I've had my fill of it.

> [*She sits in the armchair.*

BORKMAN. So have I. I had lots of time on my hands during those eight years in jail. And lots more during the time I've spent up there. I've tried that case on my own and I've re-tried it times out of number. I've been my own prosecutor, my own defender and my own judge. I've been as scrupulously fair as anyone could possibly be, and I say that quite truthfully. I've tramped that room analysing every one of my actions, I've scrutinized them from every possible angle. I've been as ruthless, as relentless as any lawyer. And every time, I've arrived at one inevitable, final judgment—the person against whom I sinned most was—myself.

> [*Ella crosses to the stove.*

MRS BORKMAN. Not me? Not your son?

BORKMAN. When I say myself I mean my family.

MRS BORKMAN. And what about the hundreds of other people you are supposed to have ruined?

BORKMAN. [*Violently.*] Once I had the power, the urge inside me grew stronger and stronger. All over the country, buried in the mountains, were veins of precious metal, treasures and riches, waiting to be released. They clamoured to be set free, but everybody was deaf to their cry. I was the only person with ears to hear them. [*He turns upstage centre.*]

MRS BORKMAN. And to use them to disgrace the name of Borkman.

BORKMAN. And wouldn't others have done what I did if they'd had the power?

MRS BORKMAN. No one—no one but you would have done it.

BORKMAN. No one else would have had the vision. And if they'd had the vision they wouldn't have had the ideals. So, on that count at least, I'm innocent.

ELLA. Are you so sure of yourself, Borkman?

BORKMAN. On that count, yes; but, on another charge, I judge myself guilty—a crushing, overwhelming charge . . .

MRS BORKMAN. What is it?

BORKMAN. Instead of going out into the world again the very day they set me free, I buried myself up there and frittered away eight precious years of my life. I should have gone out, out into the world of hard, dreamless reality. I should have started at the bottom and climbed to the heights again, higher than ever before, despite the past.

MRS BORKMAN. And you'd have done exactly the same all over again, believe me.

BORKMAN. [*Moving down centre; superior.*] There's nothing new under the sun; all the same, history never repeats itself. It's the viewer who refashions the event. He sees it in a new setting and re-shapes it in his own mind. But you wouldn't understand that.

MRS BORKMAN. I wouldn't.

BORKMAN. That's the curse of it—no one has ever understood me.

ELLA. No one, Borkman?

BORKMAN. Well yes, perhaps. One person. Long, long ago, when I didn't know I needed understanding. But since then—no one. No one to rouse me, to inspire me to start again or to convince me that there could be redemption for what I had done.

MRS BORKMAN. So you needed someone outside yourself to convince you of that?

BORKMAN. When the whole world joins together to sneer and tell me my day is over, then there are moments when I believe it myself. But they are no more than moments. My belief in myself is unconquerable—and that alone should acquit me.

MRS BORKMAN. Why didn't you ever come to me and tell me about your need for understanding?

BORKMAN. To you? What good would that have done?

[*He moves away.*

MRS BORKMAN. You've never loved anyone but yourself. That's the truth in a nutshell.

BORKMAN. [*Proudly.*] I loved power.

MRS BORKMAN. I know that.

BORKMAN. The power to make people happy, more and more people, far and wide, all round me.

MRS BORKMAN. You had the power to make me happy. Did you ever use it?

BORKMAN. Someone usually goes under in a shipwreck.

MRS BORKMAN. And your son? Did you ever use your power to make him happy? Did you ever try to bring any joy into his life?

BORKMAN. I've never known my son.

MRS BORKMAN. That's true, you've never known him.

BORKMAN. You saw to that, didn't you?

MRS BORKMAN. Oh, I've seen to much more than that.

BORKMAN. Oh?

MRS BORKMAN. I've seen to it that no trace, no memory of you, will survive you.

BORKMAN. My memory? It sounds as if I were dead already.

[*He moves away left.*

MRS BORKMAN. You are, you are!

BORKMAN. Perhaps you are right. [*Angrily.*] But no! Not yet! I've been close to death, but not now! I'm myself again now. There's a whole new life surging up before me, beckoning me, a new life resplendent with promise. And you're going to see it too.

MRS BORKMAN. Don't dream of life again! Lie still where you are!

ELLA. [*Moves quickly to Mrs Borkman's right.*] Gunhild! Gunhild, how can you . . .

MRS BORKMAN. I will erect a memorial over your grave.

BORKMAN. A pillar of shame? Is that what you mean?

MRS BORKMAN. Oh no, it won't be a marble monument; no insulting phrases will be carved into it. But I'll train a green hedge to grow over you, and it'll close you in so tightly, so tightly, that all the misery you brought on us will be hidden away for ever. For you there will be oblivion. Men will never again be haunted by the memory of John Gabriel Borkman.

BORKMAN. And you will carry out this labour of love yourself?

MRS BORKMAN. Not with my own hands. That would be too much. I've delegated the task to someone else. It will be his mission on earth. His life will be so good and pure and radiant that he will obliterate all memory of your dark deeds.

BORKMAN. If it's Erhart you're referring to, you'd better tell me at once.

MRS BORKMAN. Yes, it's Erhart, my son, whom you're willing to renounce to atone for your own crimes.

BORKMAN. To atone for the most contemptible crime I ever committed.

MRS BORKMAN. A crime against a stranger! Remember the crime against me! But Erhart won't listen to you. When he knows how much I need him he will come to me. And he'll remain with me. With me and no one else. [*She stops and listens.*] Here he is, here he is! Erhart!   [*She moves towards the door.*

[*The door is thrown open and Erhart enters on Mrs Borkman's right.*

ERHART. [*Anxiously.*] Mother! For God's sake, what. . . .[*He sees Borkman and takes off his hat.*] Why did you send for me? What has happened?

MRS BORKMAN. I had to see you, Erhart, I had to see you. I want you to tell them you will stay with me, always.

ERHART. Stay with you? Always? What are you talking about, Mother?

MRS BORKMAN. I won't let you go, I tell you. There's someone who's trying to get you to go away with her.

ERHART. Then you know!

MRS BORKMAN. Yes. Do you know, too?

ERHART. Well, of course I know.

MRS BORKMAN. So you've planned it already! Behind my back! Erhart!

ERHART. Mother, what is it you know? Tell me!

MRS BORKMAN. I know everything. I know your aunt has come here to take you away from me.

ERHART. Aunt Ella?

ELLA. [*Moving downstage right.*] Listen to me first, Erhart.

MRS BORKMAN. She wants me to give you up so that she can take my place. She wants you to be her son and not mine. She wants you to inherit everything from her. She wants you to abandon your own name and take hers instead.

ERHART. Is this true, Aunt Ella?

ELLA. Yes.

ERHART. It's the first I've heard of it. Why do you want me to go back with you?

ELLA. Because I'm losing you here.

MRS BORKMAN. You're losing him to me. That's as it should be.

ELLA. Erhart, I mustn't lose you now. I'm a sick, lonely woman. If I were to tell you that I am dying . . .

ERHART. Dying?

ELLA. Yes, dying. Will you come and stay with me? Be with me when the end comes? Stay at my side and cherish me as though you were my only child?

[*There is a pause. Erhart steps towards Ella, the armchair between them.*]

MRS BORKMAN. And forsake your mother and your mission in life? Well, Erhart?

ELLA. I am dying, Erhart. Answer me.

ERHART. [*Crossing to Ella and taking her hands.*] Aunt Ella, I can't tell you how good you've been to me. I grew up in your home and I don't believe anyone could have been happier than I was.

MRS BORKMAN. Erhart, Erhart!

ELLA. I'm glad you can still look at it like that.

ERHART. But I can't sacrifice myself for you now. I can't go back to you now.

MRS BORKMAN. Ah, I knew it. You see! He'll never go back to you again. Never!

ELLA. Yes, you've won. He's yours again.

MRS BORKMAN. [*Coming down centre.*] Yes, yes! Mine he is and mine he's going to remain. It's true, isn't it, Erhart? We've still a long way to go together, haven't we?

ERHART. Mother, I think I'd better tell you plainly . . .

MRS BORKMAN. [*Eagerly.*] Yes, yes?

ERHART. I'm afraid it's only a short way we can go together now.

MRS BORKMAN. [*Thunderstruck.*] What? What's that you're saying?

ERHART. [*Plucking up his courage.*] Good God, Mother, can't you understand—I'm still young. I'd be suffocated if I stayed here much longer.

MRS BORKMAN. Suffocated? Here, with me?

ERHART. Yes, here with you, Mother.

ELLA. Then come with me, Erhart.

ERHART. But it's no better with you, Aunt Ella; it's different but no better. Not for me, anyway. All roses and lavender! It's just as stuffy there as it is here.

MRS BORKMAN. Stuffy here?

ERHART. [*More and more impatient.*] It's the only way I can describe it. All this mawkish watching over me, all this adoration—I can't stand it any more.

MRS BORKMAN. Have you forgotten what you've dedicated your life to, Erhart?

ERHART. You mean what *you*'ve dedicated my life to. It never belonged to me. It was yours and you did what you liked with it. But not now. I've got my whole life before me. [*He looks at his mother and then at his father; then he crosses past his father to stage centre.*] And I'm not going to use it to atone for someone else's misdeeds, whoever he may be.

MRS BORKMAN. Who has given you these ideas? Who is it? Tell me, Erhart.

ERHART. Who is it? Do you find it incredible that it can be myself?

MRS BORKMAN. Someone is influencing you. [*She sits in the armchair.*] It's not I and it's not your foster-mother.

                    [*Borkman moves thoughtfully to the window.*

ERHART. I've come into my own, that's all, Mother. I'm making my own decisions.

BORKMAN. Then perhaps my time has come again, after all.

ERHART. [*Formally.*] How do you mean, sir?

MRS BORKMAN. [*With contempt.*] I'd like to know that too.

BORKMAN. [*Crossing above the settee to the left of Erhart.*] Listen to me, Erhart. If you lived as pure a life as all the saints in history it would do nothing to restore your father's good name. That's one of those silly stories you were taught in this stuffy room.

ERHART. I agree.

BORKMAN. And it wouldn't do any good, either, if I pined away for the rest of my life doing penance. For years now I've kept myself going on hopes and dreams. But I've finished with that now.

ERHART. And what do you intend to do now, sir?

BORKMAN. I'm going to work out my own salvation. I'll start at the bottom again and raise myself by sheer work. It's a man's present and his future that make up for the past. And it's work and only work that gives life a meaning. I discovered that when I was no more than a boy, and now it seems a thousand times clearer. Erhart, will you join forces with me and help me start life again?

MRS BORKMAN. Don't listen to him, Erhart.

[*Erhart moves away left.*

ELLA. Yes, yes, Erhart, you must do it.

MRS BORKMAN. Advice like that from you? The lonely, dying woman!

ELLA. I'm not thinking about myself now.

MRS BORKMAN. No, as long as *I* don't take Erhart away from you.

ELLA. Exactly.

BORKMAN. Well, Erhart?

ERHART. Father, I can't. It's impossible now.

BORKMAN. [*Moving towards Erhart.*] What are you going to do then?

ERHART. I'm going to live my own life. I'm young, Father. I've never realized it before, but now I can feel it coursing right through my body. I don't want to work! I want to live, live, live!

MRS BORKMAN. [*Suspecting the truth.*] What are you going to live for?

ERHART. For happiness, Mother.

MRS BORKMAN. And where in the world do you think you'll find it?

ERHART. I've found it already.

MRS BORKMAN. [*Rising from her chair and crying out.*] Erhart!

ERHART. [*Goes to the door and opens it.*] You can come in now, darling.

[*Mrs Wilton appears, dressed for travelling.*

MRS BORKMAN. Mrs Wilton!

MRS WILTON. [*Shyly; her eyes on Erhart.*] May I . . .?

ERHART. Yes, you may come in now. I've told them everything.

[*Mrs Wilton comes into the room and hesitates to right of the settee. Erhart closes the door behind her and comes to right of her. She bows formally to Borkman, who greets her in silence. There is a pause.*

MRS WILTON. So Erhart has told you—and you must all be thinking I've brought a great disaster on you.

MRS BORKMAN. [*Slowly.*] You've destroyed any interest in life that was left in me. [*With an outburst.*] But it can't happen! It mustn't happen!

MRS WILTON. I knew you would think that, Mrs Borkman.

MRS BORKMAN. But surely you can see it's impossible . . .

MRS WILTON. Well, it seemed unlikely. But it happened, nevertheless.

MRS BORKMAN. Are you really serious about this, Erhart?

ERHART. It's happiness, Mother—it's everything that's wonderful in life. That's all I can tell you.

MRS BORKMAN. [*To Mrs Wilton.*] You've blinded him, blinded him and bewitched him.

MRS WILTON. [*Proudly.*] I've done nothing of the kind, Mrs Borkman.

MRS BORKMAN. Do you dare deny it?

MRS WILTON. I've neither blinded him nor bewitched him. Erhart came to me because he loved me; and, because I loved him, I went out half way to meet him.

MRS BORKMAN. [*Contemptuously.*] I believe that, of course!

MRS WILTON. Mrs Borkman, there are forces in nature about which you seem to be astonishingly ignorant.

MRS BORKMAN. And will you deign to tell me what they are?

MRS WILTON. The forces which dictate that two people, man and woman, shall join their lives together indissolubly—and unashamedly.

MRS BORKMAN. But you're joined indissolubly already—to another man.

MRS WILTON. The other man deserted me.

MRS BORKMAN. But he's still alive, isn't he?

MRS WILTON. To me he's dead.

ERHART. I know all about him, Mother, and I don't care whether he's alive or dead.

MRS BORKMAN. So you know all about him?

ERHART. Yes.

MRS BORKMAN. And still you don't care?

ERHART. I've told you before—all I want is happiness. I'm still young and I want to live, live, live!

MRS BORKMAN. Yes, you're young! [*She sinks into the armchair.*] Too young for this.

MRS WILTON. Please don't think I haven't tried to dissuade him, Mrs Borkman. I've told him everything about myself. I've reminded him again and again that I'm seven years older than he is——

ERHART. *Touches Mrs Wilton's arm and makes her sit on the settee; he sits right of her.*] I knew it before you told me.

MRS WILTON. —but nothing I could say would make him change his mind.

MRS BORKMAN. Oh? Then why didn't you refuse to see him? You could have shut your door in his face, couldn't you?

MRS WILTON. [*Quietly.*] No, Mrs Borkman, that's something I could never have done.

MRS BORKMAN. Why not?

MRS WILTON. Because this meant happiness for me as well as Erhart.

MRS BORKMAN. Oh, happiness, happiness . . .

MRS WILTON. I've never known real happiness before, and I'm not going to shut it out now just because it's been so late in coming.

MRS BORKMAN. And how long do you think it'll last?

ERHART. Whether it lasts or not doesn't matter. It's now that matters.

MRS BORKMAN. [*Angrily.*] You fool, you blind fool, can't you see where all this will end?

ERHART. [*Rising; to his mother.*] I don't want to see. I don't want to look anywhere, certainly not into the future. All I know is I'm going to live from now on.

MRS BORKMAN. [*Distressed.*] And is this what you call living?

ERHART. [*Standing over his mother.*] Yes. Can't you see how wonderful she is?

MRS BORKMAN. As though I haven't had enough shame to put up with!

BORKMAN. [*Harshly.*] You should be used to it by now.

ELLA. Borkman!

ERHART. Father!

MRS BORKMAN. Every day I'll have to put up with the sight of my son in the company of a—a . . .

ERHART. You may make your mind easy on that point, Mother. I won't be staying here.

MRS WILTON. We're going away, Mrs Borkman.

MRS BORKMAN. You're going too, are you? Then you're going together, I presume?

MRS WILTON. Yes, I'm going abroad. I'm taking a companion with me. She's quite a young girl. And Erhart is coming with us.

MRS BORKMAN. With you—and a young girl?

MRS WILTON. Yes, Frida Foldal. I'm taking her with me so that she can continue with her music.

MRS BORKMAN. Did you say music, Mrs Wilton?

MRS WILTON. Yes, I did, Mrs Borkman.

MRS BORKMAN. So you are taking her with you so that she can go on studying?

MRS WILTON. I can hardly let her go out into the world alone.

MRS BORKMAN. [*Suppressing a smile.*] And what do you say to that arrangement, Erhart?

ERHART. Well, Mother, if that's what Fanny wants . . .

MRS BORKMAN. And when does this gallant little troupe set off, may I ask?

MRS WILTON. Tonight. In fact my sledge is waiting for us now, outside the Hinkels.

MRS BORKMAN. So the party at the Hinkels was just—this?

MRS WILTON. Yes, Erhart and I were the party. And little Frida, of course.

MRS BORKMAN. And where is little Frida now?

MRS WILTON. Sitting in the sledge.

ERHART. [*Embarrassed.*] Mother, please try to understand. I wanted to spare you from this—all of you.

MRS BORKMAN. You'd have gone away without even saying goodbye?

ERHART. It would have been best for all of us. Our bags were packed; we were all ready to go. But when you sent for me . . . Well, goodbye, Mother.   [*He holds out his hands to her.*

MRS BORKMAN. Don't touch me.

ERHART. Is that your last word?

MRS BORKMAN. Yes.

ERHART. [*Crosses to Ella.*] Goodbye then, Aunt Ella.

ELLA. [*Taking his hands.*] Goodbye, Erhart, live your own life and be happy—as happy as you can.

ERHART. Thank you, my dear. [*Bowing to Borkman.*] Goodbye, Father. [*Whispering to Mrs Wilton.*] Let's go. The sooner the better.

MRS WILTON. [*Rising; in a low voice.*] I'm ready.

                                        [*Mrs Borkman also rises.*

MRS BORKMAN. [*Smiling sarcastically.*] Mrs Wilton, do you think it's wise to take your little chaperone with you?

MRS WILTON. [*Returning the smile.*] Oh yes. You see, men are so fickle. And women too, for that matter. Erhart might get tired of me, and I of him, so it will be a good thing for both of us if he has a second string—poor dear!

MRS BORKMAN. But what about you?

MRS WILTON. Oh, I'm never at a loss. Goodbye, all of you!

[*She bows and goes.*

[*Erhart stands for a moment uncertain what to do, then follows Mrs Wilton.*

MRS BORKMAN. He's gone!

BORKMAN. There's only one thing left for me to do. I'll fight on alone.   [*He goes to the door.*

ELLA. [*Frightened.*] John Gabriel, where are you going?

BORKMAN. Out there—to start fighting all over again.

[*Ella clings to him.*

Let go, Ella.

ELLA. No, no, you can't. You're not fit. I won't let you go.

BORKMAN. Let me go, I tell you.   [*He tears himself away and goes.*

ELLA. [*Running to the doorway.*] We mustn't let him go. Help me, Gunhild.

[*The jingling of the horses' harness is heard.*

MRS BORKMAN. [*Harshly.*] I wouldn't hold anyone in the world against his will, not anyone. Let them go, let them both go. As far, as far away as they like. [*Suddenly breaking down.*] Erhart, don't leave me!

[*She runs blindly to the door. Ella Rentheim bars her way as—*

THE CURTAIN FALLS

An open space outside the house. The porch and front door of the house are down left, the door is approached by two stone steps. Down right is a tree wing and there is a backcloth of snow-covered fir trees. The moon gleams fitfully.

When the Curtain rises, Borkman is leaning wearily against the porch; there is a cape around his shoulders and he is holding his hat in one hand and a gnarled stick in the other.

ELLA. [*Indoors; off.*] Don't try to follow him, Gunhild.

MRS BORKMAN. [*Off.*] Let me pass, Ella—I won't let him go!

ELLA. [*Off.*] You're wasting your time. You'll never catch him up.

MRS BORKMAN. [*Appears on the porch followed by Ella.*] Let me go! I'll shout after him all the way down the road. He'll hear me, he's sure to hear me.

[*The women cross past Borkman, Mrs Borkman to stage centre, Ella to the bottom of the porch steps.*]

ELLA. He'll never hear you. He'll be in the sledge by now.

MRS BORKMAN. No, no, he can't be. Not yet.

ELLA. They've probably started off already.

MRS BORKMAN. If he's in the sledge he'll be there with her, with her!

BORKMAN. [*With a sepulchral laugh.*] And he'll have no ears for his mother!

MRS BORKMAN. No, he won't listen to me any more. [*Listening.*] What's that?

[*Tinkling sledge bells are heard distantly.*

ELLA. Sledge bells.

MRS BORKMAN. It's her sledge.

ELLA. It may be someone else's.

MRS BORKMAN. No, no, it's Mrs Wilton's sledge. I know the sound of the silver bells. Listen! They're going past here now at the bottom of the hill.

ELLA. If you want him to hear you you must shout now. You never know, he might . . .

[*The bells are now quite close.*

Now, Gunhild, now! They're right beneath us now!

MRS BORKMAN. [*She stands for a moment, uncertain, then she stiffens.*] No. Let Erhart Borkman go on his way—as far as he can go—let him search somewhere else for what he calls life and happiness.

> [*The sounds of the bells die away.*

ELLA. [*Listening.*] I can't hear the bells any more.

MRS BORKMAN. They sounded like funeral bells.

BORKMAN. [*With a laugh.*] And they weren't tolling for me either.

MRS BORKMAN. No, they're tolling for me and for my son who has left me.

ELLA. They may be proclaiming a new life and happiness for him.

MRS BORKMAN. Life and happiness?

ELLA. For a time, anyway.

MRS BORKMAN. Can you bear the thought that life with her will make him happy?

ELLA. Of course I can. With all my heart.

MRS BORKMAN. Then you must be much better endowed than I am with the capacity to love.

ELLA. It must be the absence of love that keeps the capacity alive.

MRS BORKMAN. If that's true, I shall soon be as well endowed as you, Ella.

> [*She goes back into the house. Ella stands for a while looking at Borkman, then she takes his arm cautiously.*

ELLA. [*Standing right of Borkman.*] Come, John, let's go in.

BORKMAN. [*Starting.*] I?

ELLA. It's so cold out here. Come inside, into the warmth.

BORKMAN. Up to that room again?

ELLA. No, no, we'll stay downstairs.

BORKMAN. [*Angrily.*] I'll never set foot in that house again.

ELLA. Well, where else can you go at this time of night?

BORKMAN. First of all, I want to feast my eyes on my hidden treasure.

ELLA. John, I don't understand you.

BORKMAN. [*Laughs; then he breaks off to cough. He crosses to stage centre.*] Oh, it's not stolen property in a secret hiding-place. You needn't be afraid of that. [*Stopping and pointing.*] Who's that over there? Do you see him?

> [*Vilhelm Foldal appears down right stumbling towards them through the snow. He is limping.*

Vilhelm! What have you come back for?

FOLDAL. [*Standing right centre.*] Good God, are you out here, John Gabriel? [*Bowing.*] And your wife, too, I see.

BORKMAN. It's not my wife.

FOLDAL. Oh dear, I do apologize. I've just lost my glasses in the snow. But what are you doing out here? You never put your nose outside the door.

BORKMAN. Don't you think it's time I took a turn in the fresh air? Eight years in a state prison, another eight years in prison up there . . .

ELLA. Borkman, please . . .

FOLDAL. Oh yes, yes, of course . . .

BORKMAN. What I want to know is—why have you come back?

FOLDAL. I simply had to come back, John Gabriel. I simply had to see you again.

BORKMAN. Even though I showed you the door?

FOLDAL. Oh, a little thing like that wouldn't influence me.

BORKMAN. What's the matter with your foot? You're limping.

FOLDAL. Would you believe it, I've been run over.

ELLA. Run over?

FOLDAL. Yes, by a sledge.

BORKMAN. Aha!

FOLDAL. A sledge with two horses. They came charging down the hill. I couldn't get out of the way in time.

ELLA. So they ran you over?

FOLDAL. They landed on top of me. I went head over heels in the snow. I lost my glasses and broke my umbrella. [*Rubbing his leg.*] And sprained my ankle.

BORKMAN. [*Suppressing a laugh.*] Do you know who was inside that sledge, Vilhelm?

FOLDAL. I couldn't see. It was a closed sledge and the curtains were drawn. And the driver didn't stop, not even to see what he'd done to me. But I don't mind—because—oh, I'm so happy, so happy!

BORKMAN. Happy?

FOLDAL. Well, perhaps happy isn't the right word, but if it isn't I'd like to know what is. Something astonishing has happened, John Gabriel, and I just had to come back and share the good news with you.

BORKMAN. Well, come on then, share it.

ELLA. Why don't you take your friend inside first, Borkman?

BORKMAN. I've told you already—I'll never go inside that house.

ELLA. But the man's hurt.

BORKMAN. We all get hurt sooner or later in life. The only thing to do is start working again and pretend nothing's happened.

FOLDAL. That's a very profound piece of philosophy, John Gabriel. But I can tell you everything out here. It won't take a minute.

BORKMAN. Do that then, will you, Vilhelm?

FOLDAL. Well now, listen to this. When I got home this evening after I left here, what do you think I found waiting for me? A letter! And can you guess who sent it?

BORKMAN. Could it have been your little Frida?

FOLDAL. It could. Guessed first go! It was a long letter—well, rather a long letter. A servant had delivered it! And can you guess what she had to say to me?

BORKMAN. Could she have written to say goodbye to her parents?

FOLDAL. She could! Aren't you clever at guessing, John Gabriel? Well, to cut a long story short, Mrs Wilton has taken such a liking to my little Frida that she's taking her abroad to study music. What's more, Mrs Wilton has engaged a tutor to go with them, a very clever person. Frida's education is sadly lacking in some ways, you know.

BORKMAN. [*Rippling with laughter.*] Yes, I do know, Vilhelm.

FOLDAL. And just imagine! It was all kept as a big surprise for her. She didn't know a thing till she went to that party this evening. And yet, she found time to write to me. Such a lovely letter! Full of warmth and affection! Very respectful too. And wasn't it a nice gesture to write and say goodbye even before she's gone? [*Laughing.*] But, of course, I wouldn't dream of letting her go off like that!

BORKMAN. Wouldn't you?

FOLDAL. She tells me they'll be leaving first thing in the morning.

BORKMAN. Is that what she says?

FOLDAL. [*Laughing and rubbing his hands together.*] Yes, but I've got a little card up my sleeve. I'm going along to Mrs Wilton's first thing tonight.

BORKMAN. Tonight?

FOLDAL. Yes, tonight. It's not so late, after all. And, if the place is bolted up, I shall ring, there and then. I simply must see my Frida before she goes off. Good night, good night.

[*He moves away right.*

BORKMAN. Just a minute, Vilhelm, you can save yourself the journey.

FOLDAL. If you're worrying about my ankle . . .

BORKMAN. I am, but quite apart from that you'll be wasting your time trying to get in at Mrs Wilton's.

FOLDAL. Oh no, I won't. I'll go on ringing that bell till they have to open up. I must and will see Frida.

ELLA. Mr Foldal, your daughter has left already.

FOLDAL. [*Dumbfounded.*] Left already? Are you sure? Who told you?

BORKMAN. The tutor.

FOLDAL. Oh? Who *is* the tutor?

BORKMAN. His name is Erhart Borkman.

FOLDAL. [*Beaming.*] Your son, John Gabriel? Is *he* going with them?

BORKMAN. Yes, he and Mrs Wilton are going to educate little Frida between them.

FOLDAL. Thank Heaven for that! The child couldn't be in better hands. But are you quite sure they're gone?

BORKMAN. They were in the sledge that ran you over.

FOLDAL. Just imagine my little Frida in that luxurious sledge!

BORKMAN. Well, Vilhelm, she certainly *was* in it and she was in it with Erhart Borkman. Did you notice the silver bells?

FOLDAL. Were they real silver? Genuine silver bells?

BORKMAN. Everything was genuine. Inside and out.

FOLDAL. [*With quiet wonder.*] The ways of Fate are mysterious, aren't they? My little gift of poetry has been reborn in Frida as music. So I wasn't a poet for nothing, after all. Here's my little Frida venturing out into the great big world that I always longed to see. My little Frida goes off in a closed sledge with silver bells on the harness . . .

BORKMAN. And promptly runs over her father.

FOLDAL. Pshaw! Who cares about me so long as my daughter . . . Well, if I'm too late, I'm too late. I'll go home instead and try to comfort her mother. When I left she was crying her heart out into the sink.

BORKMAN. Crying her heart out?

FOLDAL. Yes. Would you believe it, John Gabriel?

BORKMAN. And here are you splitting your sides.

FOLDAL. Yes, I'm afraid I am. But my wife doesn't know any

better, poor thing! Well, goodbye! Lucky for me the tram's so near. Goodbye, John Gabriel; goodbye, madam.

[*He bows and limps out right.*

BORKMAN. [*Gazing after him.*] Goodbye, Vilhelm! It's not the only time in your life that you've been run over, old friend.

ELLA. [*Crosses above Borkman and comes to his right. Looking at him anxiously.*] Are you all right, John Gabriel? You're so white.

BORKMAN. That's what the prison air up there has done for me.

ELLA. I've never seen you like this before.

BORKMAN. You've never seen an escaped convict before.

ELLA. Come inside, John.

BORKMAN. Don't try to get me back into that house. I've told you already ...

ELLA. But I'm begging you, for your own sake ...

MAID. [*Opens the door.*] Excuse me, but madam's just told me to lock up.

BORKMAN. [*In a whisper.*] Did you hear that? They're trying to lock me up again.

ELLA. Mr Borkman isn't very well. He wants a breath of fresh air first.

MAID. But madam said ...

ELLA. [*Crossing to her.*] I'll lock up. Leave the key in the door.

MAID. All right then. [*She goes into the house.*

BORKMAN. [*Listening for a moment, then moving right away from the house.*] I'm outside the walls now, Ella. They'll never catch me again.

ELLA. [*Following him to his left.*] But you're a free man in there too, John. You can come and go as you please.

BORKMAN. [*Fearfully.*] Never under anyone's roof again! It's wonderful to be out here in the night. If I went up to that room again, the ceiling and the walls would close in on me and crush me—crush me flat as a fly.

ELLA. Then where will you go?

BORKMAN. I'll go on and on and on—to a new life and freedom and real human beings. Will you come with me, Ella?

ELLA. Now?

BORKMAN. Yes, now. At once.

ELLA. But how far are we going?

BORKMAN. As far as I can.

ELLA. But think a moment. Out in this wild, bleak, winter night ...

BORKMAN. So madam is worried about her health, is she? Yes, I know you're a sick woman . . .

ELLA. It's *your* health I'm worried about.

BORKMAN. A dead man's health! You're making me laugh, Ella.
                                                    [*He walks upstage.*

ELLA. [*Following him and catching him by the sleeve.*] What did you say you were?

BORKMAN. I said I was a dead man. Don't you remember Gunhild telling me to lie still where I was?

ELLA. I'll go with you, John.

BORKMAN. Yes, Ella, we two belong to each other. Come!

[*Borkman and Ella pass into the wood down right. The lights fade and in the darkness the voices of Ella and Borkman can be heard off.*

ELLA. [*Off.*] Where are we going, John? I don't know where we are.

BORKMAN. [*Off.*] Follow my footprints.

ELLA. [*Off.*] But why do we have to go on climbing?

BORKMAN. [*Off.*] We're going to the top of the path.

ELLA. [*Off.*] I can't go on much farther.

BORKMAN. [*Off.*] Just a little farther. We're close to the view now. There used to be a bench there.

ELLA. [*Off.*] You remember it still?

BORKMAN. [*Off.*] Yes. You can stop and sit down there.

[*The lights slowly come up and the scene has changed to a small plateau. The mountains are immediately behind, the fiord is below with other mountain ranges in the distance. A dead fir tree stands centre with a bench beneath it. There is deep snow. The bench is raised from the rest of the scene.*

BORKMAN. [*Standing near the bench.*] Come here, Ella, look at this.

ELLA. [*Standing left of Borkman.*] What is it, John?

BORKMAN. [*Pointing.*] Look at that countryside—free and open as far as you can see.

ELLA. We've often sat here in the past and seen much farther than this.

BORKMAN. It was a land of dreams when we used to gaze out there together.

ELLA. Our land of dreams. And now it's buried deep in the snow. And the old tree is dead.

BORKMAN. [*Not heeding her.*] Can you see the smoke from the ships in the fiord?

ELLA. Smoke? No.

BORKMAN. I can. The ships are always docking or leaving port. They carry their message of goodwill all round the world. They bring light and warmth to the hearts of men in thousands and thousands of homes. That was what I dreamed of doing.

ELLA. And it remained a dream . . .

BORKMAN. Yes, it remained a dream. [*Listening.*] Listen! Down there on the banks of the river! The factories are working full speed! My factories! The factories I would have built! Just listen! Can you hear the engines throbbing? It's the night shift. They're working night and day. Listen! The wheels are turning, the cables are humming. Round they go, round and round and round. Can you hear them, Ella?

ELLA. No, dear, I can't.

BORKMAN. I can hear them.

ELLA. [*Anxiously.*] I think you're mistaken, John.

BORKMAN. But they're nothing, no more than the little satellite states surrounding the great kingdom.

ELLA. Kingdom? Whose kingdom are you talking about?

BORKMAN. My kingdom, of course! The kingdom I was about to carve out when I—when I died.

ELLA. [*Shaken.*] Oh, John, John!

BORKMAN. And there it is—defenceless, no one to rule it, wide open to every bandit who cares to plunder it. Do you see the mountains over there in the distance? Range after range soaring and towering, one above the other? That is my kingdom, my great, boundless, inexhaustible kingdom!

ELLA. It's a kingdom of ice and gales, John, that's what it is!

BORKMAN. Those gales are the breath of life to me. Those gales are a roar of greeting from the helpless spirits of the rocks. I can almost caress them, those captive multitudes. I can see those veins of metal stretching out their sinuous, branching, beckoning hands to me. I saw them before me, like living creatures, that night when I stood in the vaults of the bank with the lantern in my hand. You begged to be freed and I tried with all my strength to set you free, but my strength was not enough and the treasure sank back deep into the earth again. But here, in the quiet of the night, I will whisper to you; I love you as you lie there, helpless, in the depths and the darkness; I love you as you lie there waiting to be born, with all your shining train of power and glory! I love you, I love you, I love you!

ELLA. Ah, John, I knew it! Your love is still down there. It has always been down there. But up here, where it is light, there was a warm, living human heart that throbbed and beat for you. And you crushed that heart! No, worse than that! Ten times worse! You sold it for—for——

BORKMAN. [*Shuddering.*] —for the kingdom—and the power—and the glory, you mean?

ELLA. Yes, that's what I *do* mean. I have told you already: you killed the love in the woman who loved you. And whom you loved in return as much as you could love anybody. [*Raising her arm.*] And therefore I warn you, John Gabriel Borkman, you will never win the reward you claimed for that murder. You will never make your triumphal entry into your dark, dank kingdom.

BORKMAN. [*Stumbling to the seat and sitting down.*] I'm afraid, Ella, I'm afraid your warning will come to pass.

ELLA. [*Going to him.*] Don't be afraid, John. It would be the best thing that could happen to you.

BORKMAN. [*With a stifled cry, clutching at his heart.*] Ah! [*Weakly.*] It's gone again!

ELLA. What was it, John?

BORKMAN. [*Sinking against the arm of the bench.*] A hand of ice. It tore at my heart.

ELLA. A hand of ice?

BORKMAN. No, not of ice. It was a hand of steel.

[*He sinks right down on the bench.*

ELLA. [*Tearing off her cloak and covering him.*] Stay here. Don't move. I'll go and get help. [*She starts to go, then stops and returns. She feels his pulse and then his face. Quietly.*] No. It's best like this, John Borkman, best for you.

[*She spreads her coat over him and sinks down in the snow in front of him.*

[*There is a pause. Voices are heard off right.*

MAID. [*Off.*] Yes, yes, ma'am, here are their footprints.

[*Mrs Borkman enters through the wood right with the Maid who carries a lamp.*

MRS BORKMAN. [*Peering round her.*] Yes, there they are! On the bench there! [*Calling.*] Ella!

ELLA. [*Getting up.*] Are you looking for us?

MRS BORKMAN. You can see I am.

ELLA. [*Pointing.*] There he is, Gunhild.

MRS BORKMAN. Is he asleep?

ELLA. A long, deep sleep, I think.

MRS BORKMAN. [*Crying out.*] Ella! [*Quietly.*] Did he—did he do it himself?

ELLA. No.

MRS BORKMAN. [*Relieved.*] Not by his own hand?

ELLA. No, it was a hand of ice and steel that tore at his heart.

MRS BORKMAN. [*To the Maid.*] Go and get help. Get the men at the farm.

MAID. Yes, ma'am. God save us.   [*She goes out left.*

MRS BORKMAN. [*Standing behind the bench.*] Then the night air killed him——

ELLA. So it seems.

MRS BORKMAN. —strong man though he was.

ELLA. [*Walking in front of the bench.*] Won't you look at him, Gunhild?

MRS BORKMAN. No, no, no. [*Quietly.*] John Gabriel Borkman! He was a miner's son. He couldn't live in the open air.

ELLA. It was the cold that killed him; the cold in our hearts.

MRS BORKMAN. The cold in our hearts. It killed him years ago.

ELLA. Yes, and it turned us two into ghosts.

MRS BORKMAN. You are right, Ella.

ELLA. A dead man and two ghosts—that's what the cold has done to us.

MRS BORKMAN. The cold in our hearts. I think we two may embrace each other now, Ella.

ELLA. Yes, I think we may now.

MRS BORKMAN. We twin sisters—over the man we both loved.

ELLA. We two ghosts—over a dead man.

   Mrs Borkman is standing behind the bench, and Ella Rentheim in front of it. They clasp each other's hands as——

THE CURTAIN FALLS